*Advance Praise for Fraternity of Silence*

Caught in a whirlwind of political twists and turns, idealistic Christine "Beth" Pullen becomes enmeshed in a romantic liaison that makes her question all her beliefs and takes her down roads she could never have imagined navigating. A real page turner!

--**Karen Stolz**, Author of *Fanny and Sue* and *World of Pies*.

FRATERNITY OF SILENCE. What's the perfect job for a journalism graduate from Michigan State University? Answer: Communications Director for the newly appointed Lieutenant Governor of Texas, of course. Especially, when he's a former TV news personality who makes her heart go pitter-patter every time he speaks. That's what happens to Christine Elizabeth Pullen, formerly known as Chrissy, now renamed Beth by her new boss. Katherine Shephard, with tongue firmly in cheek, launches Beth into a world of Texas politics, intrigue and romance. Fast paced, humorous and expressly readable, Beth's adventures will enthrall you from page one until the very end. Ms. Shephard's first full-length novel is a keeper!

-- **Randy Rawls**, author of the Ace Edwards mystery series, *Jake's Burn*, *Joseph's Kidnapping* and *Jade's Photos*.

If you're looking for an interesting story with characters to match, you need look no further than this book! **Fraternity of Silence** has just what it takes. It takes hold of your imagination and doesn't let go. Bravo!

--**Kenneth Clarke**, author of *Deadly Justice*

Ms. Shephard's impressive political background and insider's knowledge makes for a fascinating read. This is a Cinderella tale with a twist - a dark side that will keep you turning pages!

--**E. Joan Sims**, author of *Cemetery Silk* and *The Plague Doctor*

# Fraternity of Silence

*Welcome to my Heaven. . .*
*Welcome to my Hell. . .*

## Katherine Shephard

## Author's Note

Concerning the actual buildings and locations mentioned in this book: while most exist, I took a small amount of literary license in their portrayal.

—

ISBN: 0-9729071-0-6  (Softcover)
Library of Congress Control Number:  2002096690

This book is printed on acid free paper.
Printed in the United States of America

—

**Cover Design by Rebecca Price**

**Author Photo by Tacy Lee**

Animal Grooming by Chez Shampooch
Running Shoe courtesy of "Mister"

## *Acknowledgements*

This book could not have been written without the help of many. Collectively, the following persons have helped this dream come true:

Editor par excellence – Regan Brown. You are, quite simply, the best.

Cover Designer, Rebecca Price – your talent is truly amazing.

Web Designer, Linda Bingham – you captured not only the books flavor, but the "essence of Katherine" so beautifully.

The Texas Coalition of Authors – what an amazing support group!

My publicist - Sherri Rosen who shares my vision.

Debra L. Beck – Debi, you were there from the beginning. Your political savvy, insider's knowledge and remarkable humor helped conceive the "Fraternity." Thank you so much for your time and ideas.

Governor John Engler's staff, of the Great State of Michigan – especially Linda. Your candor, assistance in research and welcoming attitude provided the color for most of this novel's fictional backdrops. You represent all that is fine in politics.

The "real" Dave Hawthorne – thank you for lending me your gorgeous home for this book. Your talent is only outdone by your hospitality.

The management and staff of the Amway Grand Hotel in Grand Rapids, Michigan for opening your doors to this fledgling author. The Spirit of Michigan lives in your halls.

Janet Congo, Phd – you told me to do it – you said I could - and I have! Thank you for reading my words and encouraging my voice.

My brother, Kenn. Bubby, you are the strongest man I've ever known. I love you.

Ralph Shortt – your insight and friendship, dear big bro, epitomize the definition of loyalty. There were times I know I drove you crazy – the next beer's on me!

The entire Shephard/Gordon Family – each of you have helped me grow so much this past year. You can't imagine how your support has strengthened me. I love each of you.

My card girls, Bobbi Margolis, Katie Burns, Lauren Gelford, Diane Semrau, Terry Kuramoto, Sandi Whitten. You never let me go it alone. God Bless your faithful friendship. We <u>are</u> the Ya Yas!

Jill Reiter, you always had "medicine for me" – you truly are the Queen!

Christie Mack – you'll never know what your unconditional support has meant. We've been through a lot together. You never turned your back on me.

Marianne Senatore, the best is yet to come for you, dear friend. I hope this book makes you smile.

The "O" room and "Cloak Room" chatters – to each of you a hug. A special thanks to Tide. You never let me down!

Connie Arroyo, Denise Alamazar, Alecia Rice, BK (Laurie), Witchey (Kat), Suz – and all of you in that "Old Gang of Ours." What a special group you are.

Linda Zell, Vicki Buffalino, Cathy Ross, LuAnn Najam – you could have thought I was nuts, but you kept smiling, by my side, as true friends do. Thank you so much.

The Gulf Coasters: Shelly, Harry, Laura and Sherri – after the rain there really is a rainbow. Thank you for holding my umbrella.

Emily Baker – our chance meeting goes to prove there are no coincidences in life. Bless you and your special gift. We both know what truths lie hidden.

Teri, Ron and Sarah Malloy – still crazy after all these beers, cheers and tears. Thanks for being part of my family "forever."

The staff, student body and families of Saddleback Valley Christian School for their unwavering faith and prayers. Miracles happen!

2 Chronicles 30:27

Jimmy Lockwood – you are the epitome of a TRUE Texas gentleman. God Bless you and your wonderful family. Your patience is amazing! Lisa, Karen and Brad – you've been blessed.

I save the "best" for last . . .Bernadette Lockwood. Berni, Goofmeister, Joy – the 3 in 1! Thank you for wiping the tears, never hanging up the phone and for being my #1 cheerleader. WE DID IT! I share my success with you, dear friend.

"You can't have it all by yourself"
The present and future would be empty without my past.
I share my joy with. . .
Marcia Christoff, Bethi Ozburn, Barb Glinski, Rick Shriner, Marylou Williams, Janet Hartz, Billy Alberts, Barb & Kathy Cheney, Jill Dempster, Dave Sadoway, Mark Ammerman, Jeff Teichman, Norm McKay, Dave Kensler, Lark Reilly, Rick Benglian, Jim Harris, Pat McGrew, Marie dePutron, Gail Headapohl, The YFU Chorale of '69 and, of course, Steve O'Brien. You have helped me become what I am today.
I love you all. I always will.
-------------
If you were a part of my life during the writing of this book and I've forgotten to mention you, it's for a good reason rather than an oversight.
--------------

## This Book is Dedicated to

The loving memory of my mother, Billie Gordon, who taught me to follow my dreams and my daddy, Frank Gordon, for always telling me I was his dream come true.  This book is also dedicated to Mike Licata, Flo Williams, Daniel Malloy, and my sister, Claire, whose dreams were cut short.
I'll always be missing you.

## This Book is Written for

My son, RJ, whose dreams still lie before him, and for the "real" Bob, who never forgot how to dream.
2 Corinthians 4:8-9

"To remain silent when they
should protest makes cowards of
men."

Thomas Jefferson

# Chapter One

*There's a dead body in the dome and no one's talking.*

March 20, 1998. Robert Bentley Larken's thirty-ninth birthday. Even a non-numeric like myself could figure out his birth year to be 1959. Truth be told, I used a calculator. I'm the first to admit that I'm a wordsmith, not a number cruncher. I'm also a worrier. This dead body thing ranked right up there as number one on my fret list.

I'd spent months researching Bob Larken, the former political broadcaster who was now, by hasty Senate resolution, the new lieutenant governor of Texas. Of course there was the sticky detail of the untimely death of William Glinnis, the former lieutenant governor. He was found dead at his desk at the capitol building in Austin.

I'd heard Larken a few months back on CNN and became mesmerized by his voice and every word he spoke. Tonight, thanks to my best friend, Victoria, I was headed to his birthday party at the governor of Michigan's mansion on Mackinac Island. And I had every intention of quenching my almost insatiable curiosity concerning Larken. Going from broadcaster to lieutenant governor is quite a leap. According to Victoria, I was obsessed. Then again, that's Victoria.

As an aide for the Michigan state legislature, Victoria's not privy to insider information—unless she's heard one of our state's finest talk in their sleep or when they've had a bit too much to drink. Normally, a lieutenant governor from another state is a "who cares" scenario—except when he has the means to get on air and sweet-talk the press into spreading his own agenda. Larken's background as a well-known broadcaster gave him the inside track with the media. They'd handled him with kid gloves ever since Billy Glinnis died of an apparent heart attack and Larken two-stepped into his spot as lieutenant governor.

It was the kind of story to put a gleam in the eye of any investigative reporter. Glinnis had been in the peak of health and poised to run for governor in the fall. He had no family to speak of, no autopsy was performed and no one was talking. One day Larken was doing a brief on-air eulogy for "Billy G" and the next day he was taking the oath of office. Victoria reported the jokes going around the Michigan rotunda: "Check your coffee, you could be next." No one likes a dead body in the dome. Any dome.

Vic had garnered me a last-minute invitation to the party via some fellow in the Lansing press corps—I didn't ask how. Sometimes, I've learned, it's best not to inquire too deeply into her methods. They usually involve a lie, sex, or both. I'd discovered that Larken and the governor's son had attended the University of Houston together and had been roommates all four years. Since Larken was in Michigan for a lieutenant governors' conference, our governor decided to honor our country's newest LG as he turned another year older.

I was no Nancy Drew, but I was getting into the swing of investigative reporting. A story involving a dead lieutenant governor was not the way I thought I'd be starting my career— but there was something about Larken. I just couldn't pinpoint it, but I was inquisitive enough to play whatever role was necessary to dig deeper.

Knowing I'd only be gone a day, I threw some jeans, a few sweaters and a new Michigan State sweatshirt into my roller bag. I also included one rather professional-looking pantsuit and a deep-rust silk tunic and pants for the birthday bash. I shrugged as I closed the bag, hoping that a touch of extra mascara would detract from any major wardrobe faux pas. My curly, short auburn hair and hazel eyes make rust somewhat of a wardrobe basic. At five-foot-four and 130 pounds I'm not exactly model material, but I have one of those Pepsodent smiles. Rust goes with killer smiles. I've learned that as long as I smile continually, my outfit will be perfect.

After an uneventful four-hour drive north, I parked my red Mustang convertible, Peg, at the Mackinac City Airport and braced for the short hop to the island. Peg is short for Pegasus but I like to do my flying down interstates at ninety with the top down, not in small planes over water. I thanked St. Joseph of Cupertino, the patron saint of air travel, that the planes were taking off and landing frequently. This was the only transportation to and from the island this time of year and I was running late enough as it was. Damn I hate flying. I always turn white as a ghost. Even my knuckles turn white and white is *not* my color.

With a mere ten minutes during the flight to squelch my panic, I decided to concentrate on what I knew about the island. It's small—three miles long and two miles wide with a permanent population of around five hundred people. No motorized vehicles are permitted on the island except for a fire truck, an ambulance and one public utility truck. Personally, I think that's prejudicial—I mean, Michigan *is* the motor capital of the world. Then there's the slight problem of having to live in a place with no Bob's Big Boy or Burger King. Not happening for me.

In winter, they do allow limited taxi service; during "the season," folks get around by carriage. If this were a typical March, the method of transportation would be skis and I'd have to pull my luggage on a sled. Thank God this wasn't a typical March. I got my own Whopper in Mackinac City before getting on the plane. I couldn't concentrate on dead bodies with an empty stomach.

3

Once on terra firma, I made the sign of the cross, dashed into the small restroom at the airport and changed into my silk outfit for the bash. I'd hung my tunic and pants in a separate garment bag so they wouldn't wrinkle and it paid off. Not a wrinkle to be seen. Once changed, and after a quick makeup fix, I gave the airport transfer service what I needed to be delivered to the hotel: one suitcase, one garment bag - that now held my clothes from the flight, and my trusty typewriter. I called for the taxi I'd reserved for the short trip to the governor's mansion. It took us no time at all to reach the party. A buzz-topped, tanned young man with a chiseled jaw line and orthodontically enhanced teeth approached my side of the taxi, opened the door and extended his hand. A nice snow-skier's tan. A nice snow-skier's body. When this young Adonis closed my door I noticed the printed name of the taxi. I must have wrinkled my brow, because the young man smiled and responded.

"Each of tonight's taxis on the Island carries a Disney name. It was requested by Mrs. Melvin."

I didn't think I wanted to know why, but my taxi was named "Goofy." Please don't let this be an omen, I prayed. A second teen Adonis approached.

"Good evening, Miss. Your name?"

I kept my hand on my evening bag. Being from Detroit, my trust doesn't come easy. "Um, Christine. Christine Pullen. I'm here for the party."

He checked a clipboard and responded, "Yes, Miss—you're on the list." He crooked his elbow and smiled, which I presumed was my cue to place my arm in his and go to the entrance of the mansion with him.

"Thanks, thank you, thank you very much," I stammered as I looked up the long lilac-lined driveway. Taking in the pungent floral aroma of the just-emerging buds, I was reminded of Lilac Breeze, my mother's favorite everyday cologne. Mama had died when I was five. If she could only see me now, I know she'd be so proud. I closed my eyes briefly as I walked and asked her to help me through the night. Well, okay, I asked her spirit to help make sure I didn't trip, spill, or babble.

As we got closer, I realized this was no mere residence but rather, a full-fledged Victorian mansion. The large, painted wood door stood invitingly open. As I poked my head into the foyer, I saw a small greeting area where the dark oak floors gleamed under the light of a Sheffield chandelier. An elderly gentleman appeared out of nowhere and took my wrap, a simple shawl.

"Good evening, Miss Pullen, and welcome," a somewhat older lady greeted me instantly. I presumed she was there to take over for my young escort, who nodded his head and turned to leave.

"Hi?" It came out more like a question because I wasn't sure how she knew who I was.

"I'm Victoria Wexford's friend—the writer?" (You're babbling, Christine, quit babbling, I thought. But the words wouldn't stop.) "I'm here to meet Robert Larken—the lieutenant governor? Of Texas?"

"Yes I know who Bob is, dear. I'm Bitsy Melvin, the governor's wife. Again, welcome. Come this way. I'll introduce you to Bob."

As she guided me through the big reception room, I cringed internally at how I'd mistaken the Wolverine State's matriarch for a maid. Must have been the black wool dress.

We wove through the people milling around in the parlor, our heels clicking on the aged hardwood floors. I marveled at the way the governor's wife smiled to the left, then to the right with perfect timing. She seemed to command respect and silent admiration from everyone she passed. Do they give classes in these things?

"Did you have a pleasant trip to the Island, Miss Pullen?"

"I did, thank you. I wish I were staying longer, I'd love to walk around town. I've never been this far north."

"Are you a Michigan native?"

"Yes, an MSU grad—but I've never been further north than Traverse City. I really need to ask—how did you know my name when I walked in tonight?"

"We have two-way communications. When a guest arrives, it's announced to the doorman who, in turn, lets me know their name and what they're wearing."

"Oh, so you get the right name with the right face. All along I thought that nice gentleman was wearing a hearing aid." My admission brought a smile to both our faces.

We continued through the French doors to a glassed-in morning room where a tuxedoed pianist sat at an ebony grand Wurlitzer. Mrs. Melvin and I walked through a screened door that led to the gardens just as the beginning strains of the Moonlight Sonata filled the crisp night air.

"Follow me, dear. I think Bob's gone out to catch a breath of fresh air."

We turned the corner and I spotted him. He stood in a walkway surrounded by what would soon be blossoming rose bushes.

At six-foot-four, his presence was unmistakable among the bare branches. He must have heard us approach. As he slowly turned toward us, the moonlight struck the strands of gray in his full head of hair and I had to take a deep breath to compose myself. As Mrs. Melvin stepped back, he extended his hand in greeting.

"Hello, sir. I'm Christine Elizabeth Pullen, freelance writer." What I *wanted* to say was "Damn, you've got broad shoulders" but I contained myself. For once.

He grasped my hand firmly and repeated, "Christine Elizabeth Pullen, freelance writer." I loved how my name sounded when he pronounced it in his soft Texas drawl.

"That's a mighty long name, isn't it? Pleased to meet you." He gave that excitable chuckle that he was becoming somewhat famous for. "You know, you don't look like a Christine. You look more spirited. Like a Beth. Hmmm. Beth. May I call you Beth? I always like to be different."

"Certainly, sir," I said, as I felt my cheeks warm to what I knew must be a blush.

"Then Beth it is! Let me show you around. Where did you drive in from?"

"Just the Lansing area. It didn't take long—about four hours or so, including the plane ride. I sang most of the way." A smile must have escaped because his eyes seemed to light up in laughter.

"Ah. Singing in the car, the shower, on a roller coaster—anywhere you can't be heard. That's my motto."

There was that chuckle again.

"You're on to me!" I lifted my eyebrows and winked. I winked. I winked? At the lieutenant governor of Texas I was here to write a story about? What was I thinking? Knowing I needed to get back to a more formal conversational basis, I tried another angle.

"I have a new car and I promised my father I would be careful."

He nodded his head knowingly. "I have a son just about to get his driver's license. I know the feeling. Glad to hear that you listen to your father. I hope I'm that lucky!"

"My dad is pretty protective. It's nice and all, but I can only take it in small doses! In fact, really, it's becoming oppressive. My best friend thinks I need to break away." Here I was babbling again.

Acting like a protective father himself, and ignoring my anti-father remarks, he said, "It's starting to get chilly. I should escort you back inside." He placed his hand on my back and guided me up the rock path leading into the house just as the final chord of the Moonlight Sonata faded into the night air. I let out a deep sigh, which did not go unnoticed. The lieutenant governor turned and faced me with a quizzical expression on his face.

"I'm sorry," I explained. "It's just that music. I love Beethoven."

"Oh, I know," he said. "It seems to fit the night."

We strolled back toward the morning room and took a turn to the left. Another English-type garden stood before us. It was well tended, even for this time of year. Fresh mulch had been laid down—to keep the bulbs warm, I presumed. Beyond the hedges, stars were shining down on the Straits of Mackinac. I could hear laughter through the opened windows as we turned to enter the residence.

We passed through the kitchen and continued down a small hallway to a formal parlor.

"How about meeting your state's governor? I see you've met Bitsy. Don't let her intimidate you, though. She's harmless!" That chuckle was getting to me.

Larken pointed to a large group milling around a table of hors d'oeuvres.

"The governor is over there, by the artichokes. Don't laugh. A friend had them flown in from California just for me. I *love* fresh artichokes."

Weaving our way between several women smiling too-perfect smiles, we made our approach. I brushed the front of my tunic to make certain it was hanging smoothly, tossed back my hair to portray confidence and wet my lips with my tongue. Okay. It sounded stupid, but it worked for my glamorous friend Victoria. She always looked like her mouth had been freshly glossed.

"Ah, Governor. I have someone I'd like you to meet. Governor Melvin, this is Beth. Beth Pullen, freelance writer from down in Lansing." I was not yet comfortable with the name Beth, yet it seemed to fit with the persona and agenda of Bob Larken. Apparently, when he didn't like something, he changed it.

Good God, I thought. Here I am. Face to face with a governor! What do I do? "Hello, sir" was all I could think of to say.

"What brings you to the UP, Ms. Pullen?"

His question was accompanied by a glance down toward my left hand to check what I presumed was my marital status. His use of "Ms." was appropriately PC, but I really hated it. Not that I was particularly thrilled to be a "Miss," but I always figured that way the other players knew my exact position. I wondered if he used the abbreviation for the Upper Peninsula of Michigan in all of his conversations, or only with the home-state crowd.

"Well, I just finished my studies at Michigan State in journalism and I had done a research piece on Lieutenant Governor Larken. My best friend works for a Michigan legislator. He knows someone in your office and she arranged for me to be invited tonight because she knew I had written this story." This was all true. I'd started a feature about Larken after discussing him in a journalism class. Fascinated by his rise from network newscaster to number-two man in Texas, I'd never dreamed that I would be so charmed by the man himself—let alone find myself a guest at his birthday party or hear him introducing me to the governor of my own state.

"Quite a lengthy sentence for a journalism major," Governor Melvin responded.

"That's before editing!" I quipped.

Putting his hand on my shoulder, Bob Larken joined in the laughter and said, "Stan, I like this girl. Maybe I should take her back to Texas to write my lines!"

Stan Melvin, a twinkle in his aging eyes, paused and quietly responded, "Yes, indeed. Maybe you should.

"Excuse me please, Miss Pullen, Bob. I need to mingle. That's what governors do, you know." He nodded courteously and sauntered away.

I turned my full attention on Larken and inquired, "So, what do lieutenant governors do?"

He responded again with that characteristic chuckle. "I wake up, look at the front page to see if the governor is still alive. Other than that, not much, really. I basically drink a lot of coffee while the governor governs. Would you care to join me in a cup?"

"Oh yes, thank you. Decaf, please. I don't do the real thing."

"I didn't think you were that kind of girl," he teased.

I'd heard that Bob Larken made people feel comfortable from the get-go, but I certainly never thought he would be this personable. Several guests stopped him as he made his way toward the beverage cart, which was set up behind the sofa. I guessed that he would take a few minutes to return.

Suddenly, the pianist struck a single chord and the entire party began singing "Happy Birthday." I looked over my shoulder to see that Larken's wife, Margaret, had joined him, and someone had wheeled up a cart that held a less-than-traditional birthday cake—an oblong replica of what I presumed was the Texas state capitol building. The cake was so large that it was easy to make out the lettering along the front. The bright red icing read "Congratulations, Bob, on a capitol year! Happy 39th!" With a dead body having been found in the capitol, red wouldn't have been my choice for the icing. Then again, Glinnis had died of a heart attack. It wasn't like he was murdered.

It's a strange feeling, being on the periphery of a party. You're an outsider amid all the excitement and action going on around you. I stood there wondering if I should walk across the room and join the lieutenant governor in the coffee he had offered me, or simply disappear. I noticed two cups on the table just to his left, but Mrs. Larken was with him now. She was not at all what I'd expected. I'd only read one article that mentioned Margaret Larken, although I did see a photo of her in a feature shortly after his appointment. She looked much younger in the photo. In person, her skin was starting to show the signs of living too long in the sun. I bet that I could find surgical scars from a very adept plastic surgeon behind her ears. Margaret Larken's heavily woven blonde hair was cut short in a severe style. She was petite and well groomed, but her smile—there was something about her smile. She seemed to speak through a constant, forced smile. Tension surrounded her. To be the wife of such an enthusiastic and effervescent man—there was something that just didn't seem to fit.

As I continued my internal speculations Governor Melvin rose, holding a champagne flute in one hand.

"Friends. Before the lieutenant governor's charming wife cuts the cake, I would like to propose a toast. To Robert Bentley Larken—who has gone from covering politicians to making excuses for politicians!" Laughter broke out and I could see the second-in-command for the state of Texas looming behind the governor. Once the applause died down, I noticed Larken passing his drink to his wife. He was starting back toward me.

"Beth! Things got a little hectic over there. I'm sorry I forgot your coffee."

"You know, I never even remembered to wish you a happy birthday, sir."

"That's okay....Oh. Here comes my wife. I'll introduce you."

As Margaret Pullen approached, I noticed that she carried a piece of cake. Our eyes locked as she coolly nodded her head toward me.

"Margaret, this is Beth Pullen, a freelance writer and friend of a friend of a friend." Again, the chuckle and sly grin. "She's doing a piece on me."

"It's a pleasure...."

She interrupted me and in a testy voice said, "I'm sure it is. Bob, I know how much you love seeing your name in print."

He looked down at the piece of cake she handed him and noticed the icing letters.

"*BO—*. That's a start. Maybe if I'm in office long enough I'll get the whole name!"

Everyone around us seemed to enjoy this bit of humor, except for his wife.

I saw an opportunity and took it.

"Mrs. Larken, I'm wondering how you feel, having been thrust into the role of political wife. Rumor has it that your husband is now in position to run for governor come the fall. Governor Biltmore will be term-limited. How have you transitioned from private to public life?"

"Dear, I've been asked that a million times. I'll give you the same answer I give to everyone else. I am Bob Larken's wife. 'Whither thou goest I will go'—I stand beside my husband no matter what his choices may be. It, of course, was very unfortunate that he decided to enter the political arena this way— with the unfortunate death of our beloved Billy G."

She glanced down and attempted to look heartbroken. Instead, Mrs. Larken seemed to have a twinkle in her eyes rather than tears.

"Oh yes, I'm sure it was a great shock. There have been rumors of foul play."

"To that I have no comment!"

Turning on her ever-so-perfect heels, Mrs. Larken headed back to the cake table, picked up the knife and began cutting and delivering squares of cake. It seemed to be her mission in life.

"Excuse me, please, I need to get something," I explained as my eyes darted around the room. Margaret Larken had apparently become perturbed. I wasn't sure why but for now I needed to regroup and recapture some lightheartedness. That always puts people at ease. With their guard down you could always get more info.

I have a nasty habit of muttering to myself. Somehow it keeps me focused. "Lighten up," I told myself. Out of nowhere I started murmuring, "Get the other *B*" as I approached an elderly man standing next to Mrs. Larken. Noticing that he'd put his cake down on the table next to him, I quickly snatched up the plate and returned to the small group that had gathered around the birthday boy.

Marching right up to Larken with my find, I declared, "Investigative reporter Beth here, sir. I found the other *B*. I know how people hate to have their names misspelled in print."

With a look of amazement, the lieutenant governor asked, "Where did you get *that*?"

"Over there. That man the one walking towards us. I didn't think he'd notice."

The man appeared to be in his seventies and was rather dapper in appearance. A slender man, he stood at about six feet with a full head of gray hair. In his tailored brown tweed suit he looked like he'd walked straight off the cover of a *GQ* magazine for seniors. Heading toward us with a swaggering gait and a grim look, he bellowed, "Okay. Okay. Explain to me exactly *why* you took my cake and ran off to give it to our fine guest of honor, young lady!"

I knew I was going to ramble, but all of a sudden I was nervous.

"Well, Mrs. Larken gave the lieutenant governor the first piece of cake and the final *B* was missing from his name. I noticed she gave *you* the second piece with the missing consonant." Somehow, I felt like Vanna White.

Governor Melvin was standing right next to Mrs. Larken. Why had she crossed the room to give this man the second piece of cake, ignoring the governor?

Noticing the look of puzzlement on my face, Bob intervened. "John and I have been best of friends for years. I guess you could call him my mentor. John, this is Beth Pullen. Beth, meet John Gaynor, the person formerly in possession of the final *B*."

John Gaynor. I made a mental note of the name.

"Mr. Gaynor, I'm doing a piece on the lieutenant governor. It was nice to have met you. Would you mind if I gave you a call?"

"Certainly not, young lady. I love talking about Bob and I certainly do appreciate the boldness you showed in getting what you want!" He handed me his card and when I looked up to thank him, I noticed how his eyes sparkled. Despite the years that had weathered his once-fine features, he had a delightful, boyish grin.

"If you need anything at all, please do give me a call."

"Thank you, thank you so much. I appreciate it."

John Gaynor returned to the festivities and I walked through the crowds looking for the nearest bathroom. Walking down the hall I spotted an open door to what appeared to be a den or library. Inside I noticed walls of books lining the cozy room, which had a second door. Luckily for me, it led to a half bath. I closed the door, grateful for a reprieve from the commotion of the party. Within minutes I heard a voice that began to escalate into a fevered pitch.

"Dammit, I don't care! That woman has got to learn. I know, I know. But she's Bob's wife for God's sake. If he's going anywhere she has got to tone down that attitude. She got this ball rolling, now she'd damn well better get in the game!"

The voice was that of John Gaynor. He was obviously on the phone. He wouldn't be foolish enough to be on a cell phone, so I assumed he was on a hard line. The line would need to be secure for a private conversation. What did he mean by "She got this ball rolling?" I remained as silent as I could.

"No. Absolutely not. No more money. The matter is not open for negotiation. I'm telling you it was a heart attack!"

With that the conversation ended. I stayed, motionless for a few more minutes, to allow him to exit the room.

I needed to write an article. Any article. Just write an article and get it to Larken. Keep the lines of communication open. There was something here and it was more than his smooth drawl and handsome face. I didn't think he was involved in whatever was being hushed—but Margaret Larken might very well be another story.

Bob Larken fascinated me. There was something innocent, yet strong about him.

He was personable, approachable—everything his wife was not. I'd been somewhat sheltered but I was, if nothing else, astute.

Blending my way back among the crowd, I spotted Gaynor standing alone, looking around the room. He almost appeared to be summing up each person in attendance. I smiled and headed directly over towards him.

"Mr. Gaynor, a handsome man like you shouldn't be alone at a party."

I poured it on.

"You know, I recently graduated as a journalism major. I did my senior thesis on political broadcasters. That's how I began researching Lieutenant Governor Larken. That was, of course, while he was still with KFIX in Austin. He did quite a few broadcasts for CNN—when I saw his broadcast on daycare issues I spotted a man with great talent, perseverance and drive. I believe Texas will benefit from a man like him in government."

"That's our Bob, all right. He's headed for the top. No doubt about it."

His smile was genuine—almost boastful.

"How did you get to know him?"

"Oh that's a story in itself. Best saved for another time, or when you interview Bob he can tell you. It's quite a tale!"

"I have the entire night ahead of me, sir."

"That's too bad—a cute girl like you should be having fun, not spending it with an old codger like me." He winked. It was almost an identical wink to that of Bob Larken's.

15

"Thank you for the compliment—and we will talk another time."

At that point, he nodded his head and disappeared among the partygoers.

Walking back over to where the lieutenant governor was standing I tried to just blend in. I'd no more than arrived by his side than his wife appeared, seemingly out of nowhere.

"Miss, oh, I'm sorry, I've forgotten your name."

"Miss Pullen. Beth Pullen." I loved saying my new name, although I was not yet entirely comfortable with it.

"That's right. Miss Pullen, is there something I can help you with? My husband is a very busy man, as you can see." Why did she want to keep me away from him?

"I just wanted to ask a few questions."

"I'm sure I'd have the answers. Please feel free."

This seemed odd to me since she'd cut me off so abruptly earlier.

"All right, then. There is some speculation as to the health of the former lieutenant governor." Before I could finish my question, she again cut me off.

"Miss Pullen, I'm sorry. This is a birthday party in honor of my husband. This is not a press conference. I can assure you we are all distressed by Billy's loss. It was a great blow to the state of Texas. You can quote me as saying that."

Once again, she left with no further explanation. The lieutenant governor turned his head and glanced at me, but was unable to break away from his admirers. Perhaps it was best to leave and get started on my outline, I decided. Above all else, I needed to clear my head of the sights and sounds of the party.

This was insane. I'd heard about actors, singers and politicians—men who mesmerize women beyond their ability to cope. It was an unfathomable concept—until tonight. Now it was unnerving.

I must have looked like a fish out of water because this time John Gaynor approached *me*.

"The pianist is just about to play a medley of Bob's favorites."

"Oh. Thank you for letting me know, but it's been a long day for me. It's late and I really do need to find my way back to the hotel."

"Then let me escort you outside."

"Thank you, but I'll be fine. I don't see the governor or his wife. Someone must have nabbed them when we were discussing your stolen piece of cake."

It was easy to smile in John Gaynor's presence. Once I got over my initial fright, I noticed there was a softness to him that I imagine he wasn't comfortable showing very often. But still, it was there.

"Will you let them know the party was lovely? I really need to get going."

I admit to being superstitious so I left the way I came in—through the front door. The same young, tanned teen who had escorted me inside was waiting under the porch light. He smiled and extended his arm.

"There's a taxi waiting. It will take you back to your hotel. I hope you had a nice night."

As we walked back down the drive that would soon be rimmed with bursting lilacs, the beginning chords of Beethoven's Moonlight Sonata filled the air again. Turning to glance one last time at the Victorian home and the lovely gardens, I spotted Robert Larken standing in the bay window, looking out through the moonlight toward my waiting taxi. Our eyes seemed to meet across the distance. I smiled as my young escort opened the passenger door. I placed my hand on the taxi's door, noting the name "Cinderella."

I was glad it wasn't midnight yet.

*Katherine Shephard*

## Chapter Two

The phone was ringing as I unlocked the door to my hotel room. By the time I got to the phone, the line was dead. The message light was blinking and I started to laugh. You know, that laugh you get when you're too tired to function? My friend Victoria had probably called a half-dozen times wanting every last detail on every man in attendance.

I didn't take time to settle in. I wanted to write and return what calls I had received. My one suitcase and garment bag sat alone on the bed. They could wait. Pressing "7" to retrieve my messages I positively smirked when I heard Governor Melvin's voice.

"Miss Pullen, I'm sorry my wife and I were busy when you left. I would be happy to meet with you concerning your article on Bob Larken. If you call my office, ask for Lydia, my assistant. She'll be expecting your call."

Rack one up for the budding journalist. Vic said it couldn't be done. "Governors don't call anyone," she'd told me. Guess she didn't know *everything* about men.

Vic and I had known each other since kindergarten and we'd always been an unlikely duo. Standing erect she was a sweeping five-foot-eleven. Her jet-black hair shone to an almost blue hue.

Parted on the side, it hung over one eye to her chin with the other side cut so short you could see her scalp. I always felt as if I needed to tilt my head to even her out. Her gait, unlike mine, was smooth and fluid, her facial features almost bony, her fingers long and expertly manicured. On the contrary, my fingers were short with nails that revealed how I spent most of my days: typing notes or playing the piano.

Differences aside, we were as close as Siamese twins and as competitive as siblings. I couldn't wait to go "neener neener" with this little tidbit. Being a political science major Vic prided herself on knowing politicians, their motives and moves. Granted, she'd known more than a few politicians in her brief tenure at the capitol, but sex aside, I was the winner of this round.

Smiling, I pressed "7" again, waiting for the next message. I sat, frozen as a statue, when I heard Bob Larken's voice. The number he left was his private line—I assumed his cell phone—which I immediately dialed.

"Larken here" was all he said.

Without even identifying myself I responded, "How did you know where I was staying?"

"You're not the only investigative reporter in town, Ms. Pullen. Will you be staying on the Island long?"

"No, I plan to leave in the morning. I should have my rough draft written tonight. I'm a bit of a night owl when writing. I'm inspired, sir!" I didn't mention that my inspiration came in the form of overhearing Gaynor talk about hush money and Margaret Larken in the same breath.

"Would you like to stay another day? We're having a sixteenth birthday party for our son, David John. It might be fun. A younger crowd." He chuckled as he spoke. "If you're not having to rush back to meet some sort of deadline, maybe you'd like to meet him and enjoy a much less formal Larken event."

His voice was sincere, his mood upbeat and casual. Like an old friend, even though we'd just met. Is this how a politician tries to impress a new journalist? It's all about positive press, I'd been told. Prove me wrong, Larken. Prove me wrong.

"Wow. That would be great. Sure. I can stay one more day but I'll need to see if the room is available."

"Not to worry. It's been taken care of. A taxi will be there at four. It's just a pizza party. The kids might play some pool or go to a movie. I'm sure you didn't come with a full wardrobe—well, unless you're like my wife." He almost snorted when he laughed at his own comment. "This is just a jeans-and-a-sweater affair."

I loved the way he said "affair." Yes. I was losing it.

"Okay. Thank you, sir. I'll be ready. Thanks so much."

We said brief goodbyes and I immediately dialed Victoria. She won't believe this, I kept thinking.

"Vic, um, I would have called sooner but I got invited to the lieutenant governor's son's sixteenth birthday party tomorrow. I was wondering what color sweater to wear."

"Well my oh my. Aren't you two just the best of friends now." I could feel her smirk as she continued, "You're a quick study, girl. How'd this come about? Or shouldn't I ask?"

"Oh shut up. No. He called me."

"He did *what*? *Who* called you? Larken?" she was nearly shouting.

"Yeah. Larken. You know, the lieutenant governor of Texas?" It was my turn to smirk. "He called me but I wasn't in yet. He left his private cell number so I called him back. That was right after I picked up the message that the governor had called, too."

"The *who*?" Okay. Now she was shouting.

"The governor. Governor Melvin? Of Michigan?" I was enjoying this. Making one of those little raspberry noises into the phone I couldn't resist saying, "Told ya so!"

"You didn't. Please tell me you didn't. Did I just lose a bet?"

"Yep, Vic, you did."

"You and Mr. Dreamy Voice himself are quite the party animals now. I guess dreams *do* come true. I suppose there's some saint for this crap?"

"Vic, come on now—he's almost forty! Anyhow I was just a *little* taken with his voice."

Right. I'd spent hundreds of hours researching Bob Larken. I'd listened to tapes and seen several television broadcasts he made before jumping the journalistic ship when the incumbent LG keeled over.

Larken had been a political analyst with a station out of Austin. His voice had a unique and distinctive tenor with the smoothest drawl I'd ever heard. I had pored over pictures downloaded from the Internet and noted that his hair, in every picture, was sprayed into place with perfection. A strong jaw line gave credence to his self-confidence as he spoke every word with amazing conviction. To garner prime-time air on CNN, I knew he must have quite a story to tell. Any way you sliced it, he was easy on the eyes and, considering I hadn't had a date since bouffant skirts were in style, I'd been happy to settle for a fantasy man to dwell on my senior year of college. Okay. Maybe it hadn't been that long since I had a date, but I usually knew when the sorority house phone rang, it wasn't for me.

"Chrissy, you still there?"

"Oh, sorry, Vic, I was daydreaming." That was nothing unusual for me these days. "Listen, I have another clothing
dilemma. He told me what I wore to the governor's was too formal. I'm suppose to wear jeans and a sweater, but I don't know," I lamented.

"Apparently you *do* have a dilemma if he remembered what you were wearing. Trust me I *never* wear the same thing for night number two." This was a caustic quip on Victoria's end of the line.

"Stop it already! Now, I did bring jeans and a yellow sweater. I could wear the yellow sweater." I was starting to get nervous. I ramble when I get nervous.

"Nice. The yellow sweater. It's the one with the low neckline, right? You usually wear it with your gold chain. Good choice. Got to wear jeans—he's from Texas, you know? They're tight, right? Say, how old is Mrs. Bob?" She was getting sassy.

"It's Margaret, Vic. Margaret. I heard several of the women call her Mag."

"Oh, as in *hag*?" Vic was in quite the spirited mood.

"*No!* I mean, we'll she's just a few months younger than the lieutenant governor, I think." I was getting flustered.

"Well, enjoy yourself Chrissy. Don't forget to call, okay?"

"Oh I'll call. But my name is now Beth."

"It's *what*? And *why*?" Yes. She was shouting again.

"I'll explain later. I promise. The yellow sweater. Is that okay? I mean really okay?"

"Yes. Trust me. I'll be waiting for all the dirt."

I could feel her smile as I placed the receiver back on the phone's cradle before saying thanks or goodbye. I'd moved from dazed to more dazed to dazeder. Oh wow. Now I was making up words. This was bad.

Reaching for my suitcase, I pulled out my research notes and set up my typewriter. For now, I'd work from my previous research just to prove I knew my stuff. I'd delve deeper once I'd interviewed Larken and Gaynor.

> *In six months Robert Bentley Larken has gone from reporting the news to making the news.*
>
> *At the recent bill signing, the prevailing spirit of unity left hope—for both sides of the fence—that peaceful coexistence can prevail under the Capitol dome. The fence in question? The proposed state of Texas fencing requirement for preschools and early childhood centers. To protect the children, lawmakers wanted to couple the requirements with higher levels of private or in-house security.*

*However, the legislature was at an impasse because school owners protested that the proposed fencing and security requirements were onerous and expensive. Parents, on the other hand, considered the security issue paramount to their children's welfare.*

*As a deadlock ensued, it looked as if the bill would not make it through the first committee. At the eleventh hour Lt. Governor Larken, who has passionately testified on behalf of increased security measures where children are concerned, made a proposal that was acceptable to both sides.*

*Larken proposed that the fencing around schools and daycare centers be 10 feet high with no mention of hiring security guards. This is consistent with the current fencing requirements for swimming pools and spas. The Lt. Governor's proposal alleviated the economic and safety concerns of both sides of this debate, creating common ground that moved the bill into law with a minimum amount of opposition. Similar bills are now being considered by other states.*

*Such hands-on involvement by a lieutenant governor is rare. The simple fact that child advocates, parent groups and school administrators could all rally behind the same banner indicates that Robert Larken's skillful negotiating skills will serve not only the state of Texas, but also the entire nation for years to come.*

Now for a title. At this time of night—or morning as it were—I tended to get what Daddy affectionately called "the giggles" and suggest we go to IHOP. Since there is no IHOP on the Island, I giggled alone as I typed "Lanky Lt. Governor Looks After Kidlets" before grabbing my little vial of white correction fluid. "Luscious Larken Lures Passage." Okay. That might be over the top. What about "Beautiful Bob Beams in Spotlight"? I need coffee, I thought.

Two cups later it came to me.

*LT. GOVERNOR MENDS THE FENCE*
  *Byline: Christine Elizabeth Pullen*
  No.
*LT. GOVERNOR MENDS THE FENCE*
  *Byline: Beth Pullen*


Weary from writing, typing and the day's activities, I laid my head down on the desk and fell asleep. Suddenly my head jerked up, startled by the ringing of the phone near my right ear. I glanced at my watch. Hell. It was nearly noon.

"Hello?" I must not have sounded like myself. Might have been the crick in my neck or the caffeine headache.

"They must have rung the wrong room. I'm sorry."

Not wanting the caller to hang up, and recognizing the voice despite my groggy state I yelled into the receiver "*No! Wait!* Bob! It's me. No. I mean—no, Lieutenant Governor, it's me. Chris. I mean Beth. Good morning, sir. I mean good afternoon, sir." I shook my head hoping the cobwebs would exit and sane conversation would enter.

From the other end of the line came that familiar chuckle. Damn.

"I was just calling to verify that you remembered the party. Apparently it's a good thing I called to awaken you before the taxi arrives."

"Funny. Very funny, sir." I was beginning to feel more comfortable speaking with him and that unnerved me.

"So, you should probably start getting ready, you only have several hours. I know how you women fuss." The playful banter made my anticipation grow.

"I also need to pack up and check out. I'll take the eight or nine o'clock plane back to St. Ignace if I can get a reservation. The last plane out is at ten, I think." I was making a mental checklist as we spoke.

"Eight or nine at night? Tonight? That's not very safe. Once you get to where your car is parked that makes it a long drive alone in the dark." He definitely was sounding like a father.

"Listen, I'll arrange for another night at the hotel," he continued. "The manager owes me from the old days. Hey, I have to pick up some things for Margaret at the pharmacy near your hotel." Sure, I thought. What—wrinkle cream? I was making myself smile as he continued. "Let me swing by and pick you up myself." Heard *that* one before. "You'll recognize me. I'll be the one that looks like a politician riding in a taxi."

I wished he'd lose either the chuckle or the drawl. The combination was lethal.

"Sure. That's great. I'm in room 310." What was I doing? I just gave a married man my room number.

"I know. Remember, I found where you were in the first place and have called your room?" We both laughed. Even though my hair was auburn, sometimes I felt so blond.

"Okay, then. I'll be ready. I appreciate the invitation. Is this a social event or do you mind if I take mental notes?" Once a journalist, always a journalist.

"Miss Pullen, this can be whatever you want it to be. See you then." I was in big trouble.

Glancing around the room for the first time, I noticed it was Victorian in every sense—right down to the rose-pink, lace-trimmed bath towels and crystal bowls filled with scented bath salts. It reminded me of a bed-and-breakfast Daddy talked about on the Gulf Coast of Texas. The Queen's Inn I believe it was named. Daddy was always talking about Texas but I'd never been.

I freshened up, changed into my jeans, sweater and loafers, remembered to put on my gold chain and dangle earrings, and arrived downstairs just as the taxi turned the corner. The driver opened the back passenger door and I joined Robert Bentley Larken in the back seat.

I noticed the lieutenant governor looked much younger dressed in casual clothes. He was wearing the same style of slacks as the teenaged attendants wore the night before, except his were denim. A yellow polo shirt peeked out from beneath a multicolored tweed jacket. His loafers were polished, his hair, as always, impeccably groomed—his smile wide and bright. I finally realized where I was. Sitting next to me was one of fifty people positioned to take over if a governor left office or was unable to perform his duties for any reason. Actually, sitting next to me was the nation's newest and youngest addition to those ranks.

As I turned to look out over the water I caught a glimpse of Larken's chiseled profile and how his broad shoulders tapered to a narrow waist. It was then that I realized his golf shirt matched my sweater. We were color coordinated. Oh, Vic will *love* this.

As I smiled at the thought he said, "Something catch your fancy?"

It was difficult not to reply "You." So, I merely responded with "I finished the article!"

"You work fast," he quipped.

"So I'm told." What was I thinking, making that comment? I couldn't help it. He was so—I don't know. I really didn't know how to describe it. Like an old shoe? Comfortable. A good fit. Strange as it seemed.

Once we reached the governor's mansion, the lieutenant governor, in true Southern gentlemanly fashion, hopped out of the taxi and thanked the driver. After mumbling something else he came around to offer me his hand. My feet had barely touched the ground when the door to the home opened and Margaret appeared.

"Oh Bob, you did remember the errands, right?" she inquired with a fake smile.

It was difficult not to say, "Well, hello to *you*, too."

"Yes, of course. The pharmacy. It was right by Miss Pullen's hotel." His tone was rigid as he spoke with his wife. "Strained" was a better word, perhaps.

"Oh yes. Miss Pullen. Nice to see you again. How's that little article you're attempting to write coming along?"

I was not enjoying this exchange. I felt like a total outsider, but sometimes that could be fun. Deciding to spice it up a bit I replied, "It's done, actually and thank you for asking." My sweet smile could have melted butter.

The lieutenant governor seemed to be enjoying this banter too as he stood back, grinning.

"I love your dress, Mrs. Larken. I'm surprised it's not yellow, though, to match the lieutenant governor."

"Oh no. Yellow doesn't become me."

"Really? It's one of my better colors."

I adjusted the cuffs of my canary-colored sweater, turned on my heels and walked into the party. I immediately spotted David John Larken surrounded by a group of friends. The resemblance to his father was startling. I looked around. David's father was at the door paying the delivery boy for the pizzas; his mother had gone into another room. I took this moment of awkward strandedness to hand my gift to David.

"Hi guys! Happy birthday, David, I'm Beth, a friend of your father's. Well, I'm a journalist, really."

"Hi journalist Beth," he quipped. Same sense of humor. "Thanks for coming and for the gift. You can call me D.J. All my friends do. Dad calls me Dave. Mom calls me 'baby.' I prefer D.J.," he joked.

"Well, I know when girls turn sixteen you call them Sweet Sixteen. So what are you?" I asked.

A cute blonde responded with "How about Dynamo D.J.?'" as the rest of his friends broke into typical teenaged laughter.

It finally dawned on me. The Texas twang. All these kids had what we northerners call an "accent"—but we were in Michigan. Did they all come up here just for this party? Okay. I had to ask.

"D.J., these are you friends from Austin? Quite a trip!"

"Ayep. Good thing it's a weekend, but they flew up. It was my birthday present from my folks. Pretty great, huh?" Typical teenage comment. He was charming and personable, just like his dad.

D.J. then looked down at the bag. "The Island Resort. Looks interesting!"

He tore open the card. It was a cutout of a clown. The hotel's card selection had been slim. It was that or a sympathy card. He read out loud, "To a sweet boy on his birthday." Everyone laughed again.

The blonde girl was at it again "Oh, I get it—sweet sixteen! Yeah, and never been kissed, right D.J.?"

Only when she said his nickname it came out as "deej." I thought I spotted the younger Larken blush.

"Shhh Michelle! My folks are right over there!" he reprimanded the girl.

At the reference to his parents, I glanced back to where the lieutenant governor and his wife were now setting out the pizza buffet. Seeing that I had just given D.J. the birthday bag, the elder Larken made his way over to his son.

"So what do we have here, Dave?" The younger Larken opened the bag and pulled out a rolled-up MSU sweatshirt. Luckily the one I'd brought with me was brand-new—and the best I could do on short notice.

"Well, well, well—looks like the charming Miss Pullen is hinting that you need to set your sights on her alma mater, son." His wide smile was all the thanks I needed.

"Wow. Thanks, Miss Pullen." In typical teen style Dave turned to tear open another package.

"Beth, come and join Margaret and me for a cup of coffee. The kids will have some pizza and then head off to a movie. They'll be back later to play some pool."

He extended his arm and placed his hand on my back to lead me over to where his wife was sitting. Was that an electrical bolt I felt? Shake it off, girl.

"Beth, how do you take your coffee?" Margaret's nose-in-the-air attitude was foreign to me. I'd been raised with formality yet found her speech and manners stilted.

The lieutenant governor broke in "Cream, Margaret. She takes cream." I smiled. He remembered. That had to count for something.

I also noticed the lieutenant governor wasn't drinking from a china cup, like his wife and me. Rather he had a mug inscribed with "Never trust anyone under forty."

He noticed my quizzical look and responded, "Ah yes, the mug. It was a birthday gift, yesterday, from the lieutenant governor of *your* state. I guess he figures everyone has another year before they can trust me."

Again, Margaret didn't miss a beat. "Oh that man. Jim Parsons. He wants to be the next governor of Michigan. He's always been jealous of Bob's relationship with Stan and Bitsy. He thinks being tapped for second-in-command is his way in. He hates Democrats. Hates the fact that Bob is so enormously popular with all the governors. He's had it in for Bob ever since Bob did an interview with him—back when he was a broadcaster. He tripped that man up with a few stabbing questions. This was his way of saying 'We're watching you.' I'm sure of it."

"Well, that's a shame. But jealousy can run deep." I lamented. Lieutenant Governor Parsons. I might just need to talk with him. Hopefully Michigan's lieutenant governor wouldn't meet with the same fate as Billy G down in Texas before I could speak with him.

We ate our pizza in silence as the kids provided more than enough entertainment. I was surprised there weren't other adults in attendance, and felt oddly out of place. Perhaps I needed to make an early exit. A few coffee refills later I decided to break the silence.

"Thanks for including me today. It was wonderful meeting your son. I never expected this. Sir, when I was at the capitol last week, with my friend Victoria, I sat in on the education committee. They were discussing the school voucher initiative. It's on the floor in Texas, too, I believe. If something really interesting comes up on that, could you have someone let me know? It would make a great article."

"Absolutely, Beth. I'll see to it personally. That's a bill I find interesting myself, being a parent. Not to mention the fact that children's issues are at the top of my agenda. We are fortunate enough to be able to afford a private education for Dave. We've had the privilege of choice. But it shouldn't be a privilege. It should be a right. "

"You'd better watch it, sir, you're almost sounding Republican." I smiled and Margaret grimaced.

"Better get the mouthwash then."

Margaret didn't waste any time cutting off our laughter.

"Yes. Patricia. He'll have Patricia contact you."

I wasn't sure exactly who Patricia was but Margaret's attitude was starting to get damn annoying. I assumed Patricia was an aide of some sort. I just smiled and acted as though I knew exactly who she was and what she did.

"That would be great. Thanks so much."

"Billy G was against the initiative, wasn't he, Lieutenant Governor?"

"Yes, he was aligned entirely with the governor."

"And now," I forged on, "the governor has a formidable adversary with his new second-in-command. It must be murder working alongside someone with whom you disagree and yet must support."

I just put my coffee down on the table and stood there. Waiting.

"Bob, tell the taxi that Miss Pullen is ready to leave," Margaret said. "You can help me clean up before the kids return." The evening was suddenly abbreviated. I wondered to myself where the hired help was. I couldn't imagine Margaret cleaning.

Bob Larken did as he was told. The taxi pulled into the drive and it was time for me to say my farewells.

"Again, thank you both for everything. I'll make sure you see the article before it's submitted—and I'm looking forward to hearing from Patricia."

"I'm sure you are, dear." Margaret's words always seem to be cutting in their delivery. I really wanted to stick my tongue out at her. Wouldn't that be a kick? Instead I just smiled. No guts.

"Well, goodbye then."

Tonight's taxi would probably be orange.

Cinderella one night—a pumpkin the next.

## Chapter Three

Once again, back at the hotel, I surrounded myself with pink pillows on the raised antique bed and lay there thinking. Didn't care that my mouth felt like sandpaper and smelled like stale coffee. Didn't care that my mascara would probably rub off on the pristine linen pillowcase. I just thought.

We were so different, the lieutenant governor and the frisky freelancer. Our backgrounds couldn't have been more diverse. He, an only child, adopted by ordinary parents. Me, an only child, with anything *but* ordinary parents. Bob Larken, while of simpler means, always surrounds himself with successful people. As for me—I just tend to bumble along and rely on my dad. That has got to change, I vowed.

Larken loved to talk, which accounted for his proficiency in broadcast journalism. In fact, reflecting back on our time together, I had said comparatively few sentences. What I'd learned would give me more than enough for a second article on Robert Larken. "From Reporting the News to Making the News" is how I saw it. A profile. I had watched him carefully. I saw how he worked the crowds. Saw the effect he had on people. Saw that smile. Heard that chuckle. Okay. Maybe I *was* obsessed, but how many women have been renamed by a lieutenant governor? That was the last thought that crossed my mind before I drifted off to dreamland.

The morning came all too quickly. Luckily, with little luggage and a cup of coffee to go, I could head out the door and be on my way. Goodbye UP, hello reality.

Once comfortably on solid ground, mini-flight behind me, Peg and I hit the road. Rolling down my window, I started to sing. In my next life I hoped I'd get to be Bonnie Raitt. The words to "Something to Talk About" just burst forth with no regard for tempo, tone, or key. I pitied the poor folks sharing the highway with me today.

As I flew south, I took in the natural beauty of my state. Where else could there be such a blending of sights and aromas? Oh, Daddy would tell tales of the Hill Country in Central Texas. Said it was like Michigan with a drawl and an attitude. But I was sure it couldn't even come close to these lakes, trees and birds just on the verge of spring. I kept singing all the way back to Lansing.

Close to the city limits of the state capital, the Monday evening traffic became heavier. Cars crowded even the carpool lanes—Chryslers, Chevys and Fords for the most part. Michiganders don't take kindly to foreign makes and models. Seeing the capitol dome in the distance, I took the downtown loop and headed toward Michigan Avenue. Curiosity took over my better senses and I decided to pay a visit to Lieutenant Governor Parsons. From what I'd heard at the pizza party, Michigan's LG seemed to be holding a serious grudge against Bob Larken.

Now that I'd listened to Margaret's version, it was time to hear the other side. After all, that was good investigative journalism, right? A fair evaluation of Larken. As if that would even come close to happening with me. But I could try. Maybe Parsons would have something to share about Billy G's heart attack. It was after hours but I decided to take a risk.

I parked directly in front of the Olds Office Building and noticed a state trooper perched on the stairs to the aging brick structure. The building looked deserted, but I decided to approach the guard and do what Victoria would do. Smile.

"Excuse me, sir, could you tell me where the lieutenant governor's office is, please? He said he'd be in late this evening. We attended a party at Governor Melvin's together—two nights ago. He's not expecting me, it's kind of a surprise."

I was hoping my wink and sickeningly sweet smile would do the trick.

"The offices are closed, ma'am, but you can try back after nine tomorrow morning."

Okay. Plan Two. The pathetic look.

"Oh what a shame. You know how he loves surprises."

I cut my eyes at the young trooper, hoping that he'd take the bait. Younger woman. Older politician. Everyone knows that scenario.

"Well...since you are a friend. Sign the registry—his office is on the seventh floor. I normally would call ahead, but you said it was a surprise."

"Thank you so much. I really appreciate this, sir." I smiled coyly and headed for the elevator.

Having run out of clothes during my extended stay on Mackinac, I'd thrown on my good wool trousers this morning. I looked fairly professional for a fledgling writer. Fledgling is right, I thought—what the hell would I do or say if I found the lieutenant governor? Worries crowded my mind. How would I explain my unannounced presence? Suddenly, I knew just the scenario. When all else fails, blame Margaret!

The hallway was wide with tiled floors and high ceilings. It had the weighty feel of history. The aging walls had been painted a nondescript cream; the doorways were tall and wide, made of thick, solid wood. There was only one office down this hall with light streaming from beneath the doorway. As I looked up there it was. "Lt. Governor James W. Parsons." The official seal for the State of Michigan was above the nameplate. Impressive. Knocking, I held my breath.

"Lieutenant Governor, sir, it's Beth Pullen. I'm a friend of Bob Larken's," I called out in a loud voice, hoping to be heard beyond the solid door.

I was amazed at how easily the name Bob tripped off my tongue. I wasn't sure it was really Parsons inside but then again, my bets were pretty lucky these days.

The door opened and there stood a middle-aged man, balding and overweight. My first thought was: How could someone with such horrendous teeth get elected? Maybe politicians should be judged by their teeth, like horses. I could smell the smoke on his clothes. Disgusting habit. One thing in his favor: he was well groomed, with his moustache neatly trimmed and hair—well, what hair he had—moussed into little curls. I'd seen him on TV but nothing could compare to the real thing. Now I see why he never smiled on camera and stood behind a podium or desk during interviews.

"Well, now, I should have expected Bob to have an attractive female friend. He always did pick pretty ones."

His tone was smooth, his voice deep and mellow. If nothing else, he had a voice to die for. I would have liked to close my eyes and just listen to his voice without having to look at the spare tire around his middle.

His comment about Bob always 'picking pretty ones' made me wonder how many women Larken had used his charms on. Leave it to me to pick a playboy politician.

"I was at the lieutenant governor's birthday party, at Governor Melvin's the other night. I noticed the mug you gave him. Pretty clever."

I smiled and tried to make him comfortable. I think he must have been somewhat unnerved by my presence because he started to chew his moustache. I tried not to grimace as his face contorted, allowing his lower lip to reach up on one side.

I continued my sweet, wheedling dialogue.

"I'm taking notes for a profile on Mr. Larken. His wife, Margaret, commented that there was some bad blood between you two. Mind if we talk?"

I started to walk closer to his massive presence before he could tell me no, call security or laugh in my face. More moustache chewing. Damn ugly sight.

I noticed his office was compact and tidy. Good thing, too. Being a small room, if it were cluttered there wouldn't be room for him to move his mightiness around. There were family photos everywhere. Nice touch. From what my quick perusal could register, he had a darling little blonde wife with a killer bustline. Two sons: one heavy and, unfortunately, resembling the lieutenant governor and the other looking more like the mom. Thick hair and broad shoulders. I glanced back towards the lieutenant governor, who was still standing by the door, just in time to hear his response.

"Well, it's no secret. Bob and I haven't seen eye to eye for several years. He interviewed me when Stan and I ran last election. Brought up how the governor and I disagreed on some upcoming key issues and that perhaps I was just wanting to play second fiddle so I could go for the dome. You know, the governorship?" His tone was still smooth.

"Yes, I know what the dome is, sir. You did seem to change a few of your beliefs after being vetted for the position. It seems you were pro-casino and then you changed sides once your name was put on the A-list. And there's the matter of school vouchers." I was starting to get into the swing of this.

"That's the opinion of some, of course. But Larken purposefully attempted to humiliate me on air. That doesn't sit well in the big leagues. The fraternity. You know?" He dove right into his upper lip. Apparently another disgusting habit.

"Is there anything you'd like to add to my potential profile, sir? That I could quote you on?"

I gave him the same sweet smile that had worked on the trooper downstairs.

"Well, actually, yes. You can quote me as saying: 'The people voted me in. Can Larken say that?'" He gave a crooked smile and tilted his balding head.

"Thank you, sir. I'll be sure you get a copy if I decide to run with it. I appreciate your time."

He held the door open for me. Admittedly, that was a nice gentlemanly touch. I noticed three two-liter bottles of Pepsi on the birch credenza, along with two empty pizza boxes and one nearly empty box of diet-type cookies. Those non-fat, high-carb things. Make that three disgusting habits.

Turning back towards our state's robust number two man, I asked, "Ever wonder how Larken got tapped for LG down in Texas?"

"No. I have no idea. There are rumors, but I don't spread rumors. Especially to reporters. You might try asking his wife, though. Doesn't that old adage go 'behind every successful man...'?"

"Yes, I guess it does, sir. Thanks again for your time."

I made my way back to the elevator and pushed "L"— wondering if my low opinion of our state's lieutenant governor was because of his appearance, his habits, or the fact that he didn't like Bob Larken. Something to ponder, especially since journalists were required to be impartial. I had to keep reminding myself about that.

Clicking my way back down the marble hallway, I looked at the automotive pictures hanging on the walls. I thanked the trooper again and headed back to Peg.

Zigzagging my way through side streets, I got to my apartment with just enough energy to take my suitcase inside. How bleak my tiny place looked in comparison to the gorgeous Victorian room I'd called home the past two nights. My one bedroom, one bath, tiny kitchen and living room were filled with antiques too, just like on the Island. Okay. Maybe not just like it—*my* antiques were really leftovers from Daddy's basement. A bit of this and that to make do until I got a place of my own. Daddy wanted to buy me a condo, but I'd listened to Vic. She told me it was time for me to stand on my own. Actually, I was surprised he hadn't bought one anyhow and given it to me on National Condo Day or some such—he could find a holiday for anything. I was grateful, though, that he'd given me a new typewriter and a fax machine. He said all true journalists type their notes on typewriters, even with the advent of computers. I just liked looking like the gal on "Murder, She Wrote" sitting there at my Smith-Corona.

Now that I was back home, I knew I should fax Larken the initial story for approval before shipping it off to the Free Press. I'd told him he could see it. Nothing really personal in this one. Just the facts, ma'am. Just the facts. I had his cell number and his fax number. I figure if he didn't want me to use them, he wouldn't have given them to me. Nice rationalization, I thought.

I changed the name on my fax cover sheet from Christine E. Pullen to Beth Pullen, inserted my phone number and hit "send." The first few tries came back with busy signals—third time was the charm.

Kicking off my shoes and changing into one of my requisite evening sweatshirts, I decided to make microwave popcorn for dinner. I was too tired to go out, there was nothing in my fridge, and by the time I could order out and have something delivered I might very well be asleep. I should call Daddy and Victoria, too. First the popcorn, though, with a cup of coffee.

Before the popping stopped the phone rang. Daddy. It had to be Daddy. I hadn't checked my answer machine yet but there were probably a half a dozen messages saying "Chrissy, don't forget to call when you get in."

Maybe Victoria was right. I *was* getting restless and I did need to break away from Daddy. She said it was codependency. Whatever that meant, I'm sure it wasn't good. I couldn't make a move without him wanting to know about it. I needed to do something on my own, for once. Even if it *was* being slightly infatuated with an older man. Harmless, since he was married. Plus I never thought I'd really meet him. I could study him for days and just tell Daddy I was doing research. Clever, if you ask me.

I waited to pick up the phone, dreading the onslaught of questions I knew would come from the other end of the line.

I shook my head as I answered, "Yes I'm home. Yes it was great. Yes I wrote a killer article." I wasn't prepared for the response.

"I'm glad you're home safely. Yes it was great and yes you wrote a killer article. Want a job?" The chuckle. Oh dear God the chuckle.

"Lieutenant Governor! Oh God, it's you!" Another embarrassing moment.

"I haven't gotten a response like that out of a woman in years. You flatter me."

My face, I'm sure, was as red as Texas granite.

"I'm so sorry. I just thought you were my father."

"Nothing like taking the wind out of a man's sail, Ms. Pullen." I could feel the smirk.

"I'm sorry. Really. You liked the article?"

"I must have. I just offered you a job, young lady! Would you like to work in my communications office?"

"Really? In *Texas*?" Stunned doesn't even come close.

"Yes. Really. In Texas. Billy G's staff didn't stay on when he died. They were much more to the left than I am. Guess they weren't comfortable, and neither was I."

"Well, I don't want to leave Michigan. I mean, I do, but I don't. It's so sudden. What position? When would I start?" I was babbling again.

"We could work something out. You could live there and just fly down now and then. With telecommunications the way they are that shouldn't be a problem, especially since you'll have a staff at the capitol."

"A *what?*" Okay, this had to be a joke.

"A staff. All communication directors have staffs. Granted, not as large as the governor's, but two staffers here in Austin. One full-time and one part-time intern. What do you say?"

"I say okay and *when?* Did you say *director?*" I needed to go to the bathroom.

"Yes. I said *director.* Can you fly down tomorrow? I'll have a ticket waiting at the airport. Metro in Detroit has a non-stop. I'd have you fly out of Lansing but I'd heard you hate small planes."

"I just got in, sir. I still have to unpack from Mackinac. Okay. Well, yes. Sure. I can do that. Absolutely. No problem here." Shut up Christine, I told myself. No, wait. Shut up, Beth.

"That's wonderful. We have code names for our staffers. The ticket will be under the name Sonata, is that okay?"

"It's perfect, Bob, just perfect." I hung up the phone, not having said thank you or goodbye. Not realizing I'd just called him Bob. All I knew is that I was looking out the window and the moon was lighting the sky. Another song came to my lips. "Moonlight becomes you. It goes with your hair."

Snap out of it, Beth. Pull yourself together. Oh God I was talking to myself again. Was there a saint to help with hysteria? I thought so, but I was too hysterical to think of it. Make a mental list. Okay. Here we go. Call Daddy. Call Victoria. Check Texas weather. Unpack, do laundry, repack. Maybe get some sleep before heading to Detroit Metro airport in the morning. I wouldn't be gone long, but I needed to make sure my lighter-weight clothes were fresh for the warmer climate in Austin. They'd been hanging for months in the back of my closet. No telling what dust bunnies had found homes in my cuffs and pockets.

Dialing the phone, my stomach began feeling like worms were crawling around inside of me. Or was that butterflies? I never could remember. How would Daddy take the news? Either he'd be thrilled or he'd think I was nuts. Hopefully, he'd like to feel the money he spent on my education was paying off. Then again, he didn't really trust politicians. That's why he encouraged my journalism career. So I could dig for the truth—not cover it up by working for a pol.

He picked up on the third ring with his usual spirited "Pullen residence, may I help you?" That's Daddy. Formal and set in tradition. What you were taught in Cotillion was God's own word. My heart began to race as the words left my mouth.

"Daddy, I'm home safely. Yes, it was quite an experience. Bob Larken is interesting, intelligent, and very cordial. Uh huh." I waited as he started with the questions.

"Yes, I even finished the piece and got it to him by fax. Just about thirty minutes ago. Actually he's already called me back. Yes. Yes. Called himself. No, it wasn't an aide. Trust me, Daddy, I know that voice."

I listened patiently as my father commended me, saying it must have been an outstanding article to elicit a personal phone call during evening hours.

"Well, Daddy, that's not all. I was offered a job. Yes. Full time. No, not here in Lansing. Well, sort of in Lansing. I'll be commuting back and forth a few days a month to Austin and working the rest of the time here, right here at home."

I imagined the entire apartment complex could hear him yell *"Austin?"*

"Yes, Daddy, Austin. Texas. The Lone Star State. Giant bugs. Cowboys. High humidity. No snow." The excitement was mounting.

"I'm going to start tomorrow! *Yes* that soon! Sit down, Daddy—I am going to be the lieutenant governor's communications director. I'm going to have a staff, even." My giggle sounded like a female version of the Larken chuckle.

"Listen, I have to call Vic and get to work. If you want to come over and say hello and goodbye I'd love to see you. Well, actually I'd love to have you calm me down some. Help me think of anything I'd need to take that I might be forgetting. Great. I'll see you in about an hour. I love you, Daddy." I smiled as I put down the receiver, hoping Daddy would stop by the ATM. Not that I *expected* a monetary sendoff—but I sure could use some cash.

Pushing the "2" on my speed dial, I didn't need to wait for the second ring before Vic answered with, "This better be you, Chrissy, I'm dying, just *dying* to hear every little last detail!"

"Vic, yep, it's me. I don't have time for details, really. I'm leaving for Austin tomorrow. Uh huh. Texas. No. Come on. It's not like *that!* He's married!" I had to laugh at my best friend's one-track mind.

"The two days were incredible. He's magnificent. We hit it off perfectly. His wife's a bit much but his son is a dreamboat! When he got the article he called me. Yes, I already faxed it off and he called me. Yes. Called. As on the *phone*, Vic."

I really wished she'd quit saying "You've gotta be shittin' me."

"He offered me a job as his communications director. He doesn't have one because the staff from the LG who died quit. Or he fired them. You never know what's really true. Yes, I'm going with my eyes open, Vic. I'll make sure I make the coffee so it's not poisoned."

Vic was trying to protect me. My dad was trying to protect me. I wondered: Can I protect myself?

"A ticket is going to be at Metro for me tomorrow. No, not with the name Beth, with the name Sonata. Oh. That's another story. Seems we both love Beethoven's Moonlight Sonata so when he went to choose my political code name that's what he chose. No, Vic, it's not *romantic*—it's business! Sure you can come over. Daddy's coming too. Uh-huh. Okay. Whenever. See ya."

Now that the two requisite calls were complete I began munching away on the cooled popcorn and poured myself what was left of the Pepsi in the fridge. Seeing the Pepsi reminded me of our own lieutenant governor, Jim Parsons. How could anyone let himself or herself go like that—I mean, he's a public official.

His wife is so *cute*. Just the thought of, well, let's not even get onto *that* subject! Made me shiver to think about it.

I emptied my suitcase, put my Smith Corona by the door, sorted the clothes and started the laundry. Not many of the apartment complexes in town had stackable washers and dryers in each unit. It was one of the things I loved most about my place and it was well worth the extra cost for the convenience.

Going through the back of my closet I started getting out more springtime clothes and talking to myself. "The average temperature is about sixty-five degrees this time of year in Austin, although there's supposed to be a warming trend this coming week. Supposed to get up to eighty, maybe higher, during the days. The nights can still chill you to the bone, though." To be safe I threw in my London Fog in case of spring thunderstorms.

Carefully folding my new suit, I heard that old familiar knock. Daddy always knocked twice, waited and then knocked twice again. It was our private signal.

"Use your key, Daddy, I'm packing!" I was sure he could hear me so I continued to sort and fold.

"Hey, Ms. Communications Director—got a hug for your lowly old dad?" I heard him call back as the door opened noisily. Darn squeaky door has needed WD-40 for a few months, I thought.

"Dad, come on back, calm me down."

The sight of my father warmed my heart. He was smiling, decked out in his woolen pea coat, a bag hanging from his left wrist. Okay. Smaller than a breadbox.

"Just put your coat on the chair and what's in the bag?" I smirked, knowing he'd done something sly again.

"Take a look, Chrissy. It's not much, really." He handed me the bag then draped his overcoat on the well-worn recliner. In honor of my new job he was wearing a red, white and blue vest. Daddy loved his vests.

Looking inside I saw a folded piece of paper. On it was drawn a rough likeness of the Titanic.

"Dad, um, the Titanic? Didn't that *sink*? This can't be a good thing." I started to get worried. I took the paper out of the bag and opened it up to see my father's writing:

> *Tomorrow night, March 23, 1998*
> *The movie "Titanic" is up for an Academy Award.*
> *It's a sure winner and so are you.*
> *Unlike the Titanic, you will set sail tomorrow*
> *AND SUCCEED! Here's a little sailing money. . . .*
> *I love you—you've made me so proud!*
> *Dad*

Underneath his signature were taped enough greenbacks to see me through the next week or two, until I got my first real paycheck. A real paycheck. What a concept.

"Thanks, Daddy" was all I could seem to say. If I continued I was sure to cry.

"So, what does a communications director wear, Dad?" All at once the nervousness kicked in and I knew I needed to keep occupied.

"Well, sweetie, be professional. In my office the gals wear suits and heels. I don't know. I don't look at them."

"Yeah right, Dad. You're the vice president of process engineering at Ford Motor Company, surrounded by women every day. You're a man. You look." I gave him that knowing glance with a laugh. A single knock interrupted our banter and Daddy headed for the living room.

He had no more than opened the door than I heard a familiar voice yelling "Oh my God! Where is she?" Before I could turn around there was Vic, swinging me around just like she did back at Crary Elementary.

"Girl—you did it! You not only *met* him, you're going to get paid to be with him! Isn't there a word for that?" I just shook my head.

"And speaking of *being* with him, *Beth*, here's a little present for you! Congrats, kiddo!"

Her wicked smile led me to believe I should not open this in front of my father, but I took my chances. Out of the pink-striped Victoria's Secret bag I pulled a yellow silk negligee. Lacy, low-cut with spaghetti straps. Then I read the note:

> *Beth—*
> *Yellow is your color. Enjoy.*
> *I hear it's about to get pretty hot in Texas.*
> *I'm sure you won't be lonely in the Lone Star State.*

"I can't believe this. Vic!" I tossed back my head in utter amazement and laughed. "Thank you—but—"

Before I could finish my sentence Daddy interjected with, "Oh yes, I'm sure that's just what my little girl will need. A chamois to polish her new car. That *is* what she just pulled out of that bag, right?"

"Can we please change the subject?" I had to snicker a bit.

We all sat on the bed as I gave them a Reader's Digest Condensed Version of the last three days, including my trip to see Michigan's lieutenant governor.

"I've heard he has a bloated ego to match his stomach," Victoria commented. "Everyone pretends they like him but he has no friends. Not a one. If he wanted to go shoot pool with the guys he'd have to pay them. Have you seen that God-awful ring he wears? It's this gold nugget glob shaped like Michigan. It has this diamond chip where Lansing is on the map. Whoever got him that thing has the taste of a mule. It just proves my point. He's pompous. Plus, Chrissy, you shouldn't like him just because he can't stand your lover boy!"

"Victoria Marie Wexford! As the newly appointed communications director for the lieutenant governor of the state of Texas, I must request that you call him, quite simply, my boss!" It was wonderful to have such a close friend.

We continued to discuss the physical, emotional and psychological ills of Jim Parsons while we finished packing.

"Don't forget the nightie, *Beth*."

"Vic, you are too much. You don't have to say Beth like it was the name of some sex goddess!"

"Oh no, *Beth*, you're much too young for a goddess. Perhaps a pleasure princess though."

Okay, I was ready to slug her.

Laundry done. Suitcase packed and locked. Newly acquired currency tucked into my wallet. I'm done, I reflected. Well, actually I'm just beginning, in a sense. The reality: I have a job. Not only a full-time job—but a job only forty-nine others can lay title to. The communications director for a lieutenant governor of the United States of America. Well, more accurately, the communications director for the foremost official in the line of succession to the governor's office. That sounded even headier, I thought.

"Daddy, Vic, I hate to cut this visit short—but I need to try and get some sleep. I have to get to Metro in plenty of time to park Peg in the long-term lot, get my ticket from the counter and make sure I have a decent seat. God I hate to fly. My stomach is just recovering from that puddle jumper I took to and from Mackinac."

"Sweetie, fine time to admit that, now that you have a job that will put you in the skies every few weeks. You going to be okay?" The paternal look of concern once again swept over my father's face.

"Just be sure to park your car under a light. *Please* be careful," he begged.

"Yeah, kid, be careful. The real world is waiting." Leave it to Vic to have the last word.

We hugged, the three of us. A new era of my life was about to begin. I had no idea how my life was about to change but I was ready to find out.

## Chapter Four

Before I could say "longhorn," I found myself landing at Austin-Bergstrom International Airport. The weather, according to the captain, was a comfortable seventy-eight degrees. I shoved my jacket into the pouch of my carry-on and took a deep breath. A note attached to my ticket had instructed me to look for a redheaded female as I exited the plane. That would be Patricia— Patricia Byrne, the woman Margaret Larken said would call me. Patricia hadn't called; Margaret's husband had. Chalk one up for the writer.

Yes. Patricia was unmistakable. Tiny in stature, with piercing eyes like a tiger's—penetrating with a depth meant only for intrusion. That long, brilliant red hair appeared, amazingly, natural. It was sleek, shiny and straight as a pin, hanging well below her shoulders. It seemed an odd style for someone I presumed to be in her forties, yet it suited her apparent aloofness. She stood motionless with head held erect, nose upturned and lips pursed. She looked as if she were awaiting execution.

"Miss Byrne?" I'd hoped my smile would break the icy glare.

"Yes, I'm Patricia Byrne. I'm assuming you're Ms. Pullen?"

I had just moved into the formal political world, apparently. Tossing my hair back I tried to emulate a sophisticate. I wanted to answer, "Yep, you got it" but decided it wouldn't be a smart move.

"Yes, I'm Beth Pullen."

"Do you have many bags? I can call for a porter." Her lips went back to the pursed position.

"No, thank you—I just have one suitcase, plus my typewriter. I'll only be here a few days, I think." I kept smiling as she kept glaring.

"We'll be heading for the suite. You'll be staying there when in town every month. It's a short walk from the capitol. It's normally used for in-town guests, but we'll be certain it's unoccupied when your services are necessary."

She made it sound like I was a hooker, not a communications director.

"That sounds wonderful. As long as it has a coffeepot we're all set." She found no humor in that remark.

We exited the airport into the still, warm air of Austin. The difference in humidity was remarkable. Michigan could be humid and muggy, but not in March. Not like this. I could already feel my skin begin to bead up in droplets of perspiration. Man, this was uncomfortable. I'd heard everything was bigger and better in Texas. Guess that went for the climate, too. Bigger pools of sweat. How attractive

As we approached the limo that was waiting curbside, I hoped the air conditioner was running. The driver hopped out as soon as he spotted the red-haired wonder. My instant impression of Patricia was "Don't mess with this one." There was nary a hint of a smile.

"Once you're settled in we'll have a driver take you around town to familiarize you with the city. Point out what's safe and what's not. Nice places to eat and to order takeout. You'll be ordering a lot of takeout to eat at your desk. I hope you're a night owl."

"Oh, I can be a night owl when needed. I used to stay up many nights around the clock right before finals." I immediately regretted that statement.

"Yes, that's right. Mrs. Larken said you were young. You're a recent grad. Michigan State, correct? Frank Pullen's daughter?"

"Do you know my father, Miss Byrne?"

I didn't recall Daddy ever talking about her, or Austin, and he really wasn't into politics. He'd been to San Antonio and the Hill Country, which he loved, and Houston, which he hated.

"It's my job to know."

It would take a very tall crane to extract her upturned nose from the air.

"And yes, it is *Miss* Byrne."

I really wanted to say "No joke. Who'd have you?" I smirked and it didn't go unnoticed, so I quickly responded with, "It's my job to know." Touché.

"So, Miss Pullen, have you spoken with the lieutenant governor recently?"

"No, just when Bob phoned and offered me the position."

"We refer to him as Lieutenant Governor Larken. I suggest you get used to it."

This first verbal exchange was making me feel more than a bit uncomfortable, so I decided to just smile. When in doubt, shut up.

"Remember, you are now the communications director. You're not at some birthday party anymore." Zing. Nice below-belt hit for the redhead.

"Oh yes, ma'am. I most certainly understand."

Handling the press is going to be a piece of cake compared to this chick, I thought.

"How long will it be until we get to the hotel?" Seemed like a safe enough question.

"Oh only about five more minutes." I calculated five minutes to be an eternity with Patricia. She was as ill-tempered as any bull in a Texas rodeo. I decided to save the questions and ride in silence

Looking out the side window of the white stretch limo, I gazed in awe at the various flowers and trees. I had no idea the trees would be so different. I spotted some mesquite and pecan trees, thanks to paying attention in my horticulture elective. The grayish-green oaks—live oaks, I guessed—were different from the cedar oaks back home. It was too early for bluebonnet season, but I'd heard that was something to behold. Blankets and blankets of blue covering the ground. I paid no attention to the street names or, really, the route we were taking. I figured I'd get a map once I was settled in.

We turned left at Sixth Street and then left at the light. The hotel entrance was on the right just before the next intersection. The "Crowne," as Patricia called it, was boxy in appearance and nestled downtown right by Town Lake. Sporadic trees were lined up along the curbside, contrasting nicely with the stark angles of the architecture. A bellman greeted us, immediately retrieved my bag from the back and whisked it away. How did they know what to do with it? My quizzical expression was what finally brought a smile to Ms. Irish Ice's face.

"Don't worry, dear. They know who we are." I wanted to do a "Saturday Night Live" impression and snort, "Well *excuuuuuuuse* me!" But I refrained. For now at least.

Our doors were held open and I obediently followed Patricia to the elevator.

"I understand you've met our state's second lady?"

"Second lady?" I decided to play dumb.

"Mrs. Larken." She was starting to get huffy. Maybe I was I getting to her.

"You know, you will be working very closely with the entire family, not just the lieutenant governor. The family is very closely knit and does everything as a partnership. Fifty-fifty. Side by side."

Side by side? Right. I noticed *that* at the party when he seemed to be by *my* side more than hers. The reference made me smile

"Yes, I've made her acquaintance. I was hoping she could give me her opinion on the former lieutenant governor for an article I was researching."

"I suggest you just drop that, Miss Pullen. You're no longer doing research for some article; you are now working for us.

Billy G had a heart attack—it was unfortunate and it's history. Robert Larken is now the lieutenant governor with a full agenda if he's to be on the ballot come this fall."

I just nodded my head.

We went to the top floor—damn, I hoped my nose wouldn't start to bleed. Anything over four floors and I usually get into trouble. This was the executive level, complete with its own fitness club. Not that I'd ever go there. I was pretty sure I was allergic to fitness clubs, to be honest.

There were only a few rooms and I noticed they all had names. The door in front of us had a bronze plaque that read "The Yellow Rose." Well, yellow *is* my best color, but why that name? I'd have to look into this Yellow Rose fascination Texans have. I looked across the hall and saw another suite named "Crockett." Wonder why I didn't get that one? I loved that furry little cap he wore. Dang.

Patricia took a key from the side pocket of her purse and opened the door. No card keys here, I noticed. The door opened and so did my mouth. This was not just a suite—this was pure luxury! My eyes looked ahead to the picture windows overlooking the massive capitol dome in the distance. The décor was strictly Texas chic, artfully blending the colors of the sunset: pinks, mauves, blues and greens. Breathtaking. Texas wildlife prints adorned the walls and the tables were made of rough-hewn wood, topped with glass. My suitcase and typewriter were right inside the door.

"Oh, was this your mother's luggage?" Patricia commented as she looked at the "Christine E. Pullen" luggage tags.

"No. Christine is the name my parents gave me. Beth is the name the lieutenant governor gave me." Figuring truth was an absolute, I decided why not. Plus, I actually think I left her speechless.

"Well, then, *Beth*, rest up. Tomorrow will be your first day at the capitol. I will be detained until about one, so why don't you take that time to just walk around and accustom yourself to your new surroundings?"

She exited without a goodbye or any form of pleasantry. I was left, again, daydreaming. Daydreaming about what moonlight would be like in Texas.

After a few good sighs I walked into the living area. Everything here was strictly Texan. If nothing else, these people were filled with pride for their heritage. The walls were decorated with deer horns and cast-iron armadillos. That kind of creeped me out, but I figured if I was going to be a part-time cowgirl I should get used to horns and animal bodies covered in bony plates. There were two coffee table books, one titled *Poisonous Snakes of Texas* and the other *Texas Sized Scorpions*. How charming.

On the farthest wall, adjacent to a picture window, was a weathered, wooden shelving unit that served as a desk, complete with a phone, wall lamp and ladder back chair. On top of the desk was a box. I was hoping it was donuts. Lots of donuts.

Opening the card on the outside, I read:

> *Chrissy —*
> *Your Smith Corona is fine for freelancing, but you're a pro now. Since the first radio broadcast of "Truth or Consequences" was aired on this date in 1940, I want you remember to stay truthful —and take plenty of notes. You just never know."*
> *Love you, Dad*

This was really cryptic—so I tore into the box as if it were Christmas morning. Actually it felt like Christmas morning and I'd just been given the entire candy store! I stood in shock. There, in the box, was a laptop computer and fifty blank CDs. A smaller box, wrapped in yellow, was inside.

I opened it up to find a handheld digital tape recorder with a note saying:

> *Be wary of those so far virtuous.*
> *They always have*
> *something to hide.*
> *Be careful, my friend, and always*
> *  get it on tape. Take care, kid.*
> *I love you! Vic*

I took both of the gifts out, smashed the box down and put it in the trashcan beneath the desk. It took only a few minutes to hook the cable cords up, plug the modem line into the phone jack and boot up. My Internet provider was one of four pre-loaded on the computer. Luckily, I had their toll-free number in my day planner so all I had to do was call them for a local access number, enter my current account information and I was good to go.

The modem buzz was churning—and then *bam!* I was online. Writing Daddy and Vic chatty emails about the trip down would be just the thanks they'd love. I didn't really have it in me to call, to be honest. I was a little overwhelmed at this point by all the questions I didn't have answers for and didn't need to add any more to my collection.

A few minutes later, I hit "send now" and logged off. Next I needed to unpack—a breeze, with all the storage space. Just as I was getting used to my new once-a-month home, I heard an unexpected knock at the door.

It startled me, since I hadn't ordered takeout. A second knock was followed by that all-too-familiar voice.

"Beth, it's Bob, not an ax murderer. Really."

Even though I recognized the voice, I still checked the keyhole. Again, once a gal from Detroit, always a gal from Detroit. And I didn't have a gun. Hadn't been in Texas long enough for that. Yep. It was most definitely Bob. Broad smile to match his broad shoulders.

I swung open the door and asked, "Taking a coffee break, Lieutenant Governor?"

"Aren't we cheerful today, Ms. Communications Director?" He came in and looked around the room, then back at me. I wished I could just come right out and tell him how much his chuckle unnerved me. Well, before I did that, I guess I should figure out exactly *why* it unnerved me. Victoria thought it was sexual. Of course Victoria thought everything was sexual. Who was I to argue with a pro?

"Well, there is some Gevalia in the refrigerator," Bob said. "And I made sure the coffeepot was a twelve-cup model. So if you're offering, I can't refuse."

The way he said he couldn't refuse made me smile.

"And the smile is because...?"

"Oh, just because I love this place! It's gorgeous! My dad had a laptop delivered and Vic sent a handheld recorder. I don't know how they managed that with such short notice!"

"I can answer that. Your father asked me to call Bests and have them send the computer and tape recorder to your suite. Took all of thirty minutes. That's how." Now it was *his* turn to smile.

"My father called you?" I was somewhat upset by that. Seemed like an invasion of privacy somehow. Why did he always need to be in control?

"No, really he didn't. I called *him*. I know how fathers are. I wanted to assure him that you'd be safe and your job secure. Let him know that everything was taken care of."

I softened. This kind and gentlemanly act was testimony to everything that I'd read about Bob Larken. On the air he could come across as a pit bull, but, in reality, was humane and caring.

56

A gentle soul. The diversity in his public and private personas might be a hindrance to his political career, though. I wondered: How do you blend the two? Can you? I wanted to be able to trust him, but which was the real Bob Larken?

I had a feeling I was about to find out.

"Have you decided to become a real woman and drink *real* coffee, Beth?" His smirk was almost as debilitating to my psyche as his chuckle.

"Nah, I'm still a decaf girl. There *is* decaf, right?"

"Of course there's decaf. I did have some regular and flavored coffees delivered, just in case you decided to get bold. Not a chance, hmmm?"

This coffee exchange was starting to sound titillating. No doubt Victoria would have switched to fully caffeinated at this very moment.

"Do you always make men wait this long or are you going to start the coffeemaker?" He laughed as he leaned one elbow on the kitchen counter, legs crossed informally at the ankle. Formal clothes, informal posture. Quite a dichotomy. I began to wonder what other secrets lay beneath his public versus his personal life. My mind wandered back to Mackinac Island.

In terms of body language, Bob hadn't seem particularly tied to his wife. I'd watched plenty of politicians. They work the room. Their spouses work the room. But they still made body contact—walked hand in hand or did something that signaled: "all is well on the home front." There was nothing. Nothing at all between the Larkens. Then there was Jim Parson's comment about "all of Larken's women."

"Ahem, you do work for me, Miss. The least you can do is smile and make my coffee."

My new boss snapped me back into reality. He was putting on an affronted air that caught me off guard.

"Oh, right. Funny you should mention that. I'll need to tease Vic about that. At least I get paid to make the coffee. She does it for nothing."

"Vic is the one that sent you the tape recorder, right? Who is she again? And why would she do anything for nothing?"

That comment was accompanied by a wink. A wink? Should I pick up on that or let it go? I let it go.

"Victoria Wexford, my best friend. She is the one who procured my admittance to your birthday party at Governor Melvin's."

I chose to use journalistic jargon, the "big" words—remind him that I was, after all, the communications director. I liked the sound of my title.

"She does volunteer work at party headquarters. Makes a lot of coffee. Drinks none." I kept my professional aura. I should have gotten a minor in theater arts.

"Oh yes. I remember now. May I ask w*hich* party headquarters? She sounds like a real go-getter." He returned to being my boss.

"Republican—GOP Headquarters in Lansing. Hates it but hopes to meet enough people to get a paying position somewhere. She also works part-time at the capitol as a legislative aide. She really is brilliant. A poli sci major. Gorgeous, cunning and loyal."

I was starting to sound more like Victoria's PR agent than her best friend.

"Sounds good—except for the GOP part. Think she'd ever switch sides?"

"Well, that's doubtful. As unconservative as she is in her private life, her political views are pretty right-wing. Then again, if the money were right, you just never know."

"I'll keep that in mind. Can't do anything now, but perhaps down the road. Governors have more say in staffing."

I couldn't help but ask. "Governor?"

"Hopefully, in a few years the DNC will want me to run for governor. I'm pretty certain I'll be on this fall's ticket and will be elected lieutenant governor. Everything is running smoothly in the state. The governor is extremely popular with both sides of the aisle as well as the Hispanic and Native American populations. He stays in the limelight just enough to be remembered but not enough to make tongues wag. That's one smart and savvy politician."

"I need to know something," I said. "I've researched you for countless hours. I now work for you. How on earth *did* you get this job? Or is that classified?"

I cut my eyes and smirked. Always worked for Victoria and it sure worked on that state trooper. I just might be getting the hang of it.

"Well, it's not really classified, but it's not something that is public knowledge, either. Although I assume that once I run for governor, everything will be public knowledge.

"You met John Gaynor. He's been like a father to me. He's mentored me and taught me all I know about handling people, on and off screen. He believes in me and the issues I support. I met him, quite by accident, when I began my broadcasting career fresh out of college. He came into the studio to meet with management on a special they were going to be airing on animal rights. He funds quite a few activist organizations and wanted to pay for some private advertising. Big money man. Unbeknownst to me, he'd seen some of my documentaries. This was early on, remember. When he asked the network to use me for the commentary, I was shocked. He knew everything about me. My background, that I was adopted, that I was about to marry my long-time sweetheart—the works."

"When were you adopted? You don't mention it much, really. I came across a brief one-line comment on your parentage quite by accident. I really thought I should wait to find out more—it's rather personal. But since you brought it up.... " Quit rambling, Beth, quit rambling.

"It's no secret. It's just not something that comes up a lot. I was adopted at birth. I have no idea who my biological parents are, nor do I have a desire to search for them. I know my parents—they are the people who loved and raised me. End of story."

"So how did that end up with you as second-in-command in Texas?" I was utterly confused.

"Gaynor has immense clout, monetarily. He contributes heavily to the DNC and to those he backs ideologically. He is close to Governor Biltmore, through the party. When Billy Glinnis died, Gaynor walked into the capitol and demanded to see the governor, checkbook in hand. He told him if he tapped Bob Larken as his 'sidekick'—that's the word he used—he'd make sure that come November, Biltmore would have all the support he needed for re-election. Need I say more?"

"Ahhhhhh. Your position was bought. Now it makes sense."

"Well, saying it that way sounds seedy and unethical, but I suppose in a sense it's true. John believes I have great potential to help shape the future of Texas. He champions my causes—family and children's rights. He's an advocate of some of the adoption issues I've rallied against and for. As I said, he believes in me. We have become the closest of friends. I rely on his experience and common sense. I look up to him like a second father." His eyes became softer as he spoke of his friend.

"Does he have a family?"

I was intrigued. The answers seemed so much clearer now, and his devotion to Gaynor was apparent.

"No. He's never had children. I guess, in that sense, I'm the son he never had. We like it that way."

He turned his head towards the coffeepot, which had just quit perking.

"Is Gaynor close to your wife, as well?"

"Not particularly. They have lunch occasionally. Margaret is from old money and I think she and John have more of a working relationship—he helps her with investments and such. So, now that you know *that* story, are you going to serve me or is this a beverage buffet?"

His voice seemed softer and gentler than it had just a few minutes ago.

I opened several cabinets until I found the coffee cups. They were the plain white stoneware mug variety. Typical.

"So, Lieutenant Governor, would you like the white cup or the white cup?" My turn to break the ice.

"Oh the white cup is just fine. Next time we'll go out for coffee. Right now we need privacy—for business talk. You need to discover our wonderful town. I would like to be the one to show you around."

I could have sworn he was trying to flirt with me. A cat and mouse game? I hoped it wasn't going to be like that blind date I'd had a few weeks ago. What a fiasco. The picture I'd seen of the guy was adorable. Too bad when I met him he was a beached baby whale. Pathetic loser with a lot of smooth talk. But why was I thinking about that now?

"Oh geeeeeeeez — that's it!" My exclamation came out before I realized I was no longer thinking to myself.

"*What's* it? You look like you just had one of those light bulb moments from an Oprah show." Bob returned his full attention my way with an intent look softened by a smile.

"I just realized—your nemesis in Michigan—Lieutenant Governor Parsons. He reminds me of a blind date I had once. The similarities are amazing."

"What a shame. I would hate to think there's someone else out there as slimy as Parsons."

I just shrugged my shoulders and poured our coffee. My boss would just have to deal with decaf. I added some vanilla nut flavoring I'd spotted in the cabinet. I said a prayer that it really was flavoring and not poison and walked into the living room.

"So do fill me in on what you came to discuss. Mind if I take notes on my laptop? I don't think you want to be recorded." My turn to spar.

"Actually, if you remember, I'm quite use to a microphone, except this isn't for publication or broadcast. This job calls for fierce loyalty, total privacy—and that includes with your father and friends. What I want to be broadcast, I'll let you know. Otherwise, it's between us. You'll put out press releases as needed. They'll be submitted to the governor's office for approval before being sent out on the AP or read at a news conference. Your staff is for research. You need to know something, they find it out. Your job is to make me look good."

"I like the sound of that. Mind if I start picking out your clothes?" We both burst into laughter. I can only be serious for so long.

The lieutenant governor continued, "We'll meet daily. In person if you're in town, or via a hard line if not. No cell calls for business, only a secure line."

"Okay, sir. Where would you like me to begin?"

"First by calling me Bob. Unless we're in a professional setting, of course."

"Okay, Bob." My smile softened as our eyes met.

"I'd suggest you go and familiarize yourself with the capitol building. Here are your credentials."

He reached into his pocket and extracted a laminated badge complete with my picture.

"How did you get my picture?" I was slightly shocked to see my image in his hand. Given a few minutes I might have been able to figure it out.

"The party on Mackinac. The governor's residence has a surveillance system on the perimeter. Enter at your own risk." We'd moved on to eyebrow raising. "We had a frame of you taken as you entered the home enlarged and then cropped. Good thing you were on your best behavior that night."

"Is this room bugged? Should I start being paranoid?" I was smiling, yet all of a sudden I felt a bit uncomfortable. It was dawning on me that I was playing with the big boys now.

"No no no. You're safe. Remember, I promised your dad I'd take care of you."

How could I forget?

"Well, back to business. What's happening with the school vouchers?"

"Oh that's an interesting one. It's in the state senate and it's split. I might have to make my first tie-breaking vote. The Republicans, for the most part, believe it's a matter of choice. Helping children learn should be the intent of public education, and yet they're afraid of competition. That makes absolutely no sense to me, as a father and as a politician. It's a fact that middle-class and suburban families have better schools with more money. The inner city kids are stuck, Beth. They're just stuck with no choice. I want to be their voice. I have to be their voice. Case in point—the Sam Houston Scholarship Program. It's used to improve technological resources in religious schools—it allows vouchers for religious education. Beth, shouldn't we want what is ultimately the best for our children—for all the children of Texas and the nation?"

How could I argue with that? I just listened as he continued his impassioned prose.

"The Dems, for the most part, feel that vouchers, if used for religious-based education, would infringe on separation of church and state. But guess who sends their kids and grandchildren to private Catholic schools?"

"Let me guess—most of the Democrats?"

"You got it. It doesn't affect them because they have the money to do what they want. The teacher's union and the ACLU line their pockets. You need money to run, Beth. They aren't the voice of the children—they're the voice of the unions. Granted, we send Dave to private school, but I want all the children to have the same opportunities he does. It's only fair. It's only right."

"You're willing to buck the party for principle, Bob?" I was seeing more of the Bob Larken I had hoped existed.

"I'm adamant on this, Beth. It's not only the government's responsibility, but also our civic duty to allow kids the best education available. If it's a public school, fine. If not, they need our help. Those who disagree feel that vouchers add to the desecration of the public school system. I say, bring on the competition!'"

I sat there, staring at a man whose principles could very well end his career.

"A Democrat whose pocket has been lined by private funding, being called in to break a tie opposed to his own party—whose pockets are being lined by union money? I wouldn't want to be in your shoes, Bob."

"Beth, I didn't ask for these shoes—they were given to me. I take my position very seriously, even though I wasn't elected. What I do with this will more than likely determine if I'm *ever* elected. Believe me, I've lost plenty sleep over this."

His usual upbeat demeanor was replaced by a seriousness I'd not witnessed off-screen.

"With that, young lady, I need to go. Someone is sure to miss me by now. I'll be in my office if you need me. I'll check back later in the day. It's your first day in town!" He paused as he neared the door.

"How rude of me! What's your favorite dinner entrée?" I couldn't get a pulse on this conversation. It had flipflopped more times than a catfish just pulled out of a lake back home.

"I hear there's some great Mexican food down here. Not a lot of authentic places in Detroit."

"Great! Margaret detests Mexican food. She's out of town—care to join me this evening? We can go over staffing, I'll bring some paperwork for you to fill out—the usual. Normally Patricia would see to that but I don't wish her on anyone. When Margaret is out of town Patricia watches over me like a mother hen. She's extremely efficient, but someone needs to chip away the iceberg she lives in."

"Iceberg? Gee, I hadn't noticed."

I think he liked my caustic comment. Rarely could you see his perfect teeth when he smiled. This smile showed off all his pearly whites. He'd calmed down from his soapbox performance on school vouchers. Maybe that was part of my job—defusing the lieutenant governor's temper.

"So, check and see what time the sun sets tonight and that's when I'll pick you up."

Wasn't *he* being mysterious?

And with that the lieutenant governor of the state of Texas put his hand on my shoulder and melted my heart with one final sentence.

"Then I'll see you under the Texas moonlight, Sonata."

*Katherine Shephard*

## Chapter Five

He left. He just turned around and left. I, a communications director, found myself speechless.

Getting geared up for my first night in Austin, I needed to find out when the sun would set. Fortunately, I never left home without my dictionary, thesaurus and *Farmer's Almanac*. Today's date: Monday, March 23, 1998. The table said the sun would be setting over Austin, Texas at 6:45 p.m. Okay. I'd be ready at 6:30 to be safe. That left me a few hours to walk across to the capitol and at least find the cafeteria. With any luck they would have a piece of chocolate cake. I needed a piece of chocolate cake.

I still had on the jacket and slacks I'd worn on the plane and figured if I just freshened my makeup, brushed my hair, and spritzed on a little perfume I'd look and smell professional enough. No one knew me here anyhow. Well, except for Patricia and Bob.

One quick makeover and I flew out the door, credentials in my purse and leather-bound notepad under my arm. There was a spot for a few pens and business cards in the supple folder. I didn't have any business cards, but assumed I would soon. I wondered if they'd have the official state seal on them. Should I put "Elizabeth Pullen" on them or just "Beth"? Oops. I needed to shut my brain off. Hopefully some fresh air would do that.

I took the elevator down to the lobby level and turned to the left. There before me gleamed an expansive marble floor, with potted trees arranged around a huge, oval fountain. The trees had those little twinkle lights that I presumed would be turned on at night. On the textured stucco walls hung various Texan treasures. Lithographs depicting the Alamo defenders. Pop Art finger paintings labeled "Painted with East Texas Red Dirt." Papier-mâché armadillos of all sizes. I particularly liked one rather huge armadillo made entirely out of Texas pecans. I could have sworn it was smiling at me. It was simply entitled "Arnie." Nothing at all like you'd see in Michigan. Not an automotive sign to be found. Maybe I'd found the best of both worlds.

A bellman held the door for me and called me by name. "Have a pleasant late afternoon, Miss Pullen."

How did he know who I was? I was getting spooked again. I took a closer look at him and, sure enough, there was the earpiece.

The capitol dome could be seen from where I stood on Fifth Street. I could enter the capitol grounds on Eleventh. An easy walk. My stroll took me by the infamous Sixth Street entertainment district with billboards proclaiming it "Live Music Capital of the World." I saw shops and restaurants everywhere I turned. Once I reached the capitol grounds, I realized this was nothing at all like Michigan's state capitol building. Our capitol was just *there*. Before me stood an entire complex with the biggest damn building I'd ever seen. Bob had given me some notes that I glanced through before starting my trek through the grounds. The actual capitol building faced south toward Goliad in memory of the most horrific battle of the Texas Revolution. Keeping in tune with "Everything's bigger in Texas," it was no surprise to find out that before me stood the largest state capitol in the United States in terms of gross square footage—second only to the nation's capitol in D.C.! I shook my head. These Texans. You just gotta love them.

Sauntering into the visitor's center, I picked up a map. I acted like any other tourist and did what I do best: play dumb. I was told to head north and follow the circle around the capitol. There were seventeen monuments along the way. I passed the state library and state archives, the Sam Houston Building, and continued up one of the most beautiful paths I'd ever seen. Everything was pristine and taken care of with obvious Texas pride. I'd read where all the buildings were designed to withstand the extreme Texas heat, which could be a challenge. Extreme heat didn't even come close to describing Texas, Daddy had told me. According to him, it was a living inferno during the summer. With the combination of the temperature and the hot air of all the bragging and tall tales, guess that was understandable. I supposed not all Texans were like that, but their reputation *was* amusing. Daddy told me once "Take one percent of what a true Texan tells you and you probably have the truth."

I passed a monument to Texas cowboys. Just as I was ready pay to homage to the statutes of the Texas Rangers and the Heroes of the Alamo, I heard some heated debate from around the corner. Being naturally nosy, I stopped.

"We have got to convince the others to vote our way. We can't make it this close."

This was a deep masculine voice. An older man, I guessed, from his intonation.

"Gus, I don't know. I just don't know. The reps are just not going to buy it. Our guys really want this entire voucher scenario to disappear and you know it won't. Those right-wing nuts will just not give it up. Just won't do it. They really believe this underdog crap. It's anti-public school, Gus. Our schools will go to hell in a hand basket and our support will dry up quicker than Lake Travis in El Nino. The pressure is on. We have one helluva battle ahead of us, Gus."

His voice almost sounded panicked. His drawl so thick I had to concentrate on every word.

"Marty, listen. We have to convince them. Buy them off. Do something. I don't care what. These jackass right-wingers think they rule the damn state. We have to show some of those jerks who has the *real* power and the *real* power equates to dollar signs, lobbyists and the unions."

Marty and Gus, Marty and Gus. I'll need to look up those names. They must be state senators since the bill is on their floor. Obviously Democrats. They both sounded anxious and determined

Not wanting my presence to be discovered, I turned my back and headed towards the capitol entrance. I decided to spend a little time in there before heading back to my suite. Tonight couldn't come soon enough. Bob had to know what was going on.

Entering the massive building I tried to concentrate on anything but what I'd just heard. The first thing I noticed was the gorgeous floor of the Rotunda. The terrazzo flooring was polished to an amazing shine. How could anyone take such tiny pieces of marble and granite and embed them in mortar? I walked around to view the six seals that surrounded the Great Seal. The seals on the floor traced the history of the state—the six flags that have flown over Texas. I wondered—was that how the amusement park got its name? I'd have to look that up. No—I had my own researchers to do that now. That made me smile.

I felt that I could safely exit without running into the arguing legislators. They really hadn't seen me and even if they had, they'd have no earthly clue that I was the new kid on the block. Still, I wanted to remain in the background for now. I also didn't want them to think anyone had overheard them.

I traced my steps back to the Crowne with just enough time to shower, change and pull my thoughts together. This wasn't exactly how I wanted my new job to begin, embroiled in a political debate of such magnitude, but I figured I had to get used to the high drama. First hush-hush surrounding Billy G, now this.

I decided to wear a simple yellow sundress and jacket. Nothing see-through, although I admit the thought did briefly cross my mind. Grabbing my purse, I headed back down to the lobby and waited outside for Bob. It was precisely 6:40 when I spotted the black Lincoln turning into the drive. It had government plates so I presumed the lieutenant governor was inside. I was correct.

"Nice to see you drive around in a Ford, Lieutenant Governor."

"I normally gallop up on a white stallion, but decided you're a Yankee girl and wouldn't have riding boots. Your father would have my hide if I made you ride bareback anyhow."

His humor was so unpredictable, so off-the-cuff.

"He can't even vote for you, I wouldn't think it would matter."

We both laughed. It was easy to laugh with Bob Larken. He was so...I didn't know how to describe it, and I was supposedly the pro when it came to adjectives.

"So, you don't think I could do bareback, hmmm?" I couldn't restrain my smirk.

"Oh now, ma'am, ah didn't say that." He poured on his gorgeous drawl this time.

I took off my jacket, revealing the low-cut back on my dress. "So there, sir." I smiled.

"Well, now, ah do think ah've found me a sassy one." He made a motion as if he were tipping a hat. It felt good to laugh— really laugh.

Slipping my jacket back on I asked, "So now, where are we going?"

I felt as excited as a little girl on Christmas morning. The woman in me, however, was wondering what I'd find if I unwrapped *this* present.

"You're smirking again, Beth. Going to fill me in or is it personal?"

His voice had returned to the smooth broadcaster tone. He was on to me.

"Can we change the subject?" Again, the laughter. It was getting to me in a way that didn't feel entirely comfortable.

As we headed out of town into the hills, we were soon surrounded by live oak groves and juniper-clad slopes. About

71

fifteen minutes later, tucked away in the hills, I saw a quaint, secluded Mexican restaurant with a sign saying "Rosa's Cantina." More like a Mexican bistro, if that makes any sense. In the curved front window an elderly Hispanic woman sat making fresh tortillas.

The driver opened both rear doors and we entered Rosa's. A heavenly mixture of simmering spices—cilantro, chili peppers and oregano—filled the air the moment we walked inside. The smiling owner escorted us to the far back corner, where swinging wooden doors opened to reveal a private booth. Stucco walls surrounded the booth for extra privacy. Cushioned high-backed benches wrapped around a plank table with a tin lantern hanging overhead. Through the punched holes on the lantern, which of course formed the all-too-familiar Texas star, a candle glowed gently. Everything around here seemed to be either shaped like a star, had a star carved into it, or had a star painted on it. That pride shit again. I imagined this booth was reserved for very special patrons, as it afforded the seclusion necessary for business or a tryst. Or maybe both?

"Good evening, sir, it's nice to see you again. Ma'am." The salutation directed toward me was accompanied by a head nod.

"Juan, we'd like to start with the fried spinach tortillas and a pitcher of your frozen peach margaritas. No salt. Our entrée will be the shrimp fajitas for two, please."

Juan smiled knowingly and made a hasty exit. He knew what to do, apparently.

"You come here often, I take it?"

"Yes, it's one of my favorite spots. They make sure no one bothers me; I can talk in peace and quiet. I'm glad you like Mexican food. Margaret would never dream of coming here. This is a pleasant change for me."

The lantern provided much the same glow as moonlight would on his hair.

The music was pleasantly muted and while the atmosphere felt casual, there was an air of elegance just the same. Or was it the company? There were no blinds or drapes around the large window at the end of the table. The cantina sat high on a hill overlooking Austin—the orange lights we could see burning in the distance were from the tower on the UT campus, Bob explained. Apparently the glass was the "I can see out but you can't see in" variety, although from this location there would be no access to the window from outside. Unless of course you were a bird or Superman.

"Bob, before I forget, I have something to tell you. I overheard two men talking on the capitol grounds behind the Alamo Defender monument."

Before I could continue he said, "Oh, must be some of the senators. That's their favorite hangout. If they're spotted they look like loyal Texans but, really, they go there to hash out disagreements or to strategize. The folks from the other side of the chambers go further north, near the John Reagan Building— where the Korean War Memorial is. That's where most of the war monuments are: Pearl Harbor, WWII and a replica of the Statue of Liberty. Everyone has their own spot. Very segregated for folks who claim to work together. The journalist in me picks up on every nuance." No chuckle. He was very serious with a furrowed brow.

"Bob, do you know a Gus and a Marty? They are apparently Democrats with an attitude. They are bound and determined to kill the school voucher initiative. They really sounded anti-private school."

Bob, shaking his head, filled me in. "They aren't anti-private school, Beth. Their kids and grandkids go to the finest private schools in the state. And yet they spout off that the voucher program violates constitutional rights for free high-quality public education. If public schools were so damn high quality, why don't they send *their* kids to one? I was hoping this wouldn't happen, Beth. My own party. I'm put right in the middle. Damned if I do and damned if I don't. Parents' right to choose what is best for their children is at stake here. The education of our most precious resource is in jeopardy. This is no time to worry about lining pockets—but I suppose that's what getting reelected is all about, isn't it." This was said more as a comment than a question.

Thank God the margaritas showed up. Although I was basically a non-drinker, I really needed something strong right now.

"Are you going to make a statement, Bob? What next?"

"First I'll approach them. Gus Bingham and Marty Roth. See if I can't persuade them to back off a bit. Make them see this is not the way to gain either the Hispanic or the Native American vote. That might do the trick. Tell them it will alienate voters. Then I'll make a statement, if necessary. I pray it doesn't come to that."

With perfect timing, our appetizer arrived just as he finished his sentence. He was deep in thought, so I let him be. I was beginning to learn when not to babble for a change. My nerves kicked in and I downed two margaritas before the main course arrived. This isn't good, I thought. But I did it anyway.

"What are you going to do, Bob? I mean, if your party won't vote against the passage of the bill?"

"I'm going to propose a fair compromise. A way to empower parents in the poorest of districts is a starter. See how it works. Institute more charter schools to aid the public school system. But you know, this isn't about vouchers, really. This is about money. The Republicans have plenty of backers—but the main money in our party does come from the two unions most opposed to vouchers. Not sure how I can get around that issue. Not sure at all."

The worry lines appeared on his forehead and he looked like a little boy who had just lost his puppy. Instinctively I reached over and put my hand on his.

"Bob, whatever I can do, just let me know. If it comes to a statement, give me a quote or two and I'll write something up for your approval. If it's speaking to the press in your behalf, I'll do it. Whatever you need, okay?"

"It's great to have your support. Lord knows Margaret thinks I'm nuts. Says I'm too much of a loyalist to downtrodden children. Can you even believe that? It doesn't faze her because her son isn't in that position. She says I need to be behind 'the party.' I asked her—why? I was just thrown into this party crap—I have my core beliefs. I won't bastardize myself. I just won't. True, I do love the power. God knows *Margaret* loves it. This has always been a dream, I suppose. I know I can make a difference. I just *know* it."

"Why do politics have to be so political?"

We both smiled at my quirky statement It felt good. It felt right.

He removed his hand from beneath mine and patted my arm. Why was I disappointed? And why did I feel a knife in my heart every time he said "Margaret"?

Again, just as there was a break in our conversation, our sizzling fajitas arrived. Freshly made tortillas—whole wheat, corn and white flour—as well as rice and spicy black beans, accompanied them. Seeing the margarita pitcher nearly empty, Juan replaced it without a word. Oh great.

Nothing more was said during dinner. We ate in silence that felt as thick as the smog in L.A. I'd never been to L.A. I hadn't really been much of anywhere, but Daddy said it was next to paradise. Except, of course, for the smog. But now Houston was right up there with L.A. for junky air, supposedly. Guess that was why they have those fancy degreed air quality engineers—to fix that crap. Another margarita down the hatch. Vic preferred politicians to engineers and, Lord knows, she'd had her share of both. Remembering some of her juicier comments, I started to laugh.

"You want to share what's so amusing, or is it the way I eat?"

"Oh no, really, Bob. It was something that reminded me of Victoria, is all."

"You're not willing to share? I could use a good laugh."

"Well, it all started with me thinking about moonlight and smog and men in bed."

Oh Lord I couldn't believe I just said that.

"Moonlight, smog and sex. Seems an unlikely trio but I'll just have to trust you."

At least now the tension was broken.

"Is that like a smoky moonlight room with a lot of sweat?" he inquired.

I had to cover my mouth before I spit the margarita all over the table.

"I think maybe I need to call it quits on the tequila," I admitted.

"Why quit now? The conversation is just getting amusing. I'm through talking politics for the night."

"I thought this was a business dinner?" I tried acting professional.

"Well, it was. We talked about the initiative for a while. That should qualify this as a write-off."

Oh no. The wink. I got the wink again. This could be trouble.

"Okay, why not?" And I downed my fourth margarita.

It was either the tequila or the moonlight shining through the window. I could catch glimpses of the lunar rays mixed with the city lights in the distance. The moon cast a soft glow above Bob's head and shimmered gently off his silvering hair. Just like that first night. His eyes and teeth were set off by his deep, rich tan. His linen shirt emphasized his broad shoulders. Damn. He's gorgeous. Double damn. I'm in big trouble.

As if breaking me out of a trance, I heard his voice.

"Beth, you know all about me—well a lot about me, at least. I seem to know nothing, except that you're a fabulous writer with a lot of drive. Everything else is just supposition. I'd like to get to know you—maybe it's just the investigative reporter in me."

His smile melted me to the ground. It could have been the smile or the warmth from the tequila, but I started babbling again.

"Okay. Well, you know I was just a little girl when my mother died. I questioned the existence of God during high school and, really, well into college. I met a man, a wonderful man, my junior year. He was sexy and seemed sincere. But I found out he'd lied to me several times and the trust—well, how can you trust someone who lies? Even when they say they're sorry? The more I discovered about him, the more I realized he was scum."

He just sat there listening and waiting for more, so of course I continued.

"I decided to just not trust. Just not love. Pour myself into my studies. My sorority sisters provided the social life. And then there's always my dad."

"You're a bit of an idealist, aren't you?" he questioned.

"I suppose. And a dreamer." Munching on chips helped my nerves. I hated it, though, when they got caught in your teeth and you tried to flick them out with your tongue. Damn embarrassing.

"Do you ever want to marry or have kids?" Man, this *was* getting personal. Another gulp should get me through this answer.

"Well, sure. First I have to find Mr. Right. And kids? Well, I don't know. I wouldn't mind a baby but teenagers scare the crap out of me."

"No joke. My son, I mean *our* son; he's been great so far. But you just never know. I've seen even the best of kids go sour. His mom, Margaret, she's a bit tough on him. Expects perfection. She expects perfection out of everyone. People just aren't perfect, you know?"

Oh Lord, help me. I started to think about going on a safari—wild tigers charging me, elephants squirting water on me. Anything and everything to resist saying "You *are* perfect, Bob. She just doesn't know it."

"There you go again, getting all quiet on me. Penny for your thoughts."

His eyebrows rose, almost as if he knew I was thinking Tarzan and Jane. He Tarzan, me Jane.

"Oh, it would take more like a winning Lotto ticket to pry it out of me."

Smiling, I realized what I'd been missing in my life. A man that I could really talk to.

Get a grip. Stop with the tequila.

"So, what is this Mr. Right going to be like?"

Someone help me out here. Someone please walk in, notice us in the booth, and come over to chat. Someone. Anyone. Where's the waiter anyhow?

"Oh, he'll need to be tall. Handsome in a rugged way. I don't like skinny men."

That made him smile.

"Skinny, to me, says, I don't know, a lack of strength. I know that's not really true, but it's just a personal preference. But he can't be fat, either. He has to be strong. Pick-me-up-and-carry-me-away strong."

Yep. The babbling had kicked in. So why stop now?

"He has to be intelligent, degreed, steady job, homeowner, with a dog or two. Oh, and has to treat me like a princess." I tossed back my hair in a snooty sort of way.

"You don't ask for much, do you?" We both took a drink.

I needed to get off this topic before I said "You know, someone like you."

Food. Talk about the food.

"You were right, the fajitas are to die for."

"So is the company, Beth. Thank you. It's been a long, long time since I could be myself."

I didn't want to know.

"I should get you back to the suite before our ride turns into a pumpkin."

Hmmmm, maybe he thought I was Cinderella after all? I started to hum "Someday My Prince Will Come" but I guess I wasn't humming to myself.

"You like to sing, or are you trying to tell me I'm a real prince of a guy?"

"Oh God, I'm sorry. Oh geeez. No. I mean yes. I mean, get me some coffee."

I could barely stand up.

"Right. This isn't going to look good—getting you drunk your first night in town."

He took my arm and we both tried to maintain our composure. He was doing just fine but I wasn't sure I'd make it to the door.

The next thing I remember was the smell of coffee. I didn't pass out—thank God. I just couldn't recall getting from point A to point B.

"I'm so embarrassed. But while I'm groveling for your forgiveness, mind getting me some aspirin with that coffee?" I'd kicked off my shoes and was lying on the couch under a blanket.

"Hey, not a problem. It's good to know I've hired a cheap date."

He winked as he crossed the room and headed for the medicine chest. Oh please, I silently prayed, don't let him see the birth control pills. He'd *really* get the wrong impression then. He'd never believe they were just for cramps.

"Beth, is the aspirin in a bottle or this little disc thing?"

He was smirking. I just knew he was smirking.

"Hey you could always log onto the Internet. I hear there's this dude called 'Alamo Pal.' He sells these gel caps that will cure anything."

Yep. I could feel the smirk.

"The bottle. The one that says aspirin. Just get me the aspirin, please."

I closed my eyes hoping this was all a nightmare. I'd wake up soon. I just knew I would.

Soon came sooner than I thought.

"I suppose the medicine in the disc thing is for something more personal than a headache?" Was he doing this to torment me?

"We haven't known each other long enough to discuss it. You're my boss, remember?" Should I pretend I was angry or act normal? Or just pretend to pass out?

"Amazingly, it does feel like I've know you forever. Hey, maybe in a past life? You believe in that stuff?"

"Yeah, I guess I do. I mean I can't prove otherwise. Sometimes I have that déjà vu stuff. Right now it feels as though I was one of those tortured women in the 1600s. Please tell me you have the aspirin."

"At your service. Two aspirin and black coffee. And it's not decaf."

"Should that make me nervous?"

I smiled despite feeling like a vise was gripping my temples.

"I'll stay a while longer and make sure you're all right. I wouldn't want to be called an irresponsible employer. I can't afford to get sued this early in my career."

I put the aspirin in my mouth, slugged down the coffee and fell into never-never land.


The chain saws were going full force. Loggers by the dozen were having a field day up north. One by one they took their turn sawing down a great oak or mighty pine. The noise was deafening and the contest surely would cause a buzz among the tree-huggers in Lansing. But the state relied heavily on the furniture industry. Where would the wood come from? More buzzing. Louder and louder. A logger moaned.

My head shot up off the pillow, my eyes trying to focus in the dark. Where was I? Why was it so dark?

No loggers—a sofa, a blanket and one killer headache. And a man in a recliner. Oh God. I blinked repeatedly to get my eyes accustomed to the darkness and attempted to get my wits about me. I remember now. Texas. New job. New boss. Tequila. I took the pillow from under my head and smashed it over my face. Why couldn't this have just been a dream instead of a nightmare? I was in a hotel suite with a very married lieutenant governor, who was snoring. If I sneaked out quietly maybe I could hail a cab to the airport and forget this ever happened. It was my turn to moan.

"Beth. Beth? Are you okay?"

Please let me be appropriately covered up.

I removed the pillow from my face and ran my fingers through my hair, hoping I could make myself somewhat presentable before his eyes could focus on me.

"Yep. It's me. I'm still here. Anyone ever told you that you sound like a Lionel train come to life in surround sound?"

The pounding in my temples wouldn't stop.

"Some thanks that is for the good time."

"Spare me."

I could make out his shadow and noticed he was coming closer towards me.

"You also moan when you sleep. You snore and you moan. I thought I was having a dream about loggers in the UP."

"Sorry. Next time I'll prop my head up. I don't snore as much with my head propped up."

Next time? Well wouldn't Vic love this tidbit? I shook my head to loosen the cobwebs. Big mistake.

"My head feels like your train just collided with my brain."

"A communications director who speaks in rhyme. I suppose you want a raise?"

"Are you always so chipper when you wake up?" I wanted to laugh, I really did. But it hurt to even think about it.

"Listen, go take a shower—a good hot shower. Let the water pound on your neck. Then get in the recliner. That will do it. I promise."

"You currently have the recliner."

"I will relinquish my spot for the damsel in distress. Cover your eyes, the lights are going on. Plus, if you're going to take a shower, I really should leave. It's well past the time I should have gone. If anyone spots me leaving here, when the lights have been out, you can kiss both of our jobs goodbye. Scandal is not a word I want to see linked to my name."

"I'll try not to take offense or have a broken heart." I feigned a pout. "Really, thanks so much for not abandoning me in my time of great distress."

My head was beginning to clear and I could now smile without feeling like my entire body would shatter.

"Well, I'll remember to limit your alcohol consumption from now on."

It was more of a smart-ass chuckle this time.

"And I shall remember to keep a supply of earplugs."

"What a pair we are."

We both looked at the floor, wondering what to say next.

"Sure you don't want to make me another cup of coffee before you have to go? I mean what's another half-hour this time of night? I promise to lock the bathroom door."

I cut my eyes—and caught him off guard.

"Deal. You've got yourself a deal, Miss Pullen."

He turned toward the kitchen and I turned toward the bath.

As I let the wet heat pound on my neck I contemplated what to put on post-shower. Vic would say, "Go for the jugular, kiddo. Slip into silk." I decided to play it safe and put on a cotton seafoam-green lounger. V-neck back. I could put a sports bra on under it—feminine in a sporty way. I could smell the coffee brewing as I slipped out of the shower and into the adjoining bedroom. Luckily the bathroom had two doors—one into the living area and another directly into the bedroom. I put on the lounger, clasped my hair on top of my head with a large white clip, wet my lips with gloss and went to join my boss. I had to keep reminding myself he was my boss, *not* my date.

When he heard the door open, he turned around and smiled.

"Your coffee is made, Madame."

He gave a bow and came towards me. I hoped he couldn't hear my heart pounding.

"You were right, the shower did the trick!"

"Yes it did, you look wonderful."

Our eyes met and I was speechless once again. I took the coffee from him and sat down in the recliner, just as he had instructed.

"You know, if you came over here, to the couch, I could give your neck a massage. Then you'd be all set to go."

"Go where?" I couldn't help asking. I just couldn't.

He took my shoulders into his hands, looked again into my eyes and said, in almost a whisper, "Wherever you want to go. The coffee isn't decaf; it's the real thing. And so am I."

*Katherine Shephard*

## Chapter Six

Thursday, March 26. Three days had passed since my arrival in Austin. Three days since the lieutenant governor saved me from myself—or helped me discover myself. I hadn't decided which. Thank God only a quarter of the moon was visible that night. Lord only knows what would have happened if it had been full.

The weather was unseasonably warm—in the eighties every day. Unlike Michigan, there was barely a breeze although the nights did cool down some. The nights in Austin were magic, I was discovering. From the balcony of my suite I could hear the music rising up from Sixth Street. I'd sit outside with my coffee and laptop, taking notes on what I'd heard and seen—a journal of sorts.

I'd gotten a staff list and phone directory, met with my staff members, and toured every square inch of the Capitol building. The full-timer assigned to work for me was old enough to be my mother and at times, acted like it. She was efficient, orderly, calm and precise. In other words, she balanced me out. Her name was Jill and I think she was either a queen in a past life or was rehearsing to be one soon. She understood the rules and played by them; she knew the ropes and used them. You could either trust Jill or be afraid of her. I was glad to have her on my side. Another excellent reason to have her on staff was her fabulous cooking. One night as I was poring over *Who's Who in Our Capitol* she came over with fried chicken, buttermilk biscuits, gravy and a hot-out-of-the oven pecan pie. Though not a Texan, she'd married one. After he dumped her for a younger woman she joined the political workforce, where she'd seen many LGs come and go over the years. She admitted Larken was the best-looking. I kept my mouth shut, for once.

My part-time assistant, who would do most of my research, was an intern out of UT. As she said herself, she was "born and bred, schooled and fed" right here in Texas. She had big blonde hair, a very pronounced twang, a very loud voice and the name BertaSue. Berty was thrilled to be working with Jill. She loved to eat. All of the above qualified her, in my mind, to be a "real" Texan. Big hair, big mouth, and big appetite. It was a reputation "thang." She was, however, a real go-getter. I'd no more than ask her to find something out for me and *bam!* It was done.

After only three days I'd already discovered that my job was going to be either boring or nerve-wracking. No middle ground. I supposed that paralleled being lieutenant governor. It was either drinking coffee or battling cantankerous legislators. Hopefully there would be nothing ominous added to the coffee.

Luckily, three nights ago, Bob Larken had showed that he practiced what he preached—moral leadership. He left that night as a gentleman would. I was relieved. I was disappointed.

I'd daydreamed, since then, about the quandary of political life—the public versus private personas. I'd also thought about Bob's wife and, naturally, his son. His family. I felt that I'd gotten mixed signals from him on a personal level. I just wasn't sure if that was reality, or wishful thinking. Was my infatuation because he was older and I was trying to replace my father? Or was he toying with the idea of having a spunky ingénue to replace a rigid and aging wife? Either way, what would that say about me? Nothing good, that was for sure.

As I picked apart a cold piece of Jill's chicken, deep in thought, I heard a key in the door. The maid service had already been here. My heart stopped mid-beat. Without an invitation or announcement in walked Robert Bentley Larken, my boss, the lieutenant governor, and, heaven help me, the man with whom I was head-over-heels infatuated.

"Beth. I'm sorry. I didn't call; I didn't knock. I was afraid you wouldn't answer for some reason. It's been three days of hell."

He looked haggard and beaten down. I wanted to get up from the table and take him in my arms. Not at all the jovial knight in shining armor who took me to Rosa's Cantina just a few nights before.

"It's okay. I've been tied up getting my feet wet. Sit down. Let me make some coffee. You look like you could use it."

It was my turn to play caretaker.

As I went to the kitchen, Bob slumped down on the sofa and leaned his head back. He looked as if he hadn't slept since I saw him last. Worry lines surrounded his eyes and his skin had a shallow pallor. Even his hair seemed grayer and duller. Usually a dapper dresser, he wore rumpled clothes as though he didn't care anymore.

When I returned with our coffee his head was bent down. He pressed into his forehead with his left palm and his right arm was almost limp, lying across his lap. As a Texan would say, he looked like the back end of a mule.

"Bob? Here's your coffee. Have you eaten lately?" My normal upbeat attitude was softened by the circumstances that I felt might be surrounding this visit. Circumstances that seemed to be weighing very heavily on the lieutenant governor.

"Thanks. I think I had lunch. Everything is blurring together. How 'bout we just order a pizza? Mushroom and ham. That okay with you? We can talk in private. I can't go out. I just don't have it in me."

His voice sounded tired. The normal spark was gone. He seemed to be grasping just to find words and his speech was slow and laborious—unusual for a broadcaster and politician. He took the coffee, placed it on the table next to him and continued to sit there quietly. Motionless.

"Pizza—let me call for it. I'll have them bring Pepsi too. There are no sodas here and you just can't have pizza without a soda."

I headed for the phone as he responded, almost in a whisper.

"Just not like Margaret at all. Just not."

After I'd placed the order I turned back to him, my natural curiosity kicking in once more.

"What's not like Margaret? Is something wrong? Did something happen, Bob?"

"Oh no. No. It's just the pizza thing. Margaret would never order pizza in, except for Dave and his friends. Pizza and Pepsi in a hotel room is totally foreign to me. Not even in our college days or when we were first married. She's always been so, well, so rigid," he sighed. "I guess that's the word. No spirit of adventure."

Compared to his usual demeanor, he was practically catatonic. I was hoping the pizza would provide the carbs needed to fuel him back to normalcy.

"Ordering pizza is hardly adventurous." I let a smile cross my lips in hopes it would break the aura of doom and gloom.

"It is if you live with *her*." This was not a happy man.

"Well, then, let's be different! Different is good! You look like you need a change...."

I let the sentence drift off. Bob looked up at me. I was still standing there, my own coffee in hand.

"You have yourself a deal, Beth. We will be different. This will be uniquely us, won't it?"

It was a question, but it sounded more like a plea.

"Yep, it sure will be. Can't say as I've ever ordered pizza in a hotel suite with a lieutenant governor before."

My turn to wink. It actually brought a soft smile to his face. Uniquely us. I like that term. Two simple words, but when put together—something special. Uniquely us indeed.

I sat down next to him. He was staring nowhere in particular.

"Bob, you met with Gus and Marty, didn't you. Is that what this is about? Gus and Marty?"

He nodded his head. I couldn't tell if it was from disbelief or to clear his thought process.

"I didn't talk to you sooner about this, Beth, because I was hoping it would pass. I didn't want you to start working so soon on something that might change as quickly as the wind before a hurricane. You'll need to get used to that, though. One thing one minute—then a one-eighty turn, then back again to where you were. It's always late-breaking news in politics. But I had hoped you'd ease into it. I mean, it's not the governor's office. It's not the governor's press problem. But I suppose it could become that."

It seemed to be his turn to lessen some sort of load by talking. And my job to listen, as his employee and as his friend.

"I did talk to Marty. I talked to Gus. Individually then together. Basically, Beth, they threatened me. They *threatened* me! Said I was the new boy on the block and if I didn't support them it would spell political suicide. I'd never get elected. They meant it, Beth. They have huge war chests from those unions. They'd work in the background. They said I needed to 'join the Fraternity' and if I didn't, they would make sure that, come November, I would be nowhere near the ballot. It looks like I'll be called in to break a tie in the Senate. I either align myself with them or vote my conscience. Either way, I'm dead. Either my career dies or my spirit dies. My core beliefs, Beth—that's what this is about."

His voice had a frightening edge to it. His right hand was clasped into a fist, pounding into his open left palm as if to exaggerate every word, every beat of his heart.

"Bob, is it that important to you, to destroy you career?"

Our eyes met and I instantly knew the answer.

"And Margaret. She is furious. Says if I kill her dream she'd never forgive me. *Her* dream, Beth! She wants to be the first lady of Texas. Her platform will probably be the best makeup for every social occasion. She's pathetic. I've known it for a while now, but she despises me—the only thing she loves is money and stature. Comes before me, our marriage, or our son."

His eyes narrowed as the anger turned to pure disdain. He clenched his teeth so hard that the veins on his jaw line became pronounced.

"Bob, is it worth giving up your family, too?"

"What family? You can't call coexistence a family. It's certainly not a marriage. I tried to reason with her. Then she called in Patricia. God. That woman. She's my babysitter. She watches my every move when I'm not with Margaret, whom I hesitate, now, to call my wife."

"Oh no. She told Margaret you were here Monday night, didn't she...."

Again, I let that thought trail off. I really didn't want to hear what the response was going to be. I closed my eyes, took a deep breath and braced myself.

"Of course she did. She asked the driver what time I picked up my communications director, where we went and what time he drove me home. She said she was keeping a time card on you, as a new employee. You were paid by the hour and she wanted to be certain you were accurate in your accounting. He's new. He's gullible and he was bought. Margaret's precious money bought off his loyalty. I heard the entire recap from Margaret and Patricia, in stereo."

"I am so sorry. It was innocent—we were working." Damn. Remembering the conversation I'd overheard on Mackinac I wondered exactly how Margaret got the money she wielded so heavy-handedly. True, her family was wealthy—but there was this nagging thought surrounding Gaynor and Margaret. It was like a toothache that just wouldn't go away.

"It wasn't all that innocent and you know it, Beth. I won't deny it. I won't deny it at all."

His voice had softened and so had his eyes. Instinctively I reached over to place my hand on his. This time he didn't remove it.

"Now what?"

My heart was racing. I was torn. Should I resign or stay the course? As I contemplated my next action, Bob continued.

"Beth, here I am, spouting morality and standing up for what I believe is right on one hand. On the other hand, I'm sitting here next to you, wishing we were alone on some remote island. Yes. Okay. I said it. You have to know I have feelings for you."

A nervous laugh escaped. "Lieutenant Governor, have you been drinking or did someone pay you to trip me up, see what I'd do under pressure?"

I was halfway serious. You just never know in politics.

"I'm stone sober."

I shifted position out of nerves and my thigh touched his.

"What next, Lieutenant Governor?"

"Well, the lieutenant governor says there is no way he will sell out. But Bob is more a man of action."

With that, the lieutenant governor of the Great State of Texas leaned over and kissed me.

"Bob—please, please don't do anything you will eventually regret. Your entire life is at stake here." I felt the need for someone here to say sensible things. Whether I believed them or not.

"Yes, my entire life *is* at stake. It's time *I* make the decision how I want to live it. Are you with me or not?"

"Well, as your communications director I suppose I really need to ask—will I be out of a job?"

I looked directly into his eyes, which seemed dazed. The sparkle that always lit up his face was gone; the apparently sleepless nights had taken their toll. He stared at me without answering.

My heart rose into my throat. Heartbreak was something I'd become accustomed to. Was I feeling this way because my short-lived dream job was about to end? No, probably because another dream, far more personal, might never come true if I didn't follow my heart.

Speaking with only his welfare and my dreams in mind, I responded with a simple "I'm with you, Bob."

## Chapter Seven

We sat for a while, surrounded by absolute calm. Somehow a sense of peace had dropped down and enveloped us like a dream. The pizza had been devoured, the Pepsi consumed as though we were in the lieutenant governor of Michigan's office. Instead we were here in Austin, deciding futures.

"We have a slight power problem in Texas, Beth." While his tone was more somber than usual, Bob's mood seemed much more relaxed and accepting than it had been just an hour ago. He'd tossed off his shoes, which were now strewn carelessly under the coffee table, and untucked his rumpled checkered shirt from his navy pleated pants.

"I assume you don't mean gas, electric or oil, Lieutenant Governor."

"Your assumptions, ma'am, prove correct." My sly smile was returned by a softer, more knowing glance.

"I want out but I'll need to live within the fraternity, Beth."

"The fraternity?"

My question was genuine. I knew all about fraternities in college—they were for partying and camaraderie. Somehow I didn't think this was what he meant.

Again, I asked, "The fraternity?"

"Yes. Of silence. I will have to sell my freedom for silence. Those who buck the system are given three choices. Change, be blackballed or be blackmailed. I'd heard it existed, I just never had proof until now. What can I do? Go to the press? No telling what they would do then. I'll need to get out of the formal political arena. That is one way they'll silence me. I've been thinking of alternatives. I can give speeches, lectures. I can teach. More than likely some sort of journalism or communications course. What I can teach is the truth. The truth veiled as fiction. No one will ever really know if what I'm saying comes from fact or my vivid use of metaphors, imagination and linguistics."

"Bob, did you ever read *The Good Natured Men*? I believe it was Act Three—the line 'silence gives consent.' Are you sure you can do this? If you don't fight, Bob, you'll be giving in to them." My thoughts returned to Billy Glinnis. Had he checked the box that read "none of the above?"

"Beth, I always thought I was a fighter, a crusader, somewhat like the Alamo defenders I revere. They drew the line in the sand, you know? Well, that line has been drawn for me, Beth. By the party and by Margaret. You know, it really is similar to the Alamo. If I fight, I'm sure to die. You can only fight so long and so hard. Sometimes others take your fate into their hands and there is simply nothing you can do. That's how I feel now. Is it worth it?" His eyes were pleading with me to give him the answer.

"I can't answer that for you, Bob. I just can't. There are always choices and only you can control their outcome. You know that, right? It's not up to Gus, or Marty, Patricia or Margaret—or me." I wanted desperately to hold him and tell him I'd be there for him in every way. This was happening so fast.

"Beth, you're new in the world of politics. You're young. I hate saying that, I really do. I don't mean to say it to hurt you—although it might. The choice is mine. That's true. But my freedom of choice really has been taken away. I would like to vote my conscience, stay in office, champion the causes I believe in. I could do that. But it would get very, very ugly. Ugly for me, my family and—and for you. You're just starting out in your career. You could probably write something very juicy about this whole affair."

I cut him off before he could continue. "*Affair?* This isn't an affair, Bob. I can't believe you just said that."

I was trying to maintain my composure. I wanted to remain the strong one. In any given situation, when there is a conflict or problem, someone needed to remain strong. That bit of sage advice was about the only positive thing I'd gotten from a previous relationship. Yes. I intended to be strong.

"I didn't mean affair in *that* sense of the word, Beth, although I thought we *were* entering into a relationship—other than business-related. Was that just wishful thinking?"

Again, those pleading eyes.

"Affair. Relationship," I said slowly. "Those words are so cold. I don't want to stand next to you. I want to stand *with* you. Rather than working for you, I'd rather work *with* you. I would never use what I've learned during this brief, as you call it, 'relationship' for an article or juicy piece of journalism. I'd hoped you trusted me more than that. I also know that statement was said out of desperation and hurt. I'm hereby forgetting you even said it."

With that comment I smiled before continuing.

"I know we can do this. Together, I know we can do anything." The edge had left my voice and had been replaced by sheer resolve.

"Beth, as I said, this could get ugly. The chance of your getting hired on the heels of this is slim to none. Oh, someone might pick you up hoping to use you and what you know. Capitalizing on my misfortune. You'll take a fall with me. You'll have to be at the press conferences. You'll need to field the questions that will come hurling from every direction."

I needed to break the tension somehow.

"Bob, at the Alamo, weren't there women to help out your heroes? You know. 'For every good man there's an even better woman?'"

I placed my hand on his leg and looked directly into his eyes. The twinkle was coming back.

"First of all, Miss Pullen, your leg is rubbing up against mine and it's driving me insane. This is a serious discussion and you've somehow found a way to defuse it—and me."

We both actually began to laugh.

I raised my eyebrows, turned my head and cut my eyes back towards him.

"I take it this is one of those 'uniquely us' moments?"

"Oh, yes. Yes indeed. As to the Alamo. Right off the top of my head I can't recall whether or not Crockett, Bowie and the rest of the guys had women with them. I believe they left them back home, you know those tearful farewells make for good reading. Plus back then women's roles were to cook, clean, take care of the kids. I'm sure those fighting for our independence would have had it no other way."

He cleared his throat just waiting for my response.

"Well I do know Santa Ana had a 'companion.' Her name was Emily. I'm not entirely illiterate when it comes to your great state." I smiled and tossed back my hair. That was something Victoria taught me. She swore that it totally disarmed a man.

Apparently it doesn't always work or I wasn't doing it correctly. My comment was met with a hearty laugh. "Oh. Yes. She was the Yellow Rose of Texas."

"I knew there was something juicy to this state's obsession with yellow roses. And to think, all along, it has nothing to do with real flowers but a concubine! I can't believe I'm staying in a suite named for a concubine. Did Margaret choose my room?" I had to wonder.

Bob brushed back the hair that had fallen across my face. Our eyes met again.

"I'm with you, Bob. Whatever you decide. I'll even learn to like yellow roses if I must."

"If I buy you a dog would you name her Emily?"

"A *dog*?" I was starting to wonder where this conversation was meandering.

"Well, I hate to think of you spending your nights alone. A dog could keep you company."

Okay. He appeared serious. Sometimes I just couldn't tell.

"Bob, first off, I have an apartment. I couldn't have a dog if I wanted one. Secondly, I was hoping I wouldn't spend my nights for the remainder of my life with a dog."

With that, he started to pant, tongue hanging out, head flopping from side to side. I couldn't resist. I patted his head and asked him if he wanted a treat.

"Why is it that, when I'm with you, even the most serious of moments dissolve into laughter? And, speaking of treats...."

With that, the otherwise stately and well-bred lieutenant governor leaned over and licked my nose.

"Actually, I do have something for you."

He stood up and reached deep down into the pocket of his trousers. I was getting nervous.

"Should I turn my head?" A nervous laugh escaped.

"Oh, just close your eyes and let me explain."

There I sat, eyes shut. Heart pounding. Wondering.

"Keep your eyes shut. I'm nervous enough as it is."

"You? Nervous? You're a broadcaster and politician. You speak in front of thousands every day of your life!"

I was getting suspicious now. I could tell by his voice he really *was* nervous.

"Beth, put out your hands. Here. It's just a little box. It's nothing extravagant or special. But it is significant. When I was walking through the store, I saw this in a display case. I was hoping our conversation would go the exactly way it did. I took a chance and got this for you. You can open your eyes now."

In my hands he had placed a box, tiny yet expertly wrapped. It was very light so I presumed it was delicate. I opened it carefully. Inside was a tiny crystal woven basket. In the basket sat three expertly chiseled red crystal hearts.

"Oh it's lovely! Thank you."

There were no other words forthcoming. I was utterly in shock that he would have gotten me such a beautiful little gift.

"Three hearts. They represent the three people I am to you: the broadcaster, the lieutenant governor, and just me, Bob. I hope you know my feelings are unconditional. And that's unusual for a politician. Don't just stand there, say something."

"Bob, I don't know what to say."

I wanted to trust him, I really did.

"Let's sit down and I'll tell you my plan."

His plan was simple enough, in theory. I'd leave for Michigan in the morning. I would inform Daddy and Victoria that I needed to work in privacy. I was not to tell them what was going on. He'd deal with Margaret over the weekend. He would break the tie on Monday. Simple enough. He would not sell out to anyone, for any reason. If the party didn't like his stand, he'd leave office before they could blackball him. That way he could leave with honor and on top of the game. If Margaret didn't like his stand, he'd leave her as well. His son would be fine. He was sixteen and old enough to understand. He'd have to understand. Bob knew Margaret wanted him only for his position and future. Once he gave that up she would be furious—and finished with Bob.

As he finished his outline of the upcoming few days I felt the need to discuss where we stood on a personal level, leaving politics and his marriage out of the equation.

"Bob, this certainly seems to be another 'uniquely us' scenario. I can't say as I've ever had a man give me a gift and then, in the name of decency and honor, leave his family."

He took both of my hands into his and looked me squarely in the eyes. "I've never been more serious. You leave as everyone expects you to in the morning. Life will continue as normal. Fly back Sunday evening—a quick turnaround. Say you need to be here to cover the Senate vote on Monday. Normally I'd have Patricia make the arrangements. You need to do this on your own so she can't interfere like she did before. Trust no one. Rent a car on your own Sunday evening. We'll meet at my cabin Sunday evening and I'll fill you in on what happened with Margaret. I often go to the cabin by myself to think and be alone. Margaret never goes there with me. Sometimes Dave goes but Margaret and I together—never. I'll draw out a map now since when we communicate it will have to remain completely business the next few days."

I sat, stunned, as he walked to the desk, extracted a piece of printer paper and drew a map. He brought it over to me. It looked simple enough. I folded the map and stuck it between the pages of the novel I was currently reading. Should be safe there. All this happened in silence. I imagined I might need to get used to silence.

"Bob, I'll be at the cabin Sunday night. I think you need to be going, though. We don't know who's watching, now that we've discovered Patricia is a mole."

I didn't want him to go, but knew it had to happen.

"Beth, I've never liked Patricia. She is a loyalist to no one, except to Margaret. Again, I hesitate to use the term 'my wife.' She hasn't been a real wife to me in years. I knew early on it was a mistake but needed to make it work for Dave. If it weren't for him, I would have left years ago. I never really had a reason to, before."

His hand touched the side of my face and nothing else mattered.

"I need to do what I should have done before. It's seemingly convoluted—but it's honest and it's the right thing to do. I'll talk with Margaret and walk into the Senate Monday with my head held high. That way I can continue to live with myself...and with you...."

The sentence trailed off just as the twilight outside the window gave way to moonlight.

*Katherine Shephard*

**Chap**

## Chapter Eight

There wasn't much to do now that Bob had left. It was so quiet and still. I needed to send a brief email to Dad and Vic before heading back to Michigan, so I went to my computer.

> *Hi you two! Will be home tomorrow but busy. Things have heated up here and I need to work, privately, over the weekend. I'll return to Austin on Monday. I'll be staying in seclusion to work. I know you'll honor that. Right now all I can say is it's concerning the bill before the Texas Senate that will be voted on come Monday. I love you both. Just please trust me on this one. Everything is PERFECT and we'll talk after Monday, okay? Just didn't want you to worry. ~Beth~*

It seemed strange signing a note to Daddy and Vic with my new first name, but I needed to get used to it. Since my father and my deceased mother had named me Christine it seemed somehow disrespectful to go by a shortened version of my middle name. And yet, I had quickly grown to love being called Beth. It was softer and, when pronounced by Bob Larken, sweeter. Since that night on Mackinac Island my life had underdone a huge transformation. A metamorphosis. Blossoming from a college grad with lofty dreams, I had become a woman facing an uncertain reality. All in one short week.

I considered leaving a few things in the closet so I'd have less to pack when I returned in a few days. Things like deodorant, hairspray and my favorite body lotion. I didn't, however. I took everything back to Michigan. I was somewhat superstitious. If I left things in the suite I might jinx myself. You know, assume I'd be returning for good and then *bam!*—lose my job after Monday's vote.

The maid would tend to the few coffee cups we'd left in the sink, so all I had to do was pack up and check to be certain nothing personal remained. Of course I had my new laptop and recorder, but that was just a few cords to unplug. I made certain the notes and discs were safely locked away in a side compartment of the travel briefcase I'd carry on the plane. Superstitious *and* paranoid—what a combination. But I might need both. I locked the door and turned my back on the Yellow Rose suite.

I kept looking over my shoulder—all the way back to Michigan. Of course, how would I know if someone had followed me? If they were any good, I'd never know. I did pay closer to attention to people around me to see if anyone kept "appearing" nearby. As far as I could tell, the coast was clear.

I took side streets from Detroit Metro Airport back to Lansing. The weather was consistent with the calendar. The end of March was normally gloomy and on this last Friday of the month, the clouds hung down dark and ominous from the sky. Drizzle accompanied Peg and me on our journey back to the capital. I was tempted to veer a bit off the path and go south into the Irish Hills. Having had a small taste of the Texas Hill Country when we drove out to Rosa's, I longed for the gentle terrain of my own home state. As I passed the turnoff for Highway 12, I surrendered to temptation and drove through Washtenaw County on the back roads. I smiled as I saw the cutoff for the Michigan Space Center because it made me think of Houston and NASA. Of course, in Texas. The home of Bob Larken.

Not wanting to go through a major city, I headed a bit south. Spotting a gas station with a mini mart, I filled Peg's tank and grabbed a prepackaged sandwich before the final leg home. For a while, my travels paralleled the Grand River. Winding its way through the middle of the Michigan State campus it headed west through Grand Rapids to Grand Haven, where it dumped into

Lake Michigan. Massive, majestic trees lined the edges of the Grand. The mighty oaks provided enough food for the squirrels to make it happily through the harsh winters that often dropped down on this part of the state.

I began to hum the state's anthem "Michigan, My Michigan." Strange how the tune was that of "O Tannenbaum." Made it easy to remember, at least. In my research I had discovered that the state anthem for Texas was "Texas, Our Texas." A subtle, yet remarkable, difference between the states: the use of possessive pronouns. "My" versus "our." In Michigan, it seemed, we individually had state pride: "my." In Texas, it's a plural possessive: "our." Kind of like "y'all" in reverse. The whole darn massive state bonds together. Our Texas. That damn pride.

Pulling into my carport at the apartment complex, I gave the area a once-over glance, just to be safe. Although I'd always been a worrier, the paranoia surprised me. I supposed I, too, had to be careful. My life was a new ballgame now. All seemed clear and I took my belongings out of the trunk and went inside. I was home. Or was I?

As I approached the entry to my apartment, I noticed a plant in front of my door. According to the nursery tag affixed to its trunk, I was now the proud owner of a dwarf cherry tree. I opened the card, which read:

> *Honey, the first cherry tree was planted in Washington, D.C. on this date: March 27, 1912. Here's to your blossoming career —perhaps you, too, will plant yourself at the nation's capitol. One just never knows. You are destined for greatness. I'm so proud. I know your mother is, too. Always, Dad*

Daddy always knew how to tug at my heartstrings. I decided to put the tree on my patio. Now that I'd be in Texas every month, I wasn't sure it could survive here at home. Home. It didn't feel as much like home as it did just a few days before. I couldn't pinpoint why, but I imagined it had something to do with Bob.

I checked my voice mail and, sure enough, there were calls from both Daddy and Victoria. Both assured me they would honor my privacy but wanted complete updates once I returned to Texas on Monday. Unpacking the few items I'd taken, I did my laundry and curled up on the couch to think. What was I doing? What were my motives? My feelings? The only answer that even came close to making sense was love. From that first broadcast, I'd felt an immediate pull towards Bob Larken. I remember Daddy telling me about the first time he laid eyes on Mama. He called it "being soulmates." A feeling as though you were entwined. I recalled the night, just a week ago, on Mackinac. The moonlight coupled with Beethoven...and Bob. From the start, this had been more than an article or a job. The job was simply a means of using my education and paying my bills. Bob seemed to feel I would be dragged through the mud once everything hit the fan after the vote Monday, but I chose to believe that a compromise could be worked out. I was in the big leagues now and knew that when you play the game, you gamble. I'd just as soon emerge a winner—and alive.

I was also concerned for Daddy. How would he feel about his daughter not only becoming involved with a married man, but jeopardizing our good name and everything I'd worked for? True. I was young. I had a lot of life left ahead to recover from a minor setback. But I had to wonder how minor it would be. What would be the fallout and, as I'd asked Bob, would it be worth it? With absolute resolve Bob had said yes. Yes it was. I believed him when he said his marriage had been over for years before he even knew I existed. I believed him when he said we would be together and I firmly believed we could conquer anything, as long as we could tackle it together. Call me one of those cockeyed optimists from some schmaltzy Broadway musical, but I did believe it.

It was out of my hands. I hated that. There was nothing I could do. Someone else was holding the cards. For now.

The phone interrupted my train of thought. I didn't answer. When the machine picked up I heard his voice. The voice that had mesmerized me from the very beginning.

"Miss Pullen, I was just checking to be certain you made it home safely."

I picked up the receiver and responded, "Yes, yes sir. I am safe and well. Thank you for calling."

We exchanged a few more professional comments.

"I would appreciate you preparing a few comments concerning the upcoming vote. You can bring the drafts back with you, rather than faxing, as I'll be out of the office quite a bit and would be unavailable to read them."

He was letting me know that he wouldn't be able to receive any form of communication. That made sense. He didn't want me to call or send anything for fear that Patricia, or someone else, would intercept them. We were definitely sharing the same thought process.

"Yes sir. I understand. I will work on that this weekend. Thank you again, sir."

We said business-like goodbyes and hung up. I curled up again on the couch, knowing I'd more than likely dream of him.

Unlike Daddy, who said he couldn't sleep when his mind was on overload, I drifted off for more than ten hours. The fatigue had taken more of a toll than I'd realized.

Over the rest of the weekend I used what time I had left to read more on the history of Texas, study maps of the Lone Star State and familiarize myself, via the Internet, with Gus and Marty. Their voting histories, biographical information, and who contributed to their campaigns. Interesting. Two highly financed Democrats, both with a history of repeated run-ins with the mainstream press. I knew that the press was normally kinder to the left than the right. However, these two seemed to alienate everyone. I guess it really *was* their way or the highway. Unfortunately, it seemed that Bob and I might have a one-way tickets on the bus out of town.

I was tempted to pull out John Gaynor's business card and give him a call. It was Sunday, true, but I was certain he'd have an answering machine. I had promised Bob, though, that I would lie low this weekend and remain in seclusion. I longed to hear a friendly voice—someone on the inside, someone who was on our side. John was, after all, like a father to Bob. Surely he'd know what to tell me. There was so much I didn't know. I wanted to know more about how I could support Bob in the days ahead.

The weekend felt endless. I took long walks, watered my cherry tree and watched a lot of shopping networks to pass the time. Finally I could pack again and head for the airport. I decided against the drive to Metro and headed, instead, to Grand Rapids where I'd fly out of Gerald Ford International Airport. If people *were* following me, this might throw them off the track. I used my full name when making the reservations, since my identification was under Christine Pullen. If anyone was looking for me they would, more than likely, be searching for Beth. I also called ahead for a car in Austin. I wore totally unprofessional clothes, looking more like an Austin hippie chick than someone who worked for the government. The government? The concept still shocked me. I chose to wear my tattered jeans, a long-sleeved MSU T-shirt, and a sweater coat. I could ditch the coat when I arrived in Austin. At the last minute I put a "Kiss Me, I'm from Michigan" ball cap on my head, swiped the requisite gloss across my lips and decided I looked nothing at all like the woman who'd met Patricia Byrne in Austin just one week ago.

Eight hours later, I was weaving my way out of Austin traffic and west into the Hill Country. Spreading out the map on the passenger seat of my tiny economy car, I figured I'd reach the cabin around six that evening. The roads became steeper with more curves as I headed into the high hills. The dense thickets of live oaks and cedars looked like they could swallow me whole. I

spotted the beginnings of the famed bluebonnets here and there—
it would be several more weeks before they'd be in full bloom.
After making the final right turn onto the ranch road Bob had
written down as his address, I pulled off onto the shoulder. I got
out and stretched, inhaling the fresh, crisp air. I wanted to clear
my head of all that had been on my mind. The endless questions
I'd know the answer to soon enough. Did he speak with
Margaret? Had any decision been made about their future? Was
David involved? Did he mention me at all? Did she?

Climbing back into the rental car, I drove the final mile to the
cabin. Before me stood a simple, cedar-sided building with a tin
roof. Quite nondescript for a man of means. It was surrounded on
three sides by tall cypress trees. A small front deck held two
wooden Adirondack chairs and a side table. There sat the
lieutenant governor, in jeans and plaid lumberjack shirt, coffee
cup in hand. Waiting.

The crickets had begun their evening song and the sun was
setting behind the majestic treetops. The rising moon gleamed
over the cabin's roof. Bob Larken stood up, walked toward the
car, opened my door and said softly, "Welcome home, Sonata."

## Chapter Nine

Bob extended his hand chivalrously and helped me out of the driver's seat. Good thing he did. What with the air travel, paranoia, restless nights, no lunch and seeing Bob again, I was feeling pretty weak.

"I have some things in the trunk, Bob. Do you have anything stocked in the kitchen to eat, or is it another takeout night?" Not that I'd seen any pizzerias on the way here. I could tell that he, too, was worn ragged. The fatigue showed around his puffy eyes. Instead of his normally erect posture, his shoulders stooped like they were carrying the weight of the world. I sensed, however, a new aura of serenity about him. Perhaps the trees and relative seclusion had helped to make everything seem simple and peaceful. I could see why Bob would treasure this spot.

"Let me take your things in, then we can throw some hot dogs on the grill." His casual attire, the surroundings and the mere mention of hot dogs made me realize, once again, how much more there was to Bob Larken than his public image conveyed.

I followed him, carrying only my purse. The deck was expertly constructed of some type of hardwood that I was sure came from Texas. Everything was rugged and masculine, including the overstuffed plaid couches and chairs inside. As I followed Bob, I glanced around. Living room as you entered from the front, small bath and kitchen with smaller, apartment-sized appliances and one bedroom. Small and compact. Obviously a simple hideaway. There was so much land surrounding the cabin, I wondered why he hadn't made the cabin larger.

"Bob, this is a wonderful place to relax. But with a family, why didn't you have it made bigger?" I tilted my head and tucked my hair behind my ears.

"Well, that should be your first clue. I didn't want anyone to be up here with me. Oh, my son does come up, but he'd really rather be at home with his friends. I imagine when he gets older he'll want to come up with them. We'll see. As for Margaret— it's too rustic. No mall. No sunken tub. Not enough room for her cosmetics."

"Ah, yes, I can see that." I didn't want to get into the fact that there was just *one* bedroom. Luckily the couch looked comfortable, but a bit small for Bob—perhaps I'd offer to sleep there. Perhaps.

"You like hot dogs, Beth?"

"Well, sure, what American doesn't? I didn't take you for an Oscar Mayer kind of guy. But I love them!"

"I know." There was that sly smile again. Almost impish this time.

"Why do I think my father is involved somehow?" I had one of my sneaking suspicions. Whenever Bob knew something out of the ordinary about me, it seemed like Daddy was the culprit.

"Ah, Miss Pullen, you are one astute little lady. Yes, your father leaked the information. I'm glad he's on our side." The tension was lifting from his face and my curiosity was getting the best of me.

"Okay. Spill it, Larken." We were both smiling now. A good sign, I thought.

"Well, I phoned your father to let him know you really were going to be all right, that I was overworking and underpaying you but that I'd see to it that your benefit package improved."

With that last comment he gave me a wink and slapped my butt affectionately. That startled me and I let out a yelp.

"Your dad seems like quite a colorful man."

"Eccentric is a better word for it. Always wears a vest, no matter what. He must have a hundred vests. Golf vests, dress vests, knit vests, plaid vests, cotton vests—it's amazing."

"Well, he was a bit upset that you wouldn't be home today because it's Oscar Mayer's birthday. Did you know that?"

"Oh geez. Well, that's so typical of my dad. Every time he wants to spoil me he comes up with an off-the-wall holiday. So, are you going to spoil me, Lieutenant Governor Larken, or do I head back to Detroit for the festivities?" I began to hum the Oscar Mayer wiener song.

"Well, actually, I'm probably going to spoil the night. Margaret will be over later. After we've digested our hot dogs, of course."

I felt sick just hearing her name. Suddenly all the lightheartedness disappeared from the evening.

"Margaret? Coming here? I thought she hated this place!"

Panic flooded in and I felt trapped. Bob, Margaret and me out in the middle of the woods. She didn't seem the type to pack heat so that made me feel a bit safer. But her tongue—now that was as cutting as any Bowie knife.

"We felt this was the safest place. It's been swept. There are no bugs, no hard lines to tap. If anyone follows you, they're easily spotted. Margaret will be accompanied by Patricia, who will take notes for all of our signatures."

His tone had reverted to all business.

Before I could digest all of this information and ask questions, the sound of gravel crunching under slow-moving car wheels could be heard outside. On the unpaved roads out here it was easy to discern a car's approach.

"That must be Margaret and Patricia. Damn, they're a few hours early."

Bob had the look of a deer in the headlights.

"Perhaps they think the early bird gets the worm?"

I wanted to run, to hide, but there was no place to go and certainly no graceful way to back out of the corner I'd been shoved into. Damn, I thought—all this on an empty stomach. My palms were sweating and my stomach growling from nerves and lack of food.

"I suppose this is it, Bob." I couldn't think of anything else to say.

Without a knock, Margaret Larken and Patricia Byrne walked into the cabin and sat down on the sofa. The tension that entered with them was unmistakable. As if on cue, Bob said, "Margaret, Patricia, you know Miss Pullen, my communications director. Beth, please have a seat."

I did as I was told and Bob pulled up a dinette chair to seat himself at the helm of what would, perhaps, be a sinking ship.

"Your communications director? Oh I love that, Bob. Don't you mean your lover?"

Margaret's tone was icy enough to cut a wedge out of the dense Hill Country forests.

"Margaret, please. Don't."

Bob maintained his composure. I maintained my silence.

"Beth, Margaret and I have already met and spoken about the vote that will take place tomorrow. I will not stand with the Democrats in their attempt to pass a bill that would kill any chance for school vouchers or school choice in any form. That would be voting against what I feel is best for the children, best for parents and families. I just can't do that in good conscience. I have already been told that if I side with the Republicans my party will, in essence, disown me. A smear campaign would ensue that would make the Nixon tapes look like sugar candy. They have the money to do it. They have the union backing to do it. They have the brains and the media savvy to do it. They would go underground and use every source available to ruin me."

As Bob's last sentence ended, Margaret piped in.

"And *I* will not sit by and watch my years of devotion as your wife and as mother to your only child be ruined by some cockeyed loyalty to a cause that would make your tenure in office a blip on a radar screen. If parents want to send their kids to a different school, let them find their own way to do it. I will not be the wife of a failure. I will not agree to just fade away. Bob, if you want out of politics, go. But when you return—and you will—I'll be right there by your side as I've always been, smiling and supporting you."

I could no longer remain silent as the grave.

"Wait. Back up, Bob. You're voting your conscience. Then what?"

"Then you'll be out of a job, Missy." Margaret's condescending tone made the hair rise on the back of my neck.

"Please don't call me Missy. My name is Beth."

"No it's not. It's Christine. And you will be unemployed by sundown tomorrow."

"Please, Margaret, Beth. Let's just talk like adults here."

His voice was pleading; his eyes begging me to understand.

"Adults?" Margaret was getting shrill. "You said *adults*? This *girl* is not much older than our son! And the second part of your brilliant plan, which it doesn't appear you've shared with your friend here, directly impacts her livelihood. And mine. So please, Bob, please do continue."

Her breathing was becoming heavier, as if she would soon start to hyperventilate. Patricia was dutifully taking notes with a stoic face. I wondered if she had a tiny recorder in her pocket.

"Beth, your services as my communications director will end tomorrow when I resign as lieutenant governor of Texas. I will see that you are paid, out of my pocket, for one month."

I tried not to show how horrified I was as he continued.

"I will be flying overseas for a divorce. I've found a small country where records are kept locked away and there is no public accounting whatsoever. Margaret has agreed to the divorce. However, it will be very private. To all concerned, we will still be married. She contends that I will, one day, return to politics. I absolutely disagree." Bob's resolve was loud and clear.

"Bob, it's in your blood." Margaret was trying to soften her voice now. "You love the power, the limelight, and the chance to make a difference. Broadcasting was so beneath you. When you return to the capitol, or Congress, I will be standing right next to you— your devoted wife, as always. I will not agree to a divorce unless you agree to my terms. If you don't agree, I go public with your affair. It will get ugly. Your son will suffer the humiliation of a father who is a philanderer and you'll lose monetarily in court when I do battle. Believe me, you'll lose."

Her eyes were squinting and had I not known better, I could have sworn daggers were piercing Bob Larken's heart.

"So, how does this impact me, other than not having a job?" I was befuddled, at best.

"Beth, it's no longer a secret between Margaret and me. You know how I feel about you. I want to spend the rest of my life with you."

Was this a proposal, or a proposition? I couldn't imagine anything less romantic.

"Please continue—I'm dying to hear what you have in store for my life." It was my turn to become as cold as ice.

"I didn't want it to happen this way. I'd hoped we could have talked before *they* came."

The emphasis on "they" was extremely obvious. He nodded his head towards his wife and assistant as he continued. "My married life with Margaret was over a long time ago. I stayed only because of our son. I realize, now, what I want—I want peace, laughter. I want to share what life I have left honestly. I want to do that with you. Now we have a choice, Beth. We can turn our backs on any type of future together or we can make a deal with the devil."

As he said the word "devil" he glared directly at his wife.

"Some choice," I groaned. "Exactly what is the type of future you had in mind for us?" My tone became sarcastic and cutting. My heart wanted to say yes; my mind wanted facts.

"Beth, Margaret will not let me go public with another marriage or relationship."

There it was, that word, "relationship." Despite my sigh, he continued. "I will legally be divorced from her, leaving me free to marry or date, or whatever. The catch is, it must be done within the Fraternity. In other words—done silently, not publicly. For all intents and purposes, she will still be my wife—but in name only. She'll give me up, gladly. She just won't give up the power and prestige."

"That's right," Margaret chimed in. "You can have him, Missy—it'll just have to be behind closed doors. When he returns to the political arena—and I say 'when' because *I* am the one who *really* knows him—I will be on his arm. Would you like to say something now?" She was patronizingly smug.

"Can I think about this and get back to you? Okay. I've thought about it. Go to hell."

With that, I got up and left.

*Katherine Shephard*

## Chapter Ten

One small problem with walking out in a fit of anger was that I had no way to actually leave. My purse, with the rental car keys inside, was sitting in the cabin. If this was what life as a grownup was going to be like, from now on I needed to remember to put the keys in my pocket, not my purse. That's right. Be more of a Girl Scout. Keep a credit card, a few bills and keys with me at all times. I was learning.

Having no other way to escape, I walked. I forged through the closely-knit oaks and mesquites, stepping over roots and fallen branches. I climbed over rocks and finally parked myself against a huge cypress tree in a small clearing. I let the aroma of the budding leaves fill my lungs. The cooling, crisp air sent a gentle shiver down my spine. How could they accuse us of having an *affair*? If Daddy got wind of that he'd break down. It wasn't an affair...well, not in the way they would portray it. They took something innocent and twisted the facts into folly. Well, it wasn't all that innocent. But the only intimacy was between our hearts, not our bodies. There was that kiss. Shit. They'd got us dead to rights. Out most of the night. Lights off. Too much to drink. With just that much they could buy off anyone to say we were doing something we really weren't. I'd even bet they could dummy up photos somehow. This whole Fraternity crap was more than I could even fathom, and I didn't think I was all that naïve. Vic would say "You stupid broad. Honey, how could you get yourself in this mess?" That, coming from a woman who's had more affairs than Texas has pickup trucks.

Cursing my fate, I wondered what to do next. I hadn't left a trail of crumbs, but if I turned myself around now I could stumble my way back before it was totally dark. But then what? Another confrontation with Bob Larken's razor-tongued wife  was not on my "ways to brighten your spirit and enrich your soul" list. Seeing Bob wasn't on the list either. If I saw him, I was afraid I'd melt. He had this devastating effect on me. It wasn't healthy.

On the other hand, I couldn't just stay in the woods. A breeze was kicking up, a sure sign that a storm might be approaching. That might solve my problems. I could drown in a sea of mud out here in the middle of nowhere. Or get struck by lightning. How prophetic would *that* be? I could just imagine the headlines. "'My Husband's Secret Lover Struck by Lightning Just Before Hill Country Tryst': The Second Lady's Tragic Story." Margaret would get her picture all over the tabloids. Maybe even an interview with Oprah. She would be the darling of scorned political wives. There wouldn't be a judge in the Great State of Texas that wouldn't want to hang the lieutenant governor out to dry once the "truth" was revealed. He'd lose everything. And I'd be dead. Damn depressing, so I decided I'd better get out of here and save myself. Save Bob from what that woman would do once my untimely death was discovered.

"Beth. Beth? I know you're out here somewhere—there are fresh footprints. Please. Please let me know you're okay. It's not safe out here alone."

Just his voice was enough to do me in. Double damn.

I sat motionless. If he wanted to find me, he could continue to follow the footprints, I decided. Let him be the Boy Scout. I slumped down onto the moist spring ground, thankful that I'd worn jeans and an old shirt. His walking was heavy and deliberate, as if he wanted to be heard. The walk of a man with a mission. Unlike a predator stalking its prey, he was not trying to mask his search. I knew he was closing in on me. I could smell his aftershave and hear his breathing. I stood up. Unafraid of being found, I called out towards him.

"Bob, please tell me there is no Fraternity. Please tell me I don't need to choose between you and silence. But most of all, please tell me...." Before I could finish the sentence, Bob Larken came out from behind a clump of trees, walked up to me, took my face into his hands and said, "I love you."

I laid my head on his chest. He wrapped his arms tightly around me. I was home.

"Let's get back to the cabin before it's so dark we can't see at all. Margaret and Patricia are gone. Patricia wrote up the notes from our discussion. We can look them over and sign them tonight."

He didn't yell at me for walking out. He didn't make me feel intimated or chastised. He made me feel warm and relieved to be found. And yet, I could feel my blood pressure rise with the words he chose.

"Discussion? You call what just happened a *discussion*? It was more of a unilateral decision. Your *wife* was the judge and jury—you agreed to the verdict and I was sentenced to silence. I would hardly call that a discussion."

"Beth, it's the only way we can be together and prevent the rumors, the tabloid stories, the embarrassment of scandal."

"Scandal? What have we done that is so scandalous? If something happened when I was passed out the other night, please do tell. And if it did I wouldn't brag about it. I don't even remember."

My sarcasm was not falling on deaf ears. Bob looked hurt by my cutting words but no way was I going to apologize. I was not going to be placed into the victim role.

"Beth, nothing happened. But they have threatened me—well, us—with what looked bad. They have concocted an entire scenario of what could have happened and vow to make it the world's reality if I decide to buck their plan. Margaret wants the power, the name. As I said, she doesn't really want me, just who and what I am."

"'To remain silent when they should protest makes cowards of men.' Thomas Jefferson." It was the one quote that stuck with me from poli sci. I never though it would apply to me.

119

"Okay. Fair enough. Protest. I'm still going to break the tie tomorrow. I'm still going to divorce Margaret. If you protest, then you're on your own."

This was the Bob Larken I'd seen on television. The firm, do-what-you-must-and-go-to-hell Bob Larken. I had always hoped it was the real Bob Larken. Now I wasn't so sure.

The cabin was within sight. Bob broke away from me and walked the rest of the way alone. Now I understand why Daddy told me "Don't be in such a hurry to grow up, Chrissy."

Here I was, alone in the woods with a man substantially older than me, thrust in the middle of a political and personal battle for power after a man dies at his desk, cutting deals with senators and a soon-to-be ex-wife, and about to join what felt like the witness protection program. Talk about a crappy day.

The cabin door squeaked as I opened it. "Bob, you need some WD-40 on this thing." I was still in shock. Obviously, if that was all I could think of to say.

"And you need to grow up, Beth. But I love you anyway. Now let's get back to business." His eyes were cold, his stare even icier.

"Grow up? Business? A relationship? A discussion? You're heartless. I should slap you silly, Larken."

Before I could continue with my hurtful litany he once again defused my plan.

"Go ahead, little Miss Michigan. I think I just might enjoy that."

I would have been okay except he winked.

"Lieutenant Governor, whatever am I going to do with you?"

He raised his eyebrows and gave me a Cheshire cat grin. I shook my head, rolled my eyes and simply sighed "Men." Victoria would have been proud of me.

"Let me pour you a drink and we can read these papers, sound okay? I have beer or some Hill Country wine."

"I'll take a small glass of wine. I don't need a repeat performance of the damsel-in-distress routine. You get earplugs for me, by the way?"

"Anyone ever tell you you're a brat, girl?"

He laughed as he tossed the tablet with Patricia's handwritten notes my way. He had poured himself a glass of Chablis and was taking a preliminary wine tasting before pouring my drink.

"Bob, I'm glad you're tasting that wine before I take a sip." I shuddered at the thought of how happy my demise would make Margaret right now. "Ever think Glinnis didn't have a heart attack—that he was murdered?" There. I'd said it.

"Beth—there was no autopsy. I found that strange—but no one dug deeper. No questions. He had a heart attack and that's that."

"The Fraternity?"

"But why, Beth? Why would anyone want Glinnis out of office?"

"Bob, you said he was aligned with the governor—which means Gus and Marty as well. You have a wife who sees the opportunity for you to make a huge name for yourself by bucking the mainstream and taking a stand. Think about it. You have a mentor who can buy your way into office. Seems pretty obvious to me, Bob."

"Beth—your imagination is running amuck. Margaret is power-hungry—but she's no murderer. Victoria's 'don't drink the coffee' really got to you, didn't it? Don't worry—really."

"Bob—why is his death so hushed?"

"His doctor has now come out and said he had elevated cholesterol and high blood pressure, even though he appeared to be in the best of health. Sometimes these things just happen."

"Has anyone asked to see the medical records, Bob?"

"Beth, please. Drop it. He's dead. We're not. Which can be verified by your gurgling stomach."

"We'll drop it for now—and only because I am starving. May I assume wine first, then wienies?"

Just as I finished my sentence Bob spit his wine all over himself and everything that was within a three-foot radius. Coughing and laughter accompanied the spew of Chablis. Running into the bathroom, I yanked toilet paper off the roll and began blotting up the projectile mess.

"You're quite a sight, Lieutenant Governor."

I couldn't help laughing at the casualness of the situation. Just a week ago antiques and wealth on Mackinac Island surrounded us. Now we were alone together, wearing jeans and old shirts in the rustic Hill Country woods of Texas. As I looked over Bob's shoulder, I could see, out the window, the only thing that was the same. The moonlight.

"Miss Pullen, I can't say as I've ever been propositioned quite in that fashion."

"Huh?" I suppose I was too wrapped up in the mess and moonlight to catch on.

"Your proposition. Asking me if we were going to have wine before sex."

"Sex? Who mentioned *that*?" I didn't mean for it to come out like it was a disease, but it did.

"Yes. Sex. Don't play coy with me." The smirk was there even as he used his shirtsleeve to wipe the traces of wine from his chin.

"Sex. S-E-X. Wine before wiener. I never know when you'll come up with one of your off-the-wall comments. No wonder you're a writer. You're so quick on your feet with words, even when you feign innocence." He was smiling as he continued to clean himself up.

"Well, I'm only employed for another twenty-four hours. I guess I should collect on my benefit package, hmmm?" Coy seemed to be working for me, I deduced. Why quit now?

Looking somewhat disarmed Bob picked up the papers again, and, this time, a pen.

"Let's get this over with so we can enjoy our evening. It's a gorgeous night out tonight. Maybe we can spend some time on the deck, looking at the stars."

I had a sneaking suspicion I knew what that meant. At this point I'd sign my own death warrant if it meant spending more time with Bob Larken, alone, under the Hill Country sky.

As I read the words, it *was* a type of death sentence. I'd be killing my dreams. A future of honesty. And children.

"Bob, what is this? It reads 'Any child/ren born of this union shall not bear the Larken name.' If I got pregnant it would be a bastard? This is insane."

"Beth, please. This is just a formality. I don't think, legally, she would have a leg to stand on. You can name a baby anything you want to name it. Bozo Larken works. Beth, Bob and Bozo. Alliteration. Writers love alliteration."

He smiled to break the tension that was mounting.

"Furthermore, did I ever mention anything about *babies?* I do remember mentioning a puppy...."

"Oh, that clause just hit me wrong. It's a woman thing. Plus forget the baby. I hate the name Bozo. Bowie Larken, maybe. An Alamo defender name that alliterates. Plus that child would be a knife in Margaret's back."

With that I hung my head.

"Oh, sorry. I know she's your wife and Dave's mom. I'm sorry, Bob."

"No problem. I understand. Maybe we could name a *puppy* Bowie."

He said it as a statement, not a question.

"You've got yourself a deal, Larken." I stared down at the papers. What the hell, I decided. I picked up the pen and signed away my future.

Once the formality of signing the papers was over, Bob and I took our wine and headed out to the deck. It only took a minute for the hot dogs to cook on the grill. Bob had opened up a can of barbequed beans and heated them on the tiny stove inside the cabin. I found a bag of chips in the cupboard for us to munch on. Just another perfect moment in the lives of two normal, everyday people. If anyone were to wander by they would think we were just country folk. A Currier and Ives painting come to life.

We put our food on paper plates, two plain hot dogs each. There were no condiments for the wieners. Some party this was. No ketchup and no birthday cake. I was trying to keep my thoughts on a fanciful level, making the most of our time alone. The trance was soon broken.

"Beth, I'm sorry for having dragged you through all of this ugliness. But I want to thank you, too. Really."

"Thank me? For what?" I wasn't really sure why he would be thanking me.

"You've shown me there is so much more to life. So much I've missed. In the short time I've known you I've seen a part of me that I'd hidden for a long, long time."

His voice was gentle and his eyes, locked on mine, sincere.

"What on earth could a new college grad teach an old pro like you?" I tried to lighten things up again.

"Freshness. You really are a breath of fresh air, Beth. I'd gotten so caught up in games, attitudes, how I'm perceived, that I'd lost who and what I really am and want to be. I never stopped to think about how I want to live out the days I have left on earth."

He'd finished his dinner, placed his dish and wine glass by the signed papers on the table behind us and edged his chair closer to mine. The wide expanse of the deck was mostly in front of us. On each side of the deck and cabin, the Hill Country woods separated us from the outside world. The densely compacted cedar and oaks surrounded this peaceful hideaway and seemed to keep the world at bay. And the strength represented in the sturdy trunks of those trees mirrored the strength I had recently seen in Bob.

"Beth, it's true. I love the limelight. Thinking, knowing I can make a difference. But at what cost? My personal happiness? It had gotten to be a chore, a job. I was going through the motions on sheer adrenaline—day in, day out. Margaret has worn me down for many years now. Harping and prodding me to do more, do it better, say it louder. Tells me where I should go, with whom I should be seen. She's turned out to be more of a PR agent than a wife."

"What about Dave, Bob? How is this going to affect him?" My voice started to quiver. I remember how the loss of my mother devastated me. While his dad wouldn't be dead, in a sense there would still be mourning. His father wouldn't be there, day in and day out. When they were together there would be a cloud hanging over them. I would be that cloud.

"David is a smart young man. He's so wrapped up in his own life and friends right now he hardly knows he has parents."

He smiled and I could see the love for his son shining in his eyes. "I grew up wondering who my real dad was. I know he's out there somewhere. I've known loss, too. Everyone does. It's real life. Something he will have to deal with. He didn't ask for this. He probably deserves better—but it's real life. And when the chips are down—it's *my* life. If I don't show Dave how to live happily, who will? If I'm not there to stand up and say 'Hey, this is what I want'—who will? He has his entire life ahead of him. He's smart, handsome and popular. He knows I love him."

"Isn't that being awfully selfish, Bob?" I placed my own plate and wine glass on the table and folded my arms across my chest. It was getting chillier outside in contrast with the warmth of the company.

"No. Absolutely not. If I'm not true to myself, what is that teaching him? In the end, if I didn't do what *I* truly wanted, I'd be angry. Oh, I could mask it. Go into denial mode. Get rid of all the reminders, never talk to or see you again. I could very easily deny myself—and you. I'm use to being in front of a camera, remember?"

This time his smirk had a chilling edge.

"I just want you to be certain. Absolutely certain."

"I am. When I make up my mind, I make up my mind. That's just the type of man I am. I have fallen in love with you. I finally know what that means—love. I can talk to you. Really talk. For hours on end. I can laugh. I will walk out on the past if I have to. I will leave politics, the capitol. I will do whatever I have to in order to be true to myself. For once."

The resolve was coupled with a tenderness I'd never seen in a man before. My eyes went watery with disbelief. My heart was in new territory here. How I could be so blessed while, at the same time, feel so cursed? I could no longer speak.

Not knowing what else to do, I knelt by his chair, put my head on his lap and cried. Tears of sorrow for what we'd be giving up. Tears of joy for what I'd been given. Bob stroked my hair, then lifted my head.

Wiping away the tears he said, "Don't cry, my princess. I'll make everything all right." The moonlight glistened in his eyes.

"I know you will. I trust you. I believe in you. And yes, I love you too."

I stood up, taking his hands as an invitation to stand with me.

"I'll be right back," he said. "There's something I want to get."

His smile was becoming infectious. A few warm raindrops replaced my tears and the sense of dread I'd felt earlier gave way to a rising sense of anticipation.

"Close your eyes, Miss Michigan."

I liked the latest nickname he'd come up with and couldn't possibly imagine why I had to close my eyes again. He'd taken the signed papers in with him, tossing the paper plates over the side of the deck into a large waste can on his way. The can, I noticed, had a lock on the lid. To keep the woodland creatures at bay, I guessed. I was hoping that when he returned, he'd bring me a cup of fresh coffee. Instead of smelling coffee brewing, I heard music and some indiscernible banging from inside the tiny cabin.

"Your eyes had better be closed."

There was a light chuckle accompanying these words and I turned my back to the door to resist the temptation of peeking. I always peeked. I hated surprises. My curiosity always won. On Christmas, as a little girl, I'd learned to unwrap packages so adeptly that even Santa couldn't tell I already knew exactly what was inside. It was a game. I'd find and unwrap the gifts then, on Christmas morning, see how well I could act surprised. Worked every year, too. As I was reminiscing, I heard the squeaky door open, then a loud thud on the wooden planks behind me. It startled me and, when I jumped, Bob grabbed me and pulled me down on the mattress.

"What on earth?"

My eyes opened to find the lieutenant governor smiling at his mischievous devilment.

"You dragged the bed mattress clear out here?"

We both dissolved in laughter.

Just as if on cue, the lieutenant governor began to sing.

As I listened to "Colour My World" I knew he meant every word. He took my breath away.

As the song ended, he took me into his arms.

"I have more to say, Beth, but I thought you'd like a song from Chicago, being a Midwesterner and all. But you know, I'm a Texan. Next song will be straight out of the heartland. I look refined, I play the part well, but, deep inside, I'm really a good ole boy. I care deeply, I work hard and I love pickups."

"Trucks. I do hope you mean trucks." Laughing and joking with Bob Larken was so natural.

"Hey, I didn't know you could sing! I never read that in your bio." I was genuinely shocked and quite impressed.

"You told me that, from the start, you loved my smooth voice."

There was that ornery Texas grin.

"Yes sir, you are smooth."

Before I could continue, the lieutenant governor showed me just how smooth he was. The moments became minutes, the minutes became magic as we loved one another, for the first time, on the deck under the moonlight.

## Chapter Eleven

The serenity of the night surrounded us as we drifted off to sleep. As the sun rose, it seemed to be calling us to begin anew. Today was the day of the Senate vote and here we were, tucked away in the Hill Country like we were wrapped inside a dream. My pillow was slightly damp from the morning dew. I hoped it wasn't drool. Vic always told me I drooled in my sleep. Supposedly I kind of squished my face sideways on the pillow, mouth agape. How attractive. Saying a silent prayer to the patron saint of drool, I made sure I was covered up with the blanket Bob had apparently tossed across me. Wrapped up like a burrito, I headed inside. The smell of coffee permeated every crevice of this cozy hideaway. I felt like sitting down, grabbing a cup to help shake off the cobwebs and staying forever. Hearing the shower running, I spotted Bob's suit and tie lying across the table just outside the bathroom door. There wasn't enough room in the bathroom to accommodate even one person getting dressed. Picking up his tie, I smiled. Red, white and blue—the Lone Star flag design. If nothing else, he would be making a statement. Was he, too, a lone star?

Walking into the bedroom where Bob had placed my suitcase, I looked through the few outfits I'd packed. I smiled as I gently unfolded my navy blue business suit, white camisole and red accessories. I had a pair of gold star-shaped earrings as well. If I tucked my hair back behind my ears, I too would make a statement, if only to myself. Monday, March 30. March was going out like some kind of lion.

Bob exited the shower with few words, seemingly deep in thought. I knew it was time for me to simply leave him be. I took my turn showering and, once we were both dressed, we shared a cup of early morning coffee on the deck before heading into Austin. Facing the day to come was a solemn prospect. Leave it to Bob to shake up the mood.

"Hey, do all the woman in Michigan coo and drool while they sleep, or is it uniquely you?"

He was trying to maintain a straight face.

"Good thing you're dressed to the nines, Lieutenant Governor, or I'd toss my coffee at your smarty-pants mouth." I put my nose up in the air as if I were offended. "I'll have you know that not another man has ever complained about the way I am in bed."

Zing.

"I wasn't complaining and it had nothing to do with you in bed. It was the way you slept that I found adorable."

He looked hurt, for some reason. That softened me.

"Oh. Well thank you. And for your information, no other man has ever complained... because there has been no other man."

I wanted him to know so much more, but now was not the time. With tears in my eyes I walked over to him and said, "Only you. There's only been you."

Bob inhaled deeply and luckily, changed the subject. He had a way of knowing exactly when to save me from babbling. It must be the broadcaster in him. That incredible timing with words and thoughts.

"We really need to head to the capitol, Beth."

Taking another deep breath, he glanced over his shoulder at his beloved cabin.

"I hope she doesn't take this, too."

Without another word, the lieutenant governor of the Great State of Texas walked to his car with head held high and left for Austin alone.

Going inside, I gathered what we'd left behind, turned off the coffeepot and straightened up a bit. I kept seeing Bob, standing at the end of the deck and looking back longingly as if he were saying goodbye to a dream. As I turned the lock on the cabin door and walked down the stairs, I stopped to pick up a smooth gray stone. I don't know why, I just did. Most people would say it looked like a triangle with a piece missing. But to me, it looked like a heart.

I rolled down the car windows, left the radio off and headed northeast, back to Austin. The sweet juniper-scented Hill Country air filled my lungs as I wound through the gentle hills. Although the silent serenity of the early morning hours had left me longing for more  it was time to face whatever this day would bring.

In less than an hour I was back in Austin. As I crossed back over the Colorado River on Congress Avenue, I began feeling a strong sense of dread mixed with a disconnected, indecisive kind of mood. I didn't want to get to the Rotunda too early, and really didn't know where to go or what to do with myself. I extracted my credentials from my purse, hung them around my neck and stopped at the nearest coffee house to the dome, a few blocks south of the capitol complex. I got a table on the sidewalk and watched the office workers passing by on their way to another ordinary day. My breathing was becoming heavier to match the feeling in my heart.

What had I been thinking? I'd just signed myself into purgatory, if not hell, overheard one too many ugly conversations, made love to a married man and was now about to witness political suicide. Daddy's tuition dollars at work. Shaking my head I knew what I wanted to do. I wanted to call Vic. That would have to wait because I had no clue what phone line was safe to use, if any. Mentally, I went into Pollyanna mode. I would be able to go back to my apartment soon. Maybe this would all blow over. There'd be no tiebreaker needed; Bob would admit to a major brain fart and I'd keep my dream job. Vic would move down here and we'd get a cute little apartment and hang out on

Sixth Street listening to music every night. She'd love it here—all these bubbas just waiting to impress a cute Yankee girl.

With newfound confidence, I left my car parked where it was and walked up Congress Avenue to the dome. I'd never been to the east wing of the capitol, and figured this was not exactly the way I wanted to acquaint myself with the Senate chambers. Again, not my choice. Where the hell is that American promise—freedom of choice? There was such a thing, wasn't there? Wasn't it some inalienable right? Maybe not. I didn't know. Sometimes people take our choices away. And sometimes we give up one kind of freedom to gain another.

As I followed the magnificent Great Walk through the grounds, I stopped at the statues of San Houston and Stephen Austin. Mimicking Bob's tradition of paying homage to these two great Texans, I saluted. Another superstition. Don't break tradition. I glanced, again, at the pink granite Heroes of the Alamo monument, remembering how I'd overheard the heated discussion between Gus and Marty. Entering the South Foyer of the capitol building, I let my mind continue its endless litany of whys, why-nots and what-ifs. That kept me from turning around and getting the hell out of Dodge, as they would say in cowboyspeak. When in Texas, you know? The place was rather growing on me. Like mold on old cheese. Or barnacles on a sunken ship.

Making my way to the second floor, I knew exactly which entrance led to the Senate chamber from the unmistakable presence of the media and looky-loos. They all looked the same: pens and spiral-bound tablets in hand, credentials dangling from necks, sneakers instead of dress shoes. Sneakers and journalists—a marriage made in the press box. You just never knew when something would break and you'd have to run to a phone or outside to use your cell to call your editor. I made my way past the crowds and entered the galley through the VIP entrance. Since I hadn't been in town long enough to acquaint myself with anything but the lieutenant governor's office, also on the second floor, Bob had told me exactly where to go to be the safest. Opening the door to the galley, I sat down and perused a leaflet that was handed to me by a page, along with the Senate agenda. Normally, the agenda would be delivered to me online or, when I was in town, delivered to me in the communications office. Only I hadn't had the job long enough to set up the office. Minor detail.

The history within these walls was impressive. Thirty-one original walnut desks from 1888; thirty-one senators from all over Texas. There they sat, in high-backed leather chairs. Some slumped over from too much weekend, others were looking rested and still others were reading or chatting away as if this were just another workday. For them, I guess it was. Microphones now stood where the inkwells used to be. I spotted Gus and Marty sitting there with smirks as wide as a Texas T-bone. Gus had a pencil holder on his desk made to look like longhorns. Damn. I hadn't even seen a longhorn yet. I had a Texas to-do list a mile long. I wanted to go to see an Astros game. I wanted to tour NASA, get some seafood on the Gulf Coast, go shopping in Dallas, and see Fort Worth where the West really began. I wanted to see the bluebonnets in full bloom and visit LaGrange where the famous whorehouse used to be. That last thought made me smile again.

Bob was looking completely in control, sitting at the rostrum at the front of the chamber. As President of the Senate, he commanded respect with his self-confident stance and wide, proud smile. All eyes were on him as he stood, took the gavel and began to speak.

"Ladies and gentlemen of the Senate, guests and honored citizens, today we will have the third reading of a bill for possible amendment to be returned to the House. Perhaps it will be ratified and signed. I imagine there will be chubbing. There will be those of you who will debate for stalling purposes. Please remember, however, your solemn duty as an elected official of the Great State of Texas. Remember your duties lie with your constituents and not with any personal grudge or vendetta. I am breaking with tradition today and ask that we begin our day by listening to the anthem of the State of Texas. May we stand united for this great state."

He raised his hands, inviting the senators and those in the galley to stand as well. The lieutenant governor nodded his head and, on cue, symphonic music rose from the speakers surrounding the chamber. Bob Larken began to sing, solo.

"Texas, our Texas! All hail the mighty state! Texas, our Texas! So wonderful, so great. . . ." The lieutenant governor turned, dramatically, toward the Lone Star flag. He held his head erect and his voice became even stronger on the final strains: "Texas, dear Texas! From tyrant grip now free. Shines forth in splendor your star of destiny! Mother of heroes! We come your children true. Proclaiming our allegiance, our faith, our love for you."

After a moment of total silence, he continued.

"Ladies and gentlemen of the Senate, please be seated, remembering those words."

The surprise serenade shocked the members on the floor and sent several reporters out to call their editors. The Secretary of the Senate began the roll call from his small podium in front of the rostrum. I wanted to stay, to hear the debate, but my heart wasn't sure it could control my emotions. Not being the actor that Bob was, I was fearful of breaking down. If I stumbled once, showed my emotions once, it could be extremely detrimental to the lieutenant governor's cause. I left, silently praying for God's will to be done, and walked to Bob's private office. There sat Jill, bless her heart, with a plate of freshly baked Texas pecan cookies and a hot pot of coffee. Non-decaf. Across the room was the lieutenant governor's massive mahogany desk and leather chair. The one Billy G was found sitting in, dead. It didn't strike me as a very lucky chair.

The proceedings were being piped into the office so I could keep track of their progress. 74 (R) SB was being read.

"Miss Pullen, are you all right?" Jill's life experiences made her one of the most astute women I'd ever met.

"Yes, yes thank you. Today is a very pivotal day and I need to start writing some press releases for the lieutenant governor's perusal."

"It's that amendment concerning educational vouchers, isn't it? I couldn't help but hear the scuttlebutt in the hallways and the cafeteria. Just about everywhere I go it's the topic of conversation. Seems like the lieutenant governor will have to cast his first tiebreaker. Exciting time!"

If she only knew how exciting.

"I'm really looking forward to getting to know you better, Miss Pullen. We'll have a few years in this office together and who knows, maybe even get to the governor's office. Maybe even D.C. I have great faith in him. He might have gotten here unconventionally, but I think it was God's will. He has the courage, the intelligence and the integrity we need here in Texas. Patricia says if he aligns himself right in the middle he'll stay out of trouble. I hope he does. He can be pretty stubborn. Don't know if you've seen that part of him yet or not."

Her smile was genuine, her sentiments straight from the heart.

"Oh, I've not known him all that long, Jill, but what I do know is that he won't compromise himself. If he feels as though something needs to be changed, he'll fight for it. He's strong-willed, that's apparent."

"Apparent? How so?" Her inquisitive look and tilt of her head lead me to believe she was not on the inside of this current floor debate.

"Oh, it's just about the voucher debate. He truly does not believe that school vouchers damage the public school system nor are they unconstitutional. I hope the backlash today doesn't follow him like a black cloud."

That was all I felt I could say.

"Jill, I'm going to walk the halls. Maybe head over to the west wing and see what's happening in the House. I have some excess energy to burn. I'll be back in a little bit to catch the end of the debate."

As I left the office, I looked back at the credenza next to Bob's desk. There was a grouping of family photos: one of Bob and Margaret at his swearing-in ceremony and one of Dave taken at the cabin when he was just a toddler. An empty coffee cup bearing the State Seal sat on his desk. I shut the door and headed for the west wing.

More than anything I wanted to see the original San Jacinto battle flag, which hangs in the House chambers. Bob had told me that it was one of only two flags left from the revolution. It only hangs when the House of Representatives is in session. My credentials got me into the House galley and I looked down on the largest room in the capitol. Most of the hundred and fifty members were in attendance today, along with the Speaker of the House. The paintings were magnificent and there was the flag, hanging over everything.

I listened for a while but didn't really pay attention to what was being said. I did note that the reps voted using keypads that were mounted on their desks. And unlike the senators, they didn't speak from their desks, but from podiums at the front and back of the room.

Sitting there, I couldn't shut out the words Bob had sung. "Texas, dear Texas! From tyrant grip now free."

I took one more look at the flag, turned around and left.

## Chapter Twelve

If I were the sort to have panic attacks, I'd swear I was having one now. I could barely breathe and sweat had beaded on my forehead, giving me that "glow" that women try to avoid. I couldn't focus. I just kept hearing the words Bob sang on the Senate floor, especially the part about the tyrant grip, and fearing that tyrannical grip would choke the life out of me. I felt as if I was drowning in a pile of longhorn dung.

I walked aimlessly down the halls, not seeing anyone or anything around me. I just walked. My pace quickened to keep time with the beating of my heart.

"Just leave and don't look back," the little voice kept saying.

I knew that was impossible. I had become intrinsically tied to Bob Larken. The moment I made that commitment out at the cabin, I knew the consequences would be far greater than anything I could possibly imagine. But I had done it anyway.

The noise startled me back into reality. I stopped, briefly, to catch my breath. In front of me I saw a flurry of activity, accompanied by shouts and cameras, with microphones being used by reporters while they were on camera. On instinct, I removed my credentials and began to blend in with the crowds.

"The lieutenant governor has broken the tie. After a brief debate, the Senate has voted. It was conjectured that a filibuster would ensue and yet the proceeding was quick and absolute."

"Lieutenant Governor Robert Larken, in a vote that will assuredly affect his future, voted against his party and against the bill...."

"Ladies and Gentlemen, the lieutenant governor has aligned himself with Republicans and against the teacher's union in...."

The reporters' voices were rising, clamoring for the attention of their audiences. I wondered if these were live feeds or being taped for later airing? My pace sped to almost a jog as I found my way back to the Senate chamber. Bob would exit through the private rear door and head for his office. I needed to be there, too. I began to shove my way through the throngs of reporters and guests milling around in the main hall just as all hell broke loose.

"The lieutenant governor has exited the Chamber. He is being escorted down the hall by security..."

"Lieutenant Governor, do you have a comment?"

The microphone was shoved away by a guard and I could hear his booming, confident voice. "Let me quote one of my heroes, Davy Crockett, after his defeat in 1831. 'I have acted fearless and independent and I never will regret my course. I would rather be politically buried than to be hypocritically immortalized.'"

As Bob walked down the hallway toward me, he raised his arm, motioned toward me and called out, "Miss Pullen, come with me."

He leaned toward one of the Texas Rangers that walked in front of him. The Ranger stepped aside and Bob pulled me into the circle.

"Just look down and walk, Beth," he whispered.

Moments later we were at his office. The Rangers walked inside, gave the room a once-over and left.

"We'll be right outside the door, sir," one of them told Bob.

The door closed and Bob walked deliberately across the room to his credenza. He picked up the picture of him and Margaret and threw it into the wastebasket. He snatched up the empty coffee cup that sat on his desk and with a fury ordinarily reserved for a North Texas tornado, hurled it at the wall.

"Damn them all to hell."

Sitting on the floor next to the credenza was his briefcase. He placed the picture of his son inside and said, firmly, "I didn't ask for this job. Whoever wants it can have it."

Grabbing my arm, he escorted me to the door. Looking back, he said, "Goodbye and good riddance. May God bless the next fool who sits at that desk."

We made our way through the throngs of reporters that were now gathered outside his office door. From the route we were taking through the halls, I presumed we were heading for the underground extension. During the walk, Bob made only one statement.

"If your suite isn't clear, get your things. Meet me at the airport in four hours."

He glanced at his watch, then at me. I knew better than to speak. I was learning.

Once at the lowest parking level, Bob climbed into the passenger seat of his state car as a Ranger got behind the wheel. I was escorted to a police vehicle and told I'd be driven to my car. I explained to the Ranger where I was parked, then sat in silence as I exited the employee parking lot for the first and presumably last time.

Since I'd already taken my things from the suite, I headed directly to the airport. My cell phone rang just as I arrived at the rental car return.

"Yes?" I knew it was Bob from the digital readout.

"I'm at the house, about to talk to David and Margaret. I've called into the airlines. There's a ticket for your return to Michigan. Your services as my communications director are no longer needed. If the incoming lieutenant governor wishes to hire you, that will, of course, be his or her decision. Thank you for your brief but loyal tenure."

The tone of his voice was even and businesslike. I knew that he was being cautious since we were not on a secure line. I followed his lead.

"Thank you, sir. It was an honor to serve you and the state of Texas." What else could I say? "Hey, baby, I think you're cute and can't wait to roll around on another mattress with you?" Doubtful.

We hung up. I turned in my car and took the shuttle to the Southwest terminal. Business as usual. I tried to use this time to come up with a plan. Get home, talk to daddy and Vic, find a job. Forget Bob Larken. Odds were that I could accomplish three out of four. I had flown Southwest into Austin, so I figured that was the airline Bob would book. I decided to get my ticket and wait for him by my gate. He would know the flight and where to find me, I was sure.

As I walked toward the gate, I felt suddenly ravenous. I stopped at a food stand for a salad, iced tea, and a jumbo bag of M&Ms. My one overwhelming urge was to call Vic. Passing a machine that sold telephone calling cards, I decided that would be safer than using my cell phone. I had no idea whether anyone was following me.

She answered on the first ring. "Vic, it's Beth—Chrissy. Listen, I'm coming home tonight. Can you call Daddy and be at my place around ten? Yes, ten tonight—it'll be that late by the time I get home and drive over to Lansing from GR....Okay, I'll see the two of you then and please, don't tell anyone else I'm coming home."

The hours dragged on as I kept a constant lookout for anyone remotely suspicious. No one seemed to be standing around without a purpose. Everyone had tickets or family with them. I changed seats a few times just to get views from different angles. Finally, there he was. He was wearing an Astros baseball cap, Wranglers and a UT sweatshirt, not looking at all professional. In fact, to the casual eye, he looked like just another Texan about to leave for parts unknown. Making eye contact, he motioned me toward the pre-boarding area, which was empty and would afford us privacy.

Speaking in a whisper, Bob filled me in on what was about to happen.

"The deal with the devil has been cut. I'm leaving for overseas now to get the divorce. David was the hard part. He knew his mom and I weren't a match made in heaven but he never thought it would come to this. I told him this had nothing to do with him, but I deserved to be happy. He'll live with Margaret in Austin so he can finish school with his friends. I'll see him as much as I can."

I looked into his eyes and knew the most difficult part was over for him. He had made up his mind. The hard part was always making the decision.

"You told him about the divorce?"

With all the turmoil I was in, I needed proof that he was sincere and not acting on some testosterone-related impulse.

"No! He thinks I'm just leaving politics and taking a job in another state. Falling out of the limelight. His mom and I explained we needed a time-out from each other. The stresses of the job had been overwhelming. He didn't fully understand, of course. He didn't understand why I couldn't just get another job in Texas. Go back into broadcasting or teach there."

"Bob, why aren't you staying in Texas? It's your home."

I was hoping his answer would match my own hopes and dreams.

"Because I want to—I plan to—move to Michigan and be with you. It won't be a normal life. But it will be, well, uniquely us."

That brought a smile to both of our faces.

"Bob, what will you do? Where will you live? How will we see each other? I'm so confused and feel like I've been left out of all the decisions being made for us. We can't have a partnership that is a dictatorship. I'm sorry, I know that sounds so selfish, but this has happened so suddenly. What do I tell my dad? Vic?"

My voice had started to rise from nerves and a touch of anger. I hated having control stripped from me.

"Beth, it only took a few minutes with Margaret and Dave. I really had nothing to say to her, and since Dave won't know all the details, I just told him I was going to accept a position that Stan Melvin arranged in Michigan. It's an adjunct summer professorship at Grand Valley State in Grand Rapids. Dave just assumed it was temporary. He needs to be eased into this new arrangement."

"There you go again, Bob. Arrangement—is that what this is to you? An *arrangement*?"

I couldn't hide the disappointment, the fear.

"Beth, please, please don't do this. I had to work quickly. I only had a few hours. When I left the capitol I called the governor. It was the most difficult call of my life. He knew that Gus and Marty, and other Democrats, were pressuring me. They'd gone to him as well. They'd told him to shape me up or else. I told him I was resigning effective immediately. The party, his administration, would take the brunt of my vote. There'd be no way I could run for lieutenant governor come November. The scandal would ruin my family, too. His running mate had died; I'd committed political suicide. If he has any hope at all of maintaining Democratic control of the dome he needs to find someone who can carry the votes with a clean slate. As of today, that was not me."

His face finally took on the look of a beaten man, and yet there was still that sense of inward tranquility, as if a burden had lifted.

"The media must be going wild."

I might be new in this business, but I was well aware that the vultures would be swarming around his home and anywhere else they thought he might be.

"Yep. That's why I said I was going overseas. For a much-needed rest. Unfortunately my wife and son can't accompany me. Dave has school, you know."

His mouth finally did an upturn and the devil-may-care look returned to his eyes.

"Margaret does well with the 'no comment' routine and kids are off limits for interviews."

He raised and lowered his eyebrows and then gave me that wink. How could I resist that damn wink?

"So, what are your plans for *me*?"

It was *my* turn to wink. "When will I see you? How will we manage this new life?"

I felt like my future was being carved out like a Halloween pumpkin. You're never quite sure how it will come out but you keep on cutting. Making it up as you go.

"Well, I talked with the governor, as I said. He's in meetings right now and will have a press conference tonight. I'll be well on my way out of the country by then. I did not want to face the camera. I'm good, but not that good. I've known and worked with these people for years. Many are friends. I just wasn't up to it. Margaret and Dave are taken care of. Margaret insisted on keeping Patricia on our household budget. We don't know what she'll be doing, but Margaret insists I'll return to politics one day and will need an assistant. I didn't want to nitpick, so Patricia stays. And the story about having a teaching position? That's true, Beth. I called Stan to tell him to keep his ears opened. He wondered why I wanted to relocate to a Yankee state, first off. That was easy. My two best friends live there—his son, Brad and our other college roommate, Dave Hawthorne. We named Dave after him, actually. Dave's middle name, John, is for my mentor, John Gaynor.

"So Stan said he'd poke around. Within a half hour, he called back saying I could adjunct at Grand Valley over the summer until I got my shit together."

We both laughed at the casualness of the comment.

"Well, that's how he put it!"

"That is wonderful, Bob. I'm so happy for you. Really, I am."

I was happy for him, but really scared to death for myself. I would have to explain all this to Daddy, who would be far from thrilled at what had transpired the last few weeks. How would I pay my rent? I didn't want to rely on my father forever. I could freelance. The changes had come so suddenly. So unexpectedly.

"Beth, are you okay? You got so quiet. Are you feeling okay? Tell me."

We sat on the metal benches and he placed his hand on my knee.

"How am I feeling? Blindsided. I was content and happy pursuing a killer article one month, got my dream job the next and now I'm unemployed and in the middle of a scandal. And all I did was trust. Out of nowhere all the decisions are being made for me."

I didn't want to sound hurt or resentful, so I curbed my tongue. I wanted to say I was damned mad for having been put in this position, but what purpose would it serve? Hurtful words always come back to bite you in the butt.

"First off, it *was* a killer article. Secondly, in politics dream jobs come and go. That's reality. Last, but most importantly— there is no scandal. We sidestepped that in Austin. I voted my conscience and left. They can't ruin my run for governor because I'm not running. I'm out of there. And there's more."

"Oh great. Why do I suspect this will make me throw up?"

My cutting tone was sharper than that damn Bowie knife hanging in the hallowed halls of Larken's precious Alamo.

"Beth, it's wonderful news! John flew down last night—woke up half the Democrats in the Senate. When Gaynor calls—you listen. He is very, very powerful. His money backs most of the DNC candidates across the country. And as I said, I'm the son he always wanted. He told them, in no uncertain terms, that they will join *his* fraternal organization or, come fall when they need his backing, he'll close his wallet. He locked them all in a room, held up his checkbook and said 'See this? Leave Larken alone and the zeroes will have no end. You even think of going for his throat and the money dries up.' He then told them they could leave only when they agreed. If they didn't agree, they would grow very old sitting in that locked room."

I had to admit, it was nice to see Bob smirking again.

"So, how does that stop the scandal exactly?" I had a suspicion but wanted all the details.

"Simple. Pretty black and white. Larken votes and leaves. They shut up and forget about me. I leave town, leave politics and they would leave me, Margaret and Dave alone. There was no scandal and if they tried to make one—the results would not be pretty. John got up, walked out and here we are."

"Should I go *ta-da* and take a bow? This is incredible." I was just getting the full impact of what political fraternities were.

"No bow necessary, but a kiss would be nice."

Okay. The smirking grin was doing me in.

"More details, then the kiss. Margaret and Dave are in Austin. You're getting a divorce overseas, but it's just on paper—not for public consumption. You'll be teaching in GR and that leaves me exactly where?"

I batted my eyelashes to make certain the mood remained light.

"That leaves you in Michigan with me. Go talk to your dad and Vic—we can trust them with this. The silence is between the Larkens, which includes Patricia, and the Pullens, which includes Victoria."

"Bob—I mean, how will I see you? I need details, Bob."

He must have heard the pleading in my voice even though I didn't want to appear emotionally needy.

"Beth, go home, talk to your family and start to pack. The rest is a surprise. I'll join you there in a few weeks."

"Bob! Don't you dare do this to me! I hate surprises. I have to know. When will you be there? Why am I packing?"

"Shhhhh little Miss Michigan. I'll make everything just perfect. I need to go now. Just trust me."

"I trust you."

And with those three simple words, we stood up and I kissed him goodbye.

## Chapter Thirteen

Businessmen and women crowded the Southwest flight bound for Grand Rapids. One twenty-minute stop in Cincinnati to let passengers on and off, and I would touch down around eight tonight.

Gazing out the window, I took my last look at Texas. When we lift off...oh hell. I don't want to cry and get all worked up. This was starting to feel like home. I guess it was because of what happened at the cabin. Women get all sentimental about that first-time thing. Things had been happening so fast that I'd had little time to reflect on all the transformations in my life, including my sexual initiation. But beyond that there was a familiarity, a sense of belonging about being here. Maybe everything really is better in Texas. Maybe I'd lived here in one of those past lives Bob and I had talked about. One day I hoped Bob could bring me back here to see everything I'd missed. Or maybe he could come back here to teach and he could hide me away in the cabin. Or maybe Margaret would just go *poof!* and disappear. No, I really don't want anything bad happening to her—well, maybe a little bit bad. She was Dave's mom, after all, and if something really awful happened, I'd feel like I'd put a voodoo curse on her. I wonder if there is such a thing as a *little* voodoo curse? I had to sigh at the thought that she was the mother of Bob's only child. What did that make me? I was being relegated to the mother of his dog. Margaret going *poof!* was starting to sound better.

"Pullen, Christine Elizabeth Pullen?"

The stewardess was holding a gift bag and walking down the aisle. Why was she calling my name?

"Excuse me—yes, I'm Miss Pullen. Is there a problem?"
The stewardess, dressed in the usual shorts and oxford shirt with a sweater tied around her shoulders, gave me one of those "*Awwww* isn't this gonna be so sweet" smiles as she handed me a gift bag from one of the airport stores.

"A very handsome gentleman left this at the ticket counter and asked that we deliver it to you."

She stood there, waiting for me to open it. What a nosy little thing. I guess I would be, too, in her position.

"Thank you so much." Knowing that I was dressed professionally, and remembering how casually Bob was attired, I wondered what she was thinking. My curiosity was not easily held at bay. Whatever was inside was squishy. I could tell that with one squeeze. I reached in past the tissue paper and extracted the cutest teddy bear I'd ever seen: white, furry, and dressed in pastel overalls. There was a card tied to the teddy bear's hand that read: "This little bear will keep you company when we're apart. Till then, I'll be missing you."

I knew Bob had given it a hug because I could smell his cologne.

"Oh, isn't that so cute? What are you gonna name the bear, honey?"

I love the way everyone in Texas is either "sugah" or "hone*y*." The endearments just drip from their mouths.

It didn't take me long to figure out. "Her name is Chrissy."

I smiled, knowing that I was now Beth and the bear was named for the woman who first noticed Bob Larken. Yes. Chrissy—good choice.

"Well you just hug that sweet lil ol' bear cuz ah just know that man there just loves you ta death."

Now *this* was a true Texas girl or one helluvan actress.

Chrissy and I did the travel thing together, devoured our peanuts and Pepsi, landed, found Peg and drove to Lansing without a single hitch. We chatted on the drive and I told her all about her 'daddy.' I laughed at myself. For some strange reason having that bear with me made me feel safer. She was a Texas bear, after all.

It was peaceful, driving in the dark. I knew this route like the proverbial back of my hand. I'd driven it on more than one occasion with Vic. She'd been trying to land a position at the Gerald Ford Library in GR for ages and I always came along on the interviews to lend moral support. Not to mention the fact I didn't have much else to do. That, of course, was before I'd gotten, and lost, my own first job.

The clock on the dashboard said 10:23 as I rounded the corner by my apartment. It was a nice enough neighborhood—apartment complex after apartment complex interspersed with the occasional Seven-Eleven and McDonalds. I spotted Daddy's car; I guessed he'd brought Vic. As I parked I looked up to my window and noticed that the lights were on. I said a silent prayer to the patron saint of caffeine, hoping someone had fired up the coffeemaker. Well, really, my prayer was to Saint Maximilian Mary Kolbe, the patron saint of addicts. I had memorized about a dozen saints in my earlier life when I was still religious and Mama was still alive. Saint Maximilian Mary Kolbe was the saint that came the closest to what we needed, according to the *Patron Saint Dictionary*. I inherited my love of java from Mama and she always prayed to Saint Max MK, as she called her. Some habits you just don't want to mess with.

I left my luggage and laptop locked in the car, but took Chrissy with me inside. She made me feel eerily stronger. Strength was exactly what I was going to need.

The door was unlocked. I hesitated. Why? I'm a grown woman. What was Daddy going to do—slap me on my wrist and say "No no, bad girl! You can't go out and play with Bobby anymore!'"?

At least I had good taste. I could have slept with that pig who was second in line to Stan Melvin. Great life that would be. Every other sentence would be "Honey, quit chewing your moustache." I walked in shaking my head and laughing at the repulsive thought.

"Well don't you look chipper? Tired, but chipper." Daddy walked over and gave me a big bear hug and kiss on top of my head. Vic stood back smiling.

"Don't tell me, let me guess. Uh huh. You've got the glow. It's kind of masked in exhaustion, but it's there. And what's with the teddy bear?"

I'd missed Vic's caustic but right-on-the-money observations.

"Well, you could say it's my unemployment compensation."

There. I said it. I'd lost my job.

"Chrissy, you were fired? Did Larken fire you or the governor?"

My father's blood pressure was starting to rise. I could tell because the veins on his forehead were starting to protrude.

"If that Larken fellow did anything to hurt you or your reputation I'll kill that bastard. I've never trusted politicians. I thought he was moving too fast in hiring you. Something happened. You tell me right now and I'll take care of it, honey. We saw a brief clip on CNN about that tiebreak and that Larken left the country after resigning. If he hasn't been one hundred percent a gentleman he'll pay for it."

Oh brother. This was not going well. I was wishing that Margaret would go *poof!* and now my father was threatening her husband. Well, her sort-of husband. Her ex-husband-in-waiting.

"Sit down. Both of you sit down. Well, first, Vic, get me some coffee, please."

I figured she was a go-fer by day; it wouldn't hurt to have her practice on me tonight.

"Yes ma'am! This power thing really's gotten to you."

She looked almost afraid, which is typically not an emotion Vic portrays.

Coffee in hand, the babbling began.

"Yes, the teddy bear is from Bob Larken. Yes, he broke the tie and sided with the Republicans. Yes, he resigned his position as lieutenant governor of Texas. Yes, he left the country. Yes, we love each other."

Damn. I wished the coffee had a shot of whiskey in it.

Victoria sat there, her cat eyes looking suspicious. She was savvy. She knew there was more than this brief synopsis.

"Dear Lord in heaven." That was all my dad could say. He looked angry and heartbroken. His eyes were piercing through me as if he didn't even know his own daughter.

"There's more."

I put the coffee cup down on the table next to my wing-backed chair. I clung to Chrissybear. Somehow it made me feel as if Bob were there, giving me the strength I undoubtedly would need to explain the past week. Had it only been a week since our trip to the Cantina?

"First off, what I'm about to tell you goes no further. If I can't trust you to absolute silence, let me know now. No matter how you personally feel, no matter how angry at me you become, I have to have your word that what I tell you stays between these walls."

I looked at Daddy first. Then at Victoria. They both looked dazed. Their eyes met mine and their faces reflected no emotion. The blank stares transmitted a sense of disbelief that there could possibly be more to this story, yet I was sure that inside, they must know. I have never been one to mince words. Yes, I babble. Yes, I get dramatic. But this time, they knew I was serious. Why else would I be clinging to a stuffed animal for dear life? The last time I did that was when my mother died. I was only five years old and it was the only way I could console myself.

I got up and unplugged the phone. I took the back off the phone and checked for any devices that looked suspicious. I checked underneath the tables and chairs and everywhere else Bob had taught me to look for bugs. Even though the apartment appeared "clean" I turned the sink on, full force, as well as the radio. I wasn't going to take any chances. Not now. Not ever again.

"Chrissy, what the hell are you doing?"

My father was growing impatient. As an executive, he was use to being the one in charge, in control. This, I was sure, felt extremely foreign to him.

"Vic, Dad, I love Bob Larken."

Before I could continue, my smart-ass best friend interjected "Newsflash!" and rolled her eyes.

"Stop, please. I need to explain everything. Please, don't make this any more difficult than it already is."

"Sorry" was the best response Vic could come up with.

"From that first broadcast I knew there was something about him. I was compelled to discover why I was so drawn to him. When we met, I knew it immediately and so did he. We're...I know it sounds crazy...but we're simpatico. We end up wearing the same colors—we love the same music—and we can talk and laugh for hours. So much that we do is unique for us both."

"Sorry, Chrissy, I have to interject something here. He is substantially older than you are. Either he's led a sheltered life or he's a liar."

My father's veins were becoming even more pronounced.

"Daddy, it's true. He married Margaret right out of college—no, don't say it. Don't even think it—it was doomed from the beginning. Their first night together was a nightmare. He knew right then she was not what he truly wanted but he kept thinking it might just be him, he should try harder. And then David was born. Bob's career took off and Margaret loved the power. And, above all else, she was the perfect wife for a powerful man. She said the right things, knew the right people, she made him look good. Then he ended up as the lieutenant governor and there was a whole new game to play. And it really was just a game because now he had to play by the party's rules. He couldn't editorialize anymore. He couldn't speak his mind or his own truth—unless it agreed with the party. Margaret was pressing him to do what the Democrats wanted so he could two-step into the governorship. Then we met. I encouraged him to be himself. He was able to be himself with me—he didn't have to be anyone or anything except Bob Larken. Now here comes the iffy part."

"Oh God, it gets worse?"

Daddy was starting to slump down on the couch and began rubbing his temples. He was murmuring something. I think he was cursing Texas and all things Texan.

"Get to the sex," Vic said. Daddy threw her a glare that was downright frightening.

"Do I have both of your solemn promises that what I'm about to tell you goes no further?"

"Chrissy, I don't know. Are you in harm's way? If so, I can't promise that I won't try and make it right. If he's hurt you, he'll have to pay. Dearly."

"Well, it would be too soon to know if you're pregnant....."

"Victoria, shut the hell up."

I was losing my temper. My patience was worn to a frazzle.

"You either support me or leave. But, if you leave, that's it. I need you now. I need you both. I need your support and love and understanding." On the verge of tears, and yet with newfound strength, I stood up and walked to the door. "In or out?"

"Chrissie, does this Larken fellow worship the Alamo?"

My dad's question stumped me, but I replied, "Of course. He's a Texan, Daddy. Why?"

"I want to see what kind of man he is. Most Texans literally worship and hold the Alamo right next to God in their hearts. The only thing it was important for was to tell the world they had shit for soldiers and besides, there weren't any 'good ole Texas boys' there. Chrissy, I don't know, I just don't know. I have a great disdain for those types. Not to mention that he was a broadcaster, so he knows how to be an actor. Add that to the ability to lie like a rug—since he's a politician. Excuse me if I don't trust him. And neither should you."

"Thank you for that eloquent speech, Daddy. Now, are you in or out?" For the first time in my entire life I was standing up to my father.

Vic and Daddy sat back down, looked at each other and held hands. I walked over to the couch and sat on the floor in front of them. Placing Chrissy on the floor I joined hands with my father and my best friend.

"Bob is flying overseas. He's in the air right now, actually. He is divorcing Margaret—but on paper only. We were threatened. Not physically—but with a scandal. Margaret wants power and she believes Bob will return to politics. She says it's in his blood now. Anyhow, for all intents and purposes, Margaret and Bob will appear married. If and when Bob does go back into the ring, she'll be there by his side. She concocted a story and got a pseudo-witness to what she believes was an affair. It wasn't—but it did turn into one."

With that admission, Victoria smirked. I couldn't help but return the smile.

"When Bob threatened to commit political suicide by not voting with the Democrats, several senators threatened him by saying they would ruin him and make sure he would never even make the ballot come November. It got ugly with them. It got ugly with Margaret. Bob voted his conscience and we made a deal. He made the Democrats happy by leaving politics and he made Margaret happy because she can still play wifie."

"And exactly where does that leave you? In the role of slut?"

Daddy's breathing grew heavier and beads of sweat were forming on his forehead.

"Chrissy, why did you do this?"

"Daddy, I love him. I won't deny him. I'll stand by him. I'll take him however and whenever I can. We want to be married—we just don't know all the details yet, but Bob will make it right. I know he will. He's a good man, Daddy."

I squeezed my father's hand and gave him a reassuring look.

"Can he make you happy, Chrissy? Leading this secret life?"

I knew my father wanted the best for his only child.

"Well, we have to live in silence. You, Vic, Bob and I, as well as Margaret and his former assistant, Patricia—who is also Margaret's best friend. We are the only ones, at this point, that are members of this elite group."

With that I gave them both a smile.

"It's kind of like the country club, Daddy, by invitation only. Maybe you should buy a new vest for the occasion."

I was hoping this attempt at humor would lessen what surely was a shock.

"And where will you live? What will you do for jobs?" It was Victoria's turn to be the interrogator.

"Bob will be here in a few weeks. He's taking care of it. I'll be packing. I'll continue to do freelance writing and he's gotten an adjunct professorship over at Grand Valley, at least for the summer. Most important, we'll be together."

"Well, I just want my baby to be happy. If he makes you happy, I'm all for it. But, I'll tell you right here and now, if he ever—I repeat, *ever*—breaks your heart, dumps you, turns his back on you—if he ever hurts my little girl he'll be, as they say in Texas, a deer in my sights."

With that, Daddy stood up, took Victoria's arm and left my apartment. There were no goodbyes. No "Glad you're home safely." Nothing. I didn't even get to tell him about the dog Bob wanted to get.

I watched through the dinette window as my father and my best friend walked out into the moonlit night. Looking up to the dark, star-filled sky I whispered, "Goodnight, moon. Goodnight, Bob, I love you."

*Katherine Shephard*

**Chapter Fourteen**

Living just to fill time stinks. Day in and day out all I did was putter. Putting things neatly into boxes, dumping papers from school, pawing through mementos I'd saved for too many years, while I lamented. Lamenting was my pastime of choice lately. I let the answering machine answer my calls and went on a diet. My new regime consisted of M&Ms and coffee with milk, with an occasional onion sandwich to round out the food groups. Nothing beats rye bread, deli mustard and perfectly sliced sweet onions. I hope Bob wasn't expecting me to win the Homemaker of the Year award. Amazingly, though, I was looking forward to nesting. What bugged the crap out of me was wondering what type of nest we'd build and where it would be located. Not knowing the details made me feel vulnerable.

I trusted Bob, though. I knew he'd make everything just right for us. We wouldn't have to worry about Margaret because Bob was going to be a teacher and lecturer, not a politician. She was, really, my only concern. I'd only heard from Bob once in these past two weeks and, if all had gone right, he should be in Lansing sometime today. In preparation I'd pushed the packed boxes against the wall, changed the sheets, put out new towels and put on real clothes. Up until now I'd been living in sweat-suits with my hair pulled into a knot that rested uncomfortably on top of my head.

I'd dozed off on the couch when a familiar scent woke me up. I opened my eyes to see Bob standing over me, smiling.

Wiping my mouth, the first words that spewed forth left him laughing. "Oh God, was I drooling?"

"Hello to you, too, Sleeping Beauty."

He was holding Chrissy who had, apparently, fallen onto the floor.

"Fine way to take care of a gift. I'll have to rethink the puppy thing if this is the kind of mama you're going to be."

I shook my head, stretched and stood up, touching his chest to be certain this wasn't just a dream.

"You really did come back. I missed you so much." I glanced across the room to see what time it was and how long I'd napped.

"Of course I came back. I promised, didn't I? You really need to learn to hide your key better, though."

He took me into his arms and wrapped his strong arms around me, holding me so tight I could barely breathe.

"I see you packed. You're obedient. I like that in a woman."

With that he reached down and began to tickle me so I knew he was joking.

"Ticklish too, even better."

"Stop! I mean it!"

I was trying to talk, but his tickling was making me laugh so hard I started to cough.

"Uh-oh, I have a choice to make. Either dial 911 or perform mouth-to-mouth."

He chose the later.

"God, I'm glad you're not a paramedic. I'd hate to share that mouth." His kiss took the term "breathtaking" to new heights.

"Be gentle with me, I'm young and inexperienced."

Bob Larken then fulfilled a dream of mine. Apparently he'd really paid attention when I described my dream man to him because he took me into his arms, picked me up and carried me away into the bedroom. Since it was a small apartment, he didn't have to carry me far. Good thing, since my food consumption and inactivity the past two weeks had made the scale escalate past the attractive stage.

He was a patient and gentle lover. I couldn't help but stare into his eyes as he kept saying, over and over, "Beth, I love you. I love you. I love you."

Hours passed as we grew to know each other. Finally my gurgling stomach broke the mood and we dissolved into laughter when his growled too, as if to answer mine. I laughed so hard I started to hiccup.

"Oh God, it's an IHOP moment" was all I could get out between my semi-seizures.

"An IHOP moment? Something tells me this is going to be good." He sat up, pulling the sheet up around his chest.

By doing the kind of breathing exercises a woman in labor does I finally calmed myself down.

"Yep. IHOP moment. Whenever Daddy and I get the giggles we go to IHOP. They're open round the clock for whenever the mood strikes."

"Sorry, I'm not going to get up, shower, dress and go out to eat. Got some eggs or something easy?"

He looked like a little boy, filled with anticipation of some new adventure.

"Nope. Cleaned out the pantry. You told me to pack, remember? There's always pizza. Pizza in bed would be my suggestion."

My life now felt complete. Funny, though—I felt as if I were home again here, too. Same as I felt in Texas. I suppose that had to do with Bob. It's not where you are, it's who you're with. I finally got it.

Pizza ordered and delivered; lights out; candles lit. We sat on the balcony off the bedroom and I listened to everything Bob had done since we both left Austin. I sat in wonder, hanging onto each word, as he spoke of a world that moved faster than I'd known possible.

"The divorce was painless. When I got back to Austin I gave Margaret a notarized copy of the decree to be placed in our home safe. I met with Patricia and explained that she will still get her salary, with benefits."

"What benefits?" I couldn't help but interrupt.

"Oh, a car, a credit card for her gas, cell phone. Told her if she breached our trust and agreement, she'd be sued so fast she wouldn't have time to dress for court. I hold the cards on her, Beth. Everyone has dirty secrets—she's no exception. It gets to a point where you figure out who has the most to lose. She won't double-cross us."

This was a side of Bob I'd never seen. The political negotiator.

"Go on." I was beginning to wonder what would happen if Daddy or Vic crossed the line.

"Had a good chat with Dave, too. Told him this teaching opportunity was too good to pass up. I'd be able to spend time with Brad and my friend David, too. I hate leaving my son, but he's old enough to not pry, yet young enough to be resilient. I promised I'd come see him a few times too. He asked about my staff. I explained that some were staying on in other capacities and he specifically asked about you. He thinks you're 'cool,' which I think is a compliment."

When he talked about his son his voice changed, I'd noticed. It as almost as if he was talking about a much younger child. The daddy pride was pretty obvious. Dave seemed like a great kid, but I worried about him being with Margaret exclusively. I'd hate for him to model her controlling ways or be brainwashed by her "power and money are God" attitudes.

"I told him since your home was in Michigan you'd go there and freelance. Maybe even work for me."

"Wow. I'll get paid for sleeping with you? I don't know if you can afford me. I have experience now."

A sly smirk let him know I was just teasing.

"Have I told you lately how cute you are?"

He had an adorable way of changing the subject when the heat turned up.

"Have I told you what a brat you are?" With that I stuck my tongue out.

"Hey, don't stick that thang out unless you're gonna use it."

His voice transformed to its drawl mode and his chest jaunted out like a banty rooster.

"You are such a bubba. A snoring bubba at that."

We could joke so easily, sometimes it threw me for a loop.

"We'll get to the snoring later, trust me." The wink was back!

"Okay. Well, then, continue with the saga, my dear."

"After talking with Dave I placed a few phone calls. I called Gus, then Marty, assuring them I was out of politics and a member of their elite fraternity. Against my will, mind you, but still a card-carrying member."

Seeing me roll my eyes, he took my hand and continued.

"It's okay. They got what they wanted. I'm no longer a threat to the party; a thorn has been removed from their sides. I have alienated plenty of others before, when I was in broadcasting. Your own lieutenant governor here, for instance. I hammered him during one interview and he's vowed to see me ruined ever since." He talked about Jim Parsons as though he were an ugly disease.

"He's grateful I'm not a Republican, though. As close as I am to Stan's family, he's always feared I'd leave Texas and stir up trouble for him here in Michigan. I'm sure there's more to him than we know; I just scratched the surface in my interview. Then I was tapped for LG and, well, it's history now."

He shrugged his shoulders before continuing.

"Then I called John. He was in Austin and drove over immediately. You know I can't imagine being closer to anyone than I am to John. If he were my own father I couldn't love him more than I already do. He's the reason I got into office and I felt I owed him an explanation. Between you and I he offered to make Margaret disappear permanently. Not a bad idea, if it weren't for Dave, of course. That woman is loathsome. Falling in love with her was the biggest mistake I've ever made—except, without her, Dave wouldn't exist. That's her one and only redeeming quality."

161

He gazed off into the night as if contemplating variations to the present had the past been different.

"Where does John *live*, anyhow?" This question was one that had puzzled me from day one. My question brought Bob back from his daydream state.

"Everywhere and nowhere. He has a place here, an office here, a place in California, a place in Austin, a place in Houston, and a place in D.C. Those are the ones I know about. He's entrenched in politics, making sure the right people are financed. No one—and I mean *no* one—bucks John Gaynor."

"Go on, sorry, I keep interrupting you. I'll shut up now."

"My next call was to Stan. He had, as I'd told you before, called around and secured that professorship for the summer. He also had called his son, Brad, and our friend, Dave Hawthorne—we call him Thorn—to let them know I'd be here for the summer. Brad had seen the bulletins flashed on CNN and knew his dad would call. Thorn, though, had gone right over to Stan's office in the Olds Building."

I couldn't shut up for long.

"That's the same building Parson's in. I've been there."

With that, Bob placed a finger over my lips as though to silence me so he could continue. I gave a look of "ooops" and complied.

"Thorn wanted to know the truth. He knows me almost as well as John does, to be honest. Everyone has someone—you know, like you have Vic. They can read you when no one else has a clue. Thorn told Stan it had to be another woman."

With that he gave me a broad smile. It was reassuring, because "another woman" sounded so seedy. I just sat there.

"Stan told him it wasn't just another woman—it was *the* woman. And it wasn't

just you, of course. It was political pressures, personal misery and wanting to live the life I deserved and had thought I'd never have. John had placed a call to Stan. He didn't want to place the governor in an awkward position of knowing too much, yet, as a family friend, thought he should know some of the details. Stan is a politician of utmost integrity. Beyond reproach. None of us want to place him in an awkward position."

Taking a breath, he continued. "Thorn is an artist of sorts. Artists are very much aware of their surroundings. They feel things no one else knows exists. He builds homes for a hobby. He built the cabin for me. His hands can work miracles. So he wants to meet you, of course. That's where we're going tomorrow. Okay, secret's out."

He looked at me with anticipation, knowing I'd burst out with some comment. Just to throw him off, I bit my lip to illustrate that no words were going to escape before their time.

"Say something. I know you're dying to say something."

His laugh was right from his gut. It filled the night air and broke whatever tension had previously existed. God, how had I ever been I so lucky?

"So, I get to meet your best friend tomorrow? Is he single?"

I raised my eyebrows up and down, hoping to disarm him. It didn't work.

"He's unavailable, my dear. He is involved with the governor's chief of staff. Involved isn't the right word. Committed. That's the word! So, don't get any crazy-ass ideas." He glowered at me and shook his finger as if to say, "Don't even *think* about it."

"Oh, I was thinking about Vic, actually."

"Oh yes, Victoria—that's my next proposition."

A smirk *and* a wink. This was going to be good.

"It's awfully risky having her with the legislators day in and day out—she just might talk in her sleep."

"Robert Larken!" I smacked his thigh for emphasis.

"Well.... " His laugh became even heartier before seriousness set back in.

"The Gerald Ford Library has just decided to hire a political historian. Someone to research for them, come up with ideas for new displays, and I'm not sure what all else. Think she'd be interested? It pays very well, has a complete insurance package and would start immediately."

"Wait a minute. You had a position dummied up to silence my best friend?"

I was shocked, to say the least. This type of power was totally foreign to me. It was far-reaching but now it was right here, very close to home.

"Well, when you put it that way, it sounds ugly. She's a Republican, right? So was Ford. I'm a Democrat and don't you forget it. I didn't have anything dummied up. Stan told me about it."

Vic would be thrilled, to say the least. If she had to keep our arrangement under wraps at least now she'd have a fantastic job where she could be surrounded by right-wingers and even get paid. I loved this.

"So Governor Melvin now knows. Brad and Dave Hawthorne know. The circle has grown."

"Yes. These are the people that hold our confidence. I am quite certain they all will comply. I'm sure each of them is aware that John Gaynor would have it no other way."

"I think I get the underlying message there, Bob. Now can I call Vic?"

"No, not now. There's something else I need to say. I know this isn't going to be easy for you. I'm sure it's not the life you'd planned for yourself, but believe me when I tell you that I will fight for you. I'll never let you go. Trust me. Every day with you will be worth whatever sacrifices we have to make. "

He held my gaze. We were a part of each other's souls, just as we had been on his deck in the Hill Country. Whether in Texas, Michigan or anyplace else in the world, we had become intrinsically one.

"Here, move over some. I want you to sit directly under the moon."

He was orchestrating now, much like the first movement of a never-ending symphony, I was placed precisely as he wanted before he said, "Close your eyes."

"Again? Now what?"

I was nervous, excited and amused. My hands began to sweat and my heart started to race. If nothing else, Bob Larken was predictably unpredictable. I heard the sliding door open and I think he went inside. It wasn't long before he returned.

"Okay. You can open them now."

As I opened my eyes, music came drifting outside. He'd found my tape of the Moonlight Sonata.

"Beth, I don't have much to offer you now. You deserve a better life than what I can give. You've been caught in the crosshairs, in a sense. But from the moment I saw you on Mackinac Island, I knew I'd found what I'd been missing. I've finally found someone whose actions speak volumes. You've given up so much for me, in such a short period of time. I guess what I'm trying to say is, I love you. Beth, will you be my wife? Please say yes."

With tears streaming down my cheeks, I uttered the one word that would change my life.

"Yes."

*Katherine Shephard*

## Chapter Fifteen

Hours later we were safely tucked into bed when I bolted upright in terror, wondering if a California earthquake had struck Lansing. I began to laugh when I realized it was Bob. With his body jerking violently, he snorted as loud as a bull ready to charge a rodeo clown. Sitting upright I poked at him, calling for him to wake up.

"What? What's wrong?" He was groggy, with his hair all messy and his eyes half-closed. Quite frankly, he looked drunk. I preferred to think of it as middle-aged afterglow.

"Oh my God, you scared the crap out of me. You had the jumping snorts!"

"The *what*?" That woke him up in a hurry.

"The jumping snorts. I don't know what else to call what just happened."

"You woke me up for an involuntary body movement accompanied by a minor snore? You've got a lot to learn, babe."

By now we had both come to. It was five in the morning. Sitting there looking at each other in our early-morning disarray we realized this was the real thing. Snoring, jerking legs, drool— the works.

"Hey, does this fall under 'for better or worse?' Can you go to rehab for this?" I was definitely in control now.

He took one of the numerous pillows that had cushioned his head and smacked it over my face. Pulling myself away I panted, "Great, divorce wife one and smother wife number two. You're on a roll, Larken."

"Damn, you're a smart-ass, but I'll keep you anyhow."

He leaned over, gave me a morning mouth kiss and patted my pillow.

"Dry as a whistle. Good girl!" I shook my head and began to crawl out of bed.

"Let's get a move on—I want to meet Thorn! And why did you have me pack up the apartment, anyhow?" My curiosity was back, full force.

"Wait—you hate mornings. You pride yourself on never having seen a sunrise and you want to get a move on?"

He'd managed to get out of bed and was actually pulling the sheets and covers into place.

"I'll shower, you make the coffee, then you shower and I'll get dressed—we need to get a routine going." I tossed my hair back, smiled over my shoulder and closed the bathroom door.

"Beth, come on. It's my turn." We sounded like rival siblings.

Once the morning tasks were completed we mapped out the day.

"Take a suitcase with a few changes of clothes. Something casual, some sporty clothes and maybe one dress. Wear jeans and tennies."

His militaristic tone reminded me he was used to being in charge as well as being a dad.

"Yes sir!" I snapped back with a salute. I just couldn't resist.

It was now seven. I hoped Thorn was a morning person.

We got into Bob's gleaming black BMW Z-3. He'd driven it up from Austin, and the story of how his dream car came into his life provided the entertainment as we drove through Lansing.

"I was up in Detroit—January of '96—for the Auto Show. Brad, Thorn and I try to go every year. Sometimes it's the only way we see each other. This model just was screaming for me to take her home. Just happened. There's normally quite a wait for delivery, you know? I placed an order and just a few weeks later I got the call that my car was ready. Not sure how it happened so quickly. I've taken all sorts of flak from Brad, Dave and Stan. They are 'buy Michigan' guys: if it's not GM, Ford or Chrysler, it shouldn't be on the road. I tried to explain that being a Texan, of course I have a Ford truck back home. That didn't shut them up." There was that soft smile again. "The thought of me having an import made them crazy."

When we pulled off the 96 for gas I decided to make a pit stop. Coffee did that to my bladder. Once that was complete Bob said we were going to go exploring. I just figured it was to kill time until Thorn was safely awake and ready for company. I knew I'd be plenty annoyed if folks showed up at my place this early. Then again, men didn't have all that much to do to make themselves presentable.

"Just trust me on this one, Beth, okay?"

He gave me a glance that said 'no questions allowed.' I was beginning to read his face as well as his heart. Within moments we'd turned down a dirt road that was marked "Private." That made me nervous. I didn't think getting picked up by a state trooper would be a great way for Bob to spend his first morning in town. We passed a carved wooden sign saying "Legends of the Woods," which I presumed to be the name of this cluster of home sites. The narrow road was lined with towering old white pines and wound through thickets of trees like a meandering river. I saw a few homes here and there, set well back off the road. Bob swung his Z into a gravel drive just before the road ended.

"What's this?" I didn't wait for him to open the car door—I just got out and started to explore. I spotted a small, rustic barn with a certain charm to it. No wonder there was a "**SOLD**" sign tacked to a nearby tree.

"Wow, beautiful trees, don't you think?" Bob said. Let's walk around some."

I could tell that Bob loved the woods almost as much as I did. He caught up to me and placed his arm around my shoulder. His touch felt warm and natural.

"Bob, we'd better not stay here. This is private property."

"You have no guts, ma'am. A true Texas woman has a spirit of adventure. You're part Texan now, remember."

169

I was sure that statement had to do with sex.

"Where are you taking me? There's nothing out here!"

"That's the point. Let's go back and take a look at that barn."

He led me to the weathered red barn door and kissed me.

"You're right, it is private property. But it's okay—it's *your* private property. You can write here. I had it fixed up and wired for electric and phone."

"You didn't, did you? When? How? It's charming! I love it! Oh Bob...."

Staring at him in disbelief. I couldn't fathom how he accomplished stuff like this.

"Welcome home, Beth. This is our own Legend in the Woods."

He held me tight and we savored the blessings of being here together, surrounded by nature in our very own hideaway.

"Wait! You said this is *my* private property. Then how is it *our* Legend in the Woods?"

"There's more, my dear, there's more."

His impish grin was one of those "I know something you don't know" faces.

We turned around and headed down a slope. It was heavily wooded and the trees were just starting to come back from the winter freeze. The morning sunlight was peeking through the branches, illuminating the dew that still sparkled on the ground. A perfect morning, fresh and crisp. As we approached a break in the trees Bob told me, once again, to close my eyes.

"Okay. I mean it, Beth—no peeking! I'll hold onto your arm—you'll be fine. Trust me."

Unaccustomed to walking on uneven ground, my feet felt wobbly and uncertain. I took each step tentatively and clung to Bob for dear life. I hated feeling this vulnerable. I just hated it.

"Okay—time to look."

I could hear the excitement in his voice. There was that little-boy quality again.

Before me sat a house overlooking a river.

"Oh my God, Bob, this is gorgeous. Is this where Thorn lives?"

I was in utter shock. Out in the middle of nowhere stood this absolutely breathtaking home.

"Well, I told you to pack, remember? "

His voice was entirely casual. I started to shake. Either I was cold or nervous as hell.

"Come on inside. There's more."

As we approached the door a handsomely rugged man walked out to greet us.

"Hi, you two." He gave Bob a bear hug reserved for only the closest of friends. My turn was next.

"Beth, this is my best friend, David Hawthorne. He built this place and fixed up the barn."

"Beth. I'm so glad you rescued my friend here."

His smirk was similar to Bob's, but not as disconcerting to my soul.

"This place sits on the edge of the Looking Glass River. It's a tributary to the Grand River. Bob asked me to find a place on a river—and I had just finished building this. I just knew it would be what you two would want."

Opening a double door, Thorn motioned Bob and me out onto a wooden deck off the great room. The river wound through the trees; not one bit of nature's beauty had been displaced.

"There are wild black cherry, sugar maple, bitter hickory nut and white oaks on the property." Obviously, Thorn was completely at home in this environment.

"Are these names of trees or flavors of coffee?" I joked.

"I'm no longer a lieutenant governor, if you'll remember," Bob quipped. "I don't have to be a coffee connoisseur anymore."

A tendril of hair had fallen past my brow and Bob brushed it tenderly aside. He was truly taking care of me.

"It's only twelve or fifteen minutes down the highway to the college, or I can go out Grand River Avenue. It's quiet here—you can write. No one ever needs to know we're here. There's a general store in Wacousta where you can get bread and milk. The folks there, I hear, are friendly, and Thorn says they'll leave us be."

"Wait, Bob—this is our place? Thorn's taken care of all this for us?"

I had gone from shocked to more shocked to shockeder. There I was making up words again.

"Yes ma'am. Once I called him he added a few special touches. Come here—take a look at this."

We went back through the great room to the front door where I spotted something that looked like a small, upside down gumball machine that had rusted out. Bob saw the confusion on my face and gave an explanation.

"That's a dead eye."

"Am I suppose to be impressed with this for some reason?"

"Dave has a collection of dead eyes. We used to go sailing and diving a lot in college. I found this one on an old sailing ship off of Grosse Ile. It was totally engulfed in zebra mussels. Along the port bow we found this dead eye that use to hold up the rigging. Thorn, well, he 'borrowed' it."

The two men started laughing heartily and I knew some fond memories were tied to this relic.

"I convinced him not to clean it up. He wanted to hang it by our door as a sign of friendship."

We turned back and headed up a small staircase that led to the home's solitary bedroom, a high-pitched loft with private bath. Another deck gave way to a full view of the river and trees. Looking back out toward the barn, I caught my breath once again at the splendor of the dense woods.

"Nice and convenient, Bob, We can just drag the mattress out here."

We smiled at the memory of our first night together.

"Look here." Bob turned me towards the left where a two-story rock fireplace greeted me. It was situated right in front of where a bed would be placed. A note was hanging from the fireplace mantel. Standing hand in hand we read the note out loud, together.

> *"To Beth and Bob. I split each of the stones myself. I found them at various quarries around the state. May your love for each other be as strong as these rocks and as lasting as The Ledges. This home is my gift to you.*
> *Fondly, Dave."*

Tears began to stream down my cheeks as I looked at the only man I'd ever loved. Would ever love.

"The Ledges! Let's go there, Bob. Have you ever been?"

"Can't say as I have, although Thorn talks about them all the time. Aren't they those sentinel-looking things of layered quartz-rose sandstone?

"Yes! They're along the Grand River near here. I haven't been for a long time. The city was named for the Grand River and the Ledges. Rock climbers use them for practice, but I think we can just go there to look. Rock climbing rates up there with flying in my book. Just not natural." The thought of scaling huge chunks of stone made me shudder.

"Okay then, let's get a move on!"

We walked back down the stairs to be greeted by Thorn.

"You two lovebirds do whatever. I'm going to go back to the barn and make sure everything is ready for you to move in, Beth."

I gave him a hug.

"Dave—Thorn—thank you so much. This is the most beautiful spot—and the house—it's just perfect. Really. Thank you so much."

"Not a problem, Beth," Thorn said. "My hands did the work of my heart."

He shook Bob's hand and took off through the woods on foot. We returned to the Z and headed into Grand Ledge, our new home city. On our drive Bob told me a bit more about his best friend

"Thorn is an intellect, believe it or not. He also is a woodsy kind of guy. He started in the corporate world in law, but left that to become a law professor. He'll be out at Grand Valley with me. It'll be like old home week."

It was so wonderful to see Bob beaming with happiness, hope and pride.

"He devotes all of his free time to fishing and building. I knew he'd have, find, or build the perfect hideaway for you. He can be trusted, Beth. He lives with the Dragon Lady."

"He lives with your ex-wife?" I couldn't help it. I just couldn't.

"Oh, that was choice." We both laughed before he continued.

"No. *This* Dragon Lady is Governor Melvin's executive assistant, Lydia Mayer. That's just her well-deserved nickname. No one gets to Stan except through her. It's her job to be silent and strong. She's really quite feminine, though."

I thought to myself...ah, more members of the Fraternity.

Bob had been following a hand-drawn map that Dave gave him and before us now lay Ledges Park. Rustically beautiful and full of history. It was so secluded and private. I supposed I needed to get use to this new life.

We continued on past the Victorian street lamps, Victorian homes, bridges and barns that were sprinkled throughout the little town. We passed the Old Opera House and the Rexalla Drug Store on Bridge Street and made a turn.

"Bob, my tummy is growling. Can we stop for something to eat before yours starts to grumble too?"

"Sure! Dave mentioned a place called The Log Jam. Said it was a locals' spot. Feel like a burger and a beer? It's eleven, we need a break."

Now I knew I had finally truly fallen in love. With Bob as well as our new home.

As we drove down the streets toward our chosen luncheon digs, Bob pulled over in front of one of the numerous historical homes.

"Beth! Here's 219. That's former governor Frank Fitzgerald's home! Dave told me some of the history. It's still in the Fitzgerald family—still the same red brick."

"Oh Bob, I love our place more than this. Ours is rustic and more secluded. And it's ours!"

Bob looked down. A somewhat nervous look came across his face as he stammered, "Well, not exactly. It's not really *ours*. The deed reads "Christine Elizabeth Pullen."

"What?" I admitted to being puzzled.

"Remember?" he hesitated before looking directly at me.

I was jolted back into reality.

"Yes. I remember."

*Katherine Shephard*

## Chapter Sixteen

The enormity of it all was finally sinking in. I realized I was now living a "shit happens" life, the good mixed in with the bad. With the euphoria of the morning starting to fade, I retreated back within myself a bit and became quiet. No one paid a bit of attention to us at lunch or as we drove through town. Folks waved and smiled, but the gawking that Bob had become used to was gone.

Bob's cell phone rang, startling me out of the trance the peaceful morning had lulled me into.

"Hey—Hi John! We're in Grand Ledge right now—okay. Sure. No problem—we can be there in about twenty minutes or so. Okay. Yes. Beth's with me. What's up? Okay. I'll trust you."

Without another word Bob simply clicked the phone off. I looked over at him and waited for the next bit of news.

"Mind if we head over to Grand Rapids? John wants us to meet with him. He has something for me."

"I take it he didn't say exactly what?"

"No. No he didn't."

The beer had rendered me a bit drowsy so I laid my head back for the duration of the ride. For some reason, I found myself thinking about folks who actually canoed from Lansing through Grand Ledge and over to the western coast of the state. It took them two days or so. With that thought I drifted into sleep, only to be awakened by honking.

"Oh *Lord* that's loud." I really can't drink and function.

"It's John. We're at our rendezvous spot."

He raised his eyebrows up and down to make it sound more exciting that I presumed it would be.

Once I focused my eyes I saw a sign that read "Thornwood Estates—Cascade."

John opened my door and greeted me with the exuberance of a teenager.

"Hey you two! Beth, fancy meeting you here."

John's chuckle really was just an older version of Bob's. You could tell they'd spent a lot of time together.

"Okay, boss man. Where to?"

"Follow me."

Bob waited for his mentor to get back into his own car and then followed closely behind. Taking the first left we came to a security gatehouse that was directly in front of high wrought-iron gates. The guard looked in, saw John and waved us through as the gates magically opened. Damn, I loved power. I could see how Margaret became addicted.

John pulled up next to us, rolled down his window and said, "Bob, veer to the left and follow the road alongside the river. Up ahead is an underground parking garage. Just pull up to the entrance and use this card key." He passed the card to Bob and we continued as instructed.

Stopping just inside the garage gate Bob was apparently stumped.

"I wonder where we are and what we're supposed to do now? Is this one of John's games? If so, I need to know the rules." I knew he was trying to be cute because he gave me that damn wink.

John called to Bob, "Just pull into spot fifteen."

Like an obedient son, Bob did exactly as his mentor said.

John pulled in behind us, got out and turned to the door that led directly into the building. He pulled out a key and said "Enter, my friends."

There before us was a small, yet comfortable condo. It was decorated in burgundy and navy and as we followed John through the kitchen we saw a Texas flag hanging on the wall in the living room. Turning to the right we saw a small dinette set under a framed lithograph of the Great Seal of Michigan.

"Welcome to what I call the Texigan look. A bit of Texas, a smattering of Michigan."

"Oh, you mean cordial yet arrogant?" I laughed. "Midwest hospitality with a big ego?" That made them both laugh.

"Bob, I told you, that first night at Stan's up in Mackinac—I like this girl. She has real spunk."

Having John's approval meant a lot to me because I knew how Bob felt about him.

"John, I have to ask. Why on earth did you decorate your place with Texas and Michigan memorabilia?"

Bob was looking around at the blend of Michigan cherry wood and Texas pine.

"Well, it's not mine. It's yours, Bob. The deed reads 'Robert Larken, a married man.' In Michigan you don't need to name the spouse. Good thing, huh?"

You could tell by the broad beam on his face that he was proud of himself and proud of Bob.

"John, you're joking, right? I'm just a professor now. I quit the government. I can't possibly keep up all these homes."

"Bob, didn't you hear what I said? I said this place is yours. Here are two keys. It's paid for outright. Just maintain it. If you need help, you've got it. Think of it this way. Should the need arise, and someone asks where you're living nowadays, what are you going to say, huh old pal?"

Touché.

"Thank you, John. I don't know how we'd do this without you and Thorn. I guess I hadn't completely thought this through. Hey, do they let you have dogs here?" Bob's tone changed at the mere mention of pets.

"Sure, but they have to be under twenty pounds. Sticky CC and Rs, you know. You getting a dog?"

"Wait!" I jumped in. "I thought the dog was going to be ours? Why will it be here? You really won't be here that much. No fair!"

I stomped my feet and gave a pout. That had always worked with Daddy.

"Guess we'll have to have some joint custody arrangement. A pre-nup maybe."

Bob was starting to banter with me and I wasn't about to let him get the upper hand.

"No way. I have it on tape. You promised."

"On tape? You what?" Bob looked absolutely terrified. He ran his hands through his hair and his breathing became heavier.

"That's right, Larken. Remember Vic gave me that little tape recorder? I have everything on tape. Your ass is in a sling, bud."

I kept a straight face, which wasn't easy.

"Oh God, you have *everything* on tape?"

I could have sworn there was sweat breaking out on his forehead. Those veins were starting to pop out, too

"Well, no, not everything. Unfortunately I turned the recorder off before the snoring began." I was feeling sassier with every word. Let him see who the real pro was around here.

"Beth, why the hell...."

I cut him off before he had a heart attack.

"Just kidding."

Sticking my tongue out, I watched as John Gaynor nearly lost his lunch. He was convulsing with laughter and actually fell backwards onto the sofa.

"Bob, this one's a pistol."

"I ought to smack you." Bob shook his fist at me in mock rage.

"Is that a promise or a threat?"

He was so fun to tease.

"So, when can we get a dog? When can I move into the barn and house? What about the condo? This is so exciting!" I was curious, of course, but I really needed to figure this all out so I could tell Daddy what was going on. I owed him that much. Not to mention Vic—we still had to tell her about the job at the Ford Library.

"We can't get a dog until we get married," Bob said. "It wouldn't be right. I won't have an illegitimate pup. Not gonna happen."

"So, tell me, professor, how on earth are we going to get married secretly? I'm sure that's all planned out."

John, noticing that this might be a conversation we should have in private, walked out the sliding glass door and sat down on the patio.

"Beth, we could marry ourselves. It wouldn't be legal, really, but what's a piece of paper? The house, acreage and barn are in your name. If anything happens to me, John would see to it that you're provided for. Otherwise we would have to go overseas for privacy. It's your choice."

"Bob, as long as we're married in the eyes of God, that's all that matters to me. If we make our vows in front of God, why would we care what the government says? The government has done enough damage to our lives. I say let's get John, Thorn, Brad, Stan, Daddy and Vic and do it right away."

I wasn't entirely sure I agreed with what I'd just said. I'd always dreamt of having a gorgeous white lace dress; Daddy would wear some sort of special vest we'd have tailored for the occasion and Vic would be my maid of honor. I'd had my wedding planned since I took my First Communion. Then again my dreams never included a secret life that began with a dreamy voice and dead body.

"Stan might be hard. It's not easy whisking away a governor. Plus he is one truly honest politician. Michigan's lucky, let me tell you. I don't want him involved to the point where he'd have to cover up what he knows. But we'll call everyone else. How about tomorrow night? I'll stay at the condo tonight to keep things on the up and up, and you and Vic can do whatever needs be done between now and then."

I sighed as I realized it was time to let the dreams fade and welcome in reality.

"You have a deal, Mr. Larken. We'll get married by the river in the moonlight. Then we can go back to the house for wedding cake and some coffee. I'll make the coffee."

I gave him a hug and rumbled his hair. His hair was so thick and soft.

"I hope our puppy has hair as soft as yours. Do we really have to wait to get her?"

I pouted again. It had worked the first time, so I was counting on it again

"Okay Okay Okay. You win. We can get the pup now, if you want. How can I say no to you?"

"You can't. Better get used to it."

Giggling I pulled open the patio door and blurted, "John, you're going to be a grandpa!" With jaw dropped open, John stared first at me, then at Bob. He didn't say a word. He just stood there, seemingly in shock.

Bob stood behind me, with his arms around my waist. When there was no immediate response I said, "Her name is going to be Bowie!"

"You know it's going to be a girl and you're going to name her *Bowie*? Now I know you two have lost your minds."

I was doing a good job carrying this joke to the hilt and decided—why not continue?

"Well, it's going to be Bowie Aloysia."

In stereo—from in front and behind—I got "Bowie *what?*"

"Aloysia. I have a really good friend named Bernadette Aloysia—her mom and dad didn't have a middle name for her so they named her for their priest—his name was Aloysius. Now, Aloysia, they figured was the feminine ...."

"Beth, honey, you're babbling. Sorry, John, she does that when she gets nervous."

I broke out of his bear hug, turned around and smacked him a good one in the chest.

"Children, children, children."

John was shaking his finger at us but still had a look of puzzlement on his face.

"Now, first off, I'm thrilled it's a girl. It'll be easier on David. Oh Lord. David. How are we going to keep this under wraps? God, this does complicate matters. A granddaughter."

He was beginning to get misty-eyed and had this dreamy look. I kind of hated to burst his bubble.

"Well, not *exactly* a granddaughter—more like a grand pup."

I tucked my head down in case he threw something. You just can never be too careful with men.

"You are incorrigible, Beth! I'm usually so quick. You absolutely got me on that one. Bob—you didn't help any!"

I was feeling pretty proud of myself. Daddy was going to love John.

"If we're going to pull all this off tomorrow and find a pup today, we'd better get a move on." Bob was getting into orchestration mode. "John, will you call Brad and Thorn and tell them to be at the house tomorrow at sunset? Let's say, oh, seven, judging on last night's sunset. Once again, as always, thank you. This is more than I ever imagined. I won't disappoint you."

"You never have, Bob, you never have."

Heading back towards Grand Ledge there were several signs reading "Pigs for Sale" and "Fresh Michigan Cherries—but no puppies. Bob retrieved the Michigan map he'd stuck up in his visor and pulled over to the side of the road.

"Okay. We'll take the back roads. In Texas all sorts of country folks put kittens and cows up for sale, but you have to get off the beaten path. If nothing else we can see some pretty country on the way back to Lansing."

"Lansing? We're going back to Lansing? Why? You had me pack everything up!"

"Well, that was before we decided to get married tomorrow, my dear. Don't you think we need to talk to your Dad and Vic?"

183

"I suppose you're right. As always." I was getting use to rolling my eyes when talking to Bob.

"Of course I'm always right, I'm a Texan!" No chuckle. No laugh. He was attempting to make that statement believable. Frankly, I wanted to puke.

We found our way back to Willow Highway and turned left on Clinton. Reaching Saginaw Highway I knew it would be ten minutes or less until we reached Lansing. I didn't want to take any chances.

"Beth? You awake? Everything okay?"

"I'm praying to Saint Roch."

"And that would be....?" He had one of those 'I don't believe this but I shouldn't laugh' looks—half incredulous, half joking.

"Saint Roch, the patron saint for dogs. It's a Catholic thing. I just know our puppy is waiting for us somewhere."

I was worried someone else had started praying before me and Bowie was going to be placed in a home with a dozen kids. She'd be miserable. They'd pull her tail and dress her up in ugly T-shirts.

Before Bob could condemn my selective faith, Bob yelled, "Way to go Roch!"

He maneuvered the Z into a quick spin, squealed the tires and turned right. Heading down a residential street dotted with taquerias and apparently some pastry shops, his eyes were squinting, looking for something. I could smell the bakeries, I just couldn't read the signs—they were all in Spanish.

"Bob, what on earth are you doing?"

"The sign said *perritos blancos libres* and the arrow pointed down this way. Keep your eyes open!"

"For what?"

"For puppies! *Perritos blancos libres* means 'free white puppies.'"

"Is that all it said? There wasn't an address? Oh Bob, please find the puppies." I know. I know. I was whining, but you can't mess around with Saint Roch.

Spotting a bit of commotion, we pulled into the first free spot on the street and walked up to an aging clapboard house whose front yard was filled with children and puppies. The chain link fence was gated, but not locked. As soon as we entered the yard puppies scattered—running under bushes, into the laps of children sitting on the grass and over mounds of freshly placed mulch. An attractive Hispanic woman approached Bob and he immediately began speaking to her in Spanish. I hate it when people do that.

"The only one spoken for is the one with the green ribbon around her neck. The others are fair game."

*"¿Cuál uno de usted los perritos desea ser llamado* Bowie?"

Laughing at my stunned expression Bob explained, "I just asked them which one wanted to be named Bowie."

I went from pup to pup: the one with the blue ribbon, then the one with the purple ribbon. I wasn't about to miss the perfect pup.

"Hey, looky here—this one, the one with the pink ribbon. She's a real beauty, Beth."

Bob was kneeling down with his fingers in the mouth of a tiny, scruffy ball of white fluff.

"She thinks I'm her personal chew stick."

I picked her up. Snuggling up under my chin was the sweetest little Schnauzer mix I'd ever seen. She couldn't have been more than four pounds.

"Is this a dog or a rat? She's so small—I was thinking of something bigger...."

"Bob, stop. She's perfect. Look at these eyes. She is just begging to come home with us."

"Well, we could always say she was a Rottweiler dressed in a Schnauzer suit."

He winked at me and gave the pup a pat on the head.

"Looks like we have ourselves a little girl. Hi there, Bowie."

Just then, the woman approached us. I closed my eyes again and prayed. Please don't let her decide to keep this one. I just kept talking to the pup, telling her how much she'd love her new home with all the trees and birds.

*"Los perritos entienden solamente español."*

"Uh oh," Bob muttered.

"Oh no, what's wrong?" I clung to the pup for dear life.

"The puppies only understand Spanish."

Taking Bowie from me, he held her gently and said, *"Papá habla español."*

It was love at first lick.

## Chapter Seventeen

Stopping by the Lansing Mall we picked up a pink blanket, a cute pink collar, leash, food, bowls—the works. Bob was petting Bowie under the chin and rubbing her ears.

"Did you notice how she sneezed every time we put a collar on her? What do you think *that's* all about? Do you think she has a cold? Should we take her to the vet?" I was already an overprotective parent. I had learned that lesson well from Daddy.

"She isn't sneezing now. She likes the pink collar. In fact, she told me that she's allergic to anything that's not pink." A smug look came across his face. One of those holier-than-thou routines.

"Oh really? She told you that?"

"Yes, ma'am. You just couldn't understand because you don't speak Spanish. ¿la derecha, Bowie? Isn't that right?"

As if on cue, the pup let out an affirmative bark.

Oh boy. I was in trouble. Trust us to find a dog that only communicates in Spanish and will only wear pink.

"Bob, can we just go back to the barn? I really want to show Bowie the woods. She's going to love running around. I want to play with her and see if I can start making her bilingual." I was back to whining and wheedling. I admit it.

"What about your dad and Vic? What about the ceremony tomorrow? You're confusing me, girl!"

He was talking to me but his attention was on the pup. She was sitting on my lap, looking like a little white fluffball.

"Oh, well, yeah. Them. Well, how about Plan B?"

I had been trying to come up with Plan B while he focused on the little Schnauzer. She'd found the cuff on his lightweight sweatshirt and was happily gnawing her way through not only the material, but also his heart.

"Plan B? This should be good. Go on."

His attention was still on Lil Miss Fluff Puff.

"I was thinking, since we can't tell your son, we can't put out an announcement in the paper, we can't walk around town introducing ourselves as Mr. and Mrs., why not just have something totally private and personal? We don't need anyone but the two of us—well, and Bowie—to profess our love and commit ourselves to each other. God will be our witness and that's all that matters."

I shut my eyes and began praying.

"Who's the saint this time?"

He couldn't help but notice and laugh.

"Saint John Francis Regis. I learned all about him when mama was alive. He's the patron saint of marriages."

"Maybe we could invite him." He was biting his lip to keep from totally breaking up.

"Not funny. This is serious stuff here, Larken." I feigned absolute disgust. Talking and teasing with Bob was unbelievably easy. Definitely, most definitely, uniquely us.

"You've got a deal Mrs. Larken-to-be-sort-of. We'll get married tonight, then. I don't want to wait any longer for our wedding night."

He smirked, patted Bowie and, leaning over, kissed me. It was one of those "oh my God I'm gonna stop breathing soon" kisses.

Once back at the barn, we put Plan B into action. Bob left for the house to make all the calls, and I stayed to get Bowie settled in our new digs. Since I'd be spending most of my time at the barn, I wanted her to have her bed, bowls and toys right near my desk.

Looking around the barn, I figured I'd probably need to decorate in burgundy and pink to avoid having a sneezing, snorting pup on my hands. Once I'd stowed all the puppy's belongings, I scooped Bowie into my arms and we headed to the house so she could get situated there, too. She had a leash but I wanted to hold her so she could get accustomed to my scent.

I thought about domestic arrangements as we walked. Bob would get a bed and food for the condo later. A dog with three homes. How spoiled could one pup get?

The door to the house was ajar. The two of us walked in and began looking for signs of life. I finally had time to look more closely at the woodworking Thorn had done—what an artist he was. Everything was done with such precision. Not a nail to be spotted. Every finish was flawless—no streaks, no brush marks. The workmanship was professional and intricate. All the necessities were in place. We'd need to get more furniture, of course, but at least there was a bed in the loft. Good to know Thorn had his priorities in order.

Going through the slider off the deck we found Bob leaning up against the railing, talking on the phone. His tone was firm and unwavering. This was strictly business. Turning around when he heard my footsteps, he motioned for me to come and join him. I put Bowie down, shut the door behind me and sat cross-legged on the deck.

"Vic, you're welcome. You can start as soon as you'd like. No, Mr. Pullen, I won't destroy your daughter's life. You have my word."

This was obviously a three-way call. Smart. One call, two down.

"Mr. Pullen, I fully intend to make this legal as soon as I can. You have to believe me. I love Beth and we'll be fine. It's just as I explained. We have to be safe for a while until Margaret and the others are convinced I'm a civilian forever. There's also my son. He's not privy to this information. I have to protect him. We will marry ourselves tonight, in the presence of God. He's all that really matters anyhow, don't you think?"

Bob could be very persuasive, but Daddy had been a corporate exec for years. He'd heard every excuse in the book and was used to lies and corporate shenanigans. He would become either our strongest ally or worst nightmare.

"Mr. Pullen, please don't threaten me. That's not necessary."

Oh Lord, this was getting ugly.

"Nothing, I repeat nothing, will happen to your daughter or to Victoria. We just need to play by the rules they've imposed upon us. And it's only temporary. Believe me. It's only temporary."

I guess Daddy wanted to hear it from me because, with a serious look on his face, Bob handed me the phone.

"Hi, Daddy. I'm fine. Really. I've never been so happy. And we just got a puppy! You'll love her! I know. I can't wait to have you out here. It's beautiful. I don't really know what I'll do, Daddy. I think I'll freelance and Bob wants me to do press work. I'll travel with him when he gives speeches and write recaps. That kind of thing. Yes. I'll be on his payroll."

With that I gave my usual eyeball roll to show that I was somewhat put out by Daddy's assumptions.

"Yes, Daddy, I promise. We'll have a real wedding and you can walk me down the aisle of a huge cathedral. We just need to make sure Margaret is taken care of. She'll come around. I'm sure of it. It won't be long. I promise."

My voice had risen beyond what I'd normally use when speaking to my father. I guess I *was* becoming more independent. I had a newfound resolve that felt liberating yet somewhat disconcerting.

"I love you, too, Daddy. You, too, Vic. We'll get together soon. Yes, I promise."

All these promises.

"Bye for now."

I clicked the cordless phone off and handed it back to Bob.

"Man, they're a tough crowd." Bob had been baptized by fire. I needed to change the subject. "Did you call Thorn and John?"

"Yes. It's all taken care of. What now?"

He bent down and picked up Bowie, who immediately licked his face and started to chew on his sweatshirt.

"She loves me, what can I say?"

"You might want to start teaching her the word 'no.' We can't have her eating our clothes. How do you say no in Spanish?"

"Um, 'no'? 'No' is *no* in Spanish, Beth." He was trying to keep a straight face.

"Well how was I supposed to know?"

"Don't get your feelings all hurt now. Try this—tell her *No no, mal perro.* Do it firmly though. It means 'no no, bad dog!' "

Being as firm as I could be while looking at that fuzzy white face chewing away at his sweatshirt I commanded, "No no, mal perro."

Bowie immediately stopped and hung her head.

"I'm not believing this. Will you hang out and communicate with her while I go into town for a few things? I want to get ready for tonight."

It finally dawned on me. Tonight I'm getting *married*. I began making a mental to-do list.

"I need to get going, before the bakery closes. We can't get married without a cake!"

A quick kiss for Bob, then one for Bowie when it dawned on me—I didn't have a car. Peg was still at the apartment in Lansing.

"Bob, Peg isn't here. Can I borrow the Z?"

"You want to drive my Z? No one has ever driven the Z—not even Margaret."

He looked hesitant but reached in his pocket for his key chain, which of course was shaped like Texas.

"There's always a first. Here you go. Be careful."

I drove the few miles into Grand Ledge and started my search. I knew there were supermarkets on Saginaw, a main drag in Lansing. That was only five miles or so down the road. Krogers, Randalls and Farmer Jack's, if I remembered correctly. Surely there'd be something in Grand Ledge, though. If I make my way over to Saginaw, I could head toward Lansing if need be.

Rounding the corner I spotted it. Bingo! Felspausch Food Center. Pulling the Z ever so carefully into a parking spot, I got in and out in record time. That's the nice thing about small towns. No crowds and relatively tiny stores. A pan of brownies would do just fine as a wedding cake. Who could celebrate without chocolate? Not me! I picked up a box of dog bones so Bowie could celebrate, too, and a pink sticky bow for the top of her head.

Next stop, a florist. Had to have flowers. The cashier told me there was Fox's out on Willow Highway. That was perfect because it wasn't far from Legend Woods Drive, where we now lived. It still hadn't quite sunk in.

Within thirty minutes I had everything I needed, including red Michigan tulips and yellow roses to represent Texas. The florist tied them together with white lace—a unique and startling combination. But then again, so were Bob and I.


It was getting closer to sunset and I still needed to shower and change clothes. I didn't have much to choose from but I had packed one dress, just as Bob suggested. It was a denim button-down jumper. I had a royal blue ribbed T-shirt to wear with it. I might be a bit chilly, but denim was always a good choice. The jumper would look nice with the tulips and yellow roses

Sneaking into the house wasn't easy with Bowie around. She bounded to the door with reckless energy when she heard the door open. I raised the flowers and brownies high above my head. She was tiny but quite a jumper. Bob, fresh out of the shower and wearing nothing more than boxers and a grin, accompanied her.

"Get ready, lil bride. This is our night."

I hurriedly took the brownies to the kitchen and ran upstairs with the flowers.

The anticipation was mounting. I took a few of the rose petals and placed them on our pillows. This isn't exactly what I'd dreamt of for a wedding, but I realized now that the man was far more important than the ceremony.

Showered and dressed with flowers in hand, I took a look in the bathroom mirror. I'd brushed my hair a hundred times to make sure it was shiny, and had used makeup sparingly. One day I'd have a pretty white dress and dangly pearl earrings—just not tonight. I closed my eyes and silently asked Mama to be with me and to understand.

I called down the stairs. "Bob, Bowie, you two ready to get married?"

I'd no more than gotten the words out before I heard the sound of piano music. Bob must have gotten a CD player when I was out. I wondered how, since I had the car—but he never ceased to amaze me. "Moon River" drifted through the air.

Walking down the stairs, I saw the man of my dreams holding Bowie—our very own pup. Since she was all white, she looked more like a bride than I did. I wasn't nervous at all, to my surprise. My heart was pounding but it was from anticipation, not nerves.

Robert Larken, wearing jeans and a yellow oxford shirt, extended his free arm and escorted me outside, through the clearing, to the edge of the river. There we stood, the moonlight glistening on the water—facing each other and the rest of our lives. Bob was the first to speak.

"Before God, Beth, I pledge you my love, my devotion and my heart. I'll love you alone, forever. You are my dream come true. I'll love you no matter what the future holds. I'm yours alone, till the day I die."

"Before God, Bob, I promise to be your wife. Your greatest supporter and only love. You have brought me more joy than I knew existed. I'll love you forever and I promise to be by your side always."

Tears fell from both of our eyes as we held each other for the first time as husband and wife.

"Mrs. Larken, let's go home."

Bob put Bowie down and commanded her to follow us.

Normally, laughter, toasts and applause would surround the new bride and groom. Since nothing we'd experienced thus far was normal, tonight was no exception. We walked back to the house, the music getting louder as we approached the front door.

We stopped. Bob kissed me. And Bowie peed right on his sneakers.

## Chapter Eighteen

My first job, as Bob's wife, was wiping dog pee off his Nikes. I hoped this was not a clue of some sort. A premonition. I couldn't believe I'd really agreed to get married on San Jacinto Day. What decent, God-fearing Yankee would do *that*? Well, seeing how I had no clue until today what that day was, it didn't mean a thing to me. Bob's excitement, however, was considerable. He'd told me all about the Battle of San Jacinto. How it was the last military conflict of the Texas Revolution; how they won their independence after that. Said it was prophetic because us getting married on April 21 was saying we were setting off on our own. It was, apparently, a decisive battle and Bob felt we'd won, too.

This comparison still freaked me out, though. Making such a big deal about something like a battle and then thinking that was a great day to get married. Weird, if you asked me.

Shaking off my bad vibes and setting the brownies on the counter, I summoned my new husband and pup inside. Bowie, smelling something edible, trotted right into the kitchen. Bob wasn't far behind.

"Brownies for a wedding cake? That's my Beth."

He gave me a squeeze just before I grabbed a gooey chunk of chocolate heaven and smashed it on his face. Far be it from me to break from tradition.

"A dog pisses on my wedding sneakers and I'm wearing a brownie. This is not going to be a typical marriage." With that I stuck out my tongue and began licking my husband's face.

"Do you think you're strong enough to carry me up the stairs, sir? All this face licking has made me feel incredibly playful."

"I'm a Texan. Strong is my middle name."

With that, he whisked me into his arms and just about galloped me away. Stopping at the top of the stairs, we faced the window and door that led out to the deck. We didn't have curtains. With all the trees, they weren't really needed out here. The only light in the room trickled in from the moon that was hanging between the tree branches.

"Hey, do you have a baptismal name?" I asked. I was comfortable in his arms, but curiosity won over romance.

"Sure do. Camion, for Saint Camion. I think he's the patron saint of pickup trucks. It's a Bubba Catholic thing."

"Saint who?"

Mama had made me learn plenty of saints as she tutored me through her faith, but that one never made the 'must know' list. Then again, Mama wasn't a truck-loving kind of woman.

"Camion. *Camion* is Italian for truck. Saint Camion."

He was trying to be serious but his eyes started to get that twinkle. "Well, actually I don't have a clue if Camion is a saint."

"No. Really?" The eyeball roll was his cue that I was on to him.

"Well, c*amion* really does mean truck in Italian. It's one of the only words I remember from Professor whomever. Two years of Italian and I remember *camion* and *sesso*—that's sex."

The twinkle was accompanied by that eyebrow thing he did so well.

"Truck and sex. Seems about right for a born and bred hot-blooded Texan."

I think he considered that an invitation because he let me slip gently out of his arms. Standing before him I watched as he removed his shirt, moved closer to me and laid me down on the bed.

Just as I was in the middle of being transformed from lover to wife, the mood was broken by an incredible cracking noise, then a thud. There we were, in the outfits bestowed upon us by nature, lying on the floor.

In a fit of laughter, Bob coughed out "Breaking bed slats—now *this* is uniquely us."

"Oh Lord." We laughed until our strength was gone. I think I was the first to pass out.


The phone startled me and I did a remarkable impersonation of the involuntary jump—*sans* snort—that Bob was becoming famous for in his sleep. The same trees that blocked the moon's full illumination didn't work as well with the morning light of the sun. There it was, staring directly at me. I hate mornings. There should be a law against mornings. At times like this I wished Bob still worked in government. I'm sure he could write a bill and get it passed. No phone calls before noon. No work before two pots of coffee.

Bob had picked the call up downstairs. It was his cell, of course, since we didn't have a number at the house yet. Making my way to the stairs I eavesdropped.

"Sure, that will be great. We'll be there—sure, Vic. No problem."

Bob came back upstairs, Bowie in hand.

"She's all taken care of and ready for her first road trip." He was beaming.

"That was Vic. She's invited us to the Ford Museum—she can show us around. Well, she actually wants to see the pup here, but we can tag along. I think she might be spying for your dad. Making sure I haven't done something sinister to you." That comment was accompanied by a gentle tap on the rear. His playful spirit was in full force this morning after.

Bob had also become more at ease these last few days, I'd noticed. I could tell he loved being in the woods, surrounded, at last, by serenity. His gait had gone from that of a precise and focused public figure to the easy-going stride of a man at peace.

"Let's get a move on, it's late. I've got the coffee ready and we can have leftover wedding brownies for breakfast. It's a gorgeous Tuesday morning. I'd say we started this week off just fine."

I loved the way he said 'fine'—it came out *fahn*. His voice still mesmerized me.

"Uh, can I shower and get dressed, Mr. Morning Sunshine?" One of us was going to have to give on this morning shit.

One shower, five cups of coffee and two hours later we'd crossed over the Grand River and were sitting outside a very oddly shaped glass building that was Victoria's new place of employment. Bob dropped me off on Pearl, which I think is a great name for a street.

He was going to park in the lot and unobtrusively join my best friend and me inside. Bowie would be just fine inside the Z because the April days were still cool. I, frankly, was shocked Bob that let a dog ride in the Z, but who was I to argue with the new and improved Bob Larken?

As I entered the massive glass doors, Vic came around the corner.

"Hey, you!" As my best friend hugged me she whispered in my ear, "I can't believe you did this. Everyone would expect me to be impulsive and run off with a married man, but you? Little Miss Sweetness and Light?"

"I'm a quick study. Thanks, teach."

We stood back and looked at each other. Vic was her usual 'together' self–crisp red linen suit, white silk camisole and red high heels. The pearl shoe clasps precisely matched her pearl earrings. Her hair, slicked down and sprayed with that stuff that makes your hair shine, gave her that edge that said "pro" in every sense. As usual, I was the antithesis of Victoria's elegance. Pleated denims with basic white oxford shirt over a rust tank top with my usual gold dangly earrings.

"Hey, is the pup in the car? Time for me to take a break, how about it?"

I knew Vic wanted to get out of the building–so we could talk more openly.

Wandering through the lot and down Pearl to where the Z was parked, the questions and comments began.

"Okay, is he as smooth in bed as he is on camera? Are you sure he's really divorced? What about his kid? Oh my god, you're a step-mother!" All this was said in one breath.

"Vic–you're killing me here." It was refreshing to be alone with Vic at long last. No father weighing every word. No political insiders assuming everything they said would show up in print. No Margaret.

" I'm not the experienced woman you are, Vic, but believe me, I have no complaints."

"Why am I expecting to hear 'details at eleven'? Doesn't this kind of freak you out?"

Luckily, we reach the parked Z and I was able to gracefully cut off Vic's Twenty-Question routine. I wasn't use to discussing my sex life–since I'd never had one before.

"Can you believe I actually have keys to Bob's beloved Beemer? He gave me his second set as a wedding gift."

"Along with the keys to the house, your own writer's retreat– and a puppy. Girl, you've always been so damned spoiled. It's good to see someone's keeping up the good work."

As she was editorializing about my life I was getting Bowie out of her kennel.

"Tada! Isn't she cute?"

Vic reached over and began petting the pup under the chin. Cocking her head, Bowie took Vic's suit cuff button into her mouth and began happily teething.

"Uh, excuse me you little fluff puff, but you can't gnaw on my best ever-so-Republican suit." With that she attempted to pry Bowie's mouth away from the gold button.

"That won't work Vic. And don't get her excited or she'll pee."

"Damn left-wing dog." She was cursing and laughing at the same time.

Once I'd reprimanded the pup in Spanish and placed her back in the kennel, Vic and I headed back to meet up with Bob.

"You know, Vic, that pup is really a symbol for us. She has such unconditional love. That's how I feel. My love for Bob is unconditional."

"Girl, not exactly. You have more conditions on your life now than I ever knew existed. What are you getting at?"

"I mean how I feel about him–I love him unconditionally. Otherwise I wouldn't have agreed to any of this. There is nothing I wouldn't do for him, Vic."

We continued our stroll back to the library arm in arm, just like we use to walk around the MSU campus chit chatting. Once back at the library steps our conversation came to an end. Time to find Bob.

Before I could say "I am not a crook" we saw him standing in front of a full-scale reproduction of the Oval Office. The look of longing in Bob's eyes did not escape me.

"It's not out of your blood is it, Lieutenant Governor." I phrased it as a statement, rather than a question. We both knew the answer.

Bob, head down and silent, left the room and continued to the "Betty Ford, First Lady" display. This, of course, was Vic's favorite since it contained a collection of dresses worn by the former first lady. I just stood back as the two of them walked past the wall with a picture of President and Mrs. Ford with their dog, Liberty, at Camp David. Vic and I entered the amphitheater. Since it was a Tuesday in April, the room was deserted. While the slide show ran we were able to talk again.

"I am so excited for the two of you," Victoria whispered.

She was remaining very professional and guarded.

"Chrissy, you might want to start carrying around a notebook and pen or something, in case folks wonder why you're with Bob so much, you know? You could say you're doing a 'day in the life of an ousted LG' article."

She tilted her head, making her lopsided haircut even more pronounced. Those cat-eyes narrowed, letting me know she was in the game but not sure, yet, whether or not she was enjoying the silence thrust upon her.

"Good point, Vic. And you'll need to get use to calling me Beth."

The slide presentation over, we left the second-floor galleries and headed back down the stairs.

As our time together drew to a close, Victoria's pager went off and she glanced down at the readout.

"Bob, the museum director wants to see you. Someone cancelled a speech for this weekend. The library would like to extend an invitation if you would be available to fill in. It's a luncheon for the State Republican Women's Convention." It was obvious that Victoria enjoyed playing her position to the hilt.

"How did he know I was here?"

"I put your name on the V.I.P list for today. We like to keep track of visiting dignitaries."

"Great," Bob chuckled. "My first speaking engagement as a civilian will be on the stage of a Republican stronghold, surrounded by women dressed to the nines. I spoke at a women's convention of Democrats once. They were whoopin' and hollerin' and dancing in the aisles to a gospel group. Everyone dressed in pantsuits or pretty casual. I'll bet you a dollar to a dime not so this weekend. Hey, if Jerry's in town maybe we could go play golf. My big ole Texas mouth can yell "fore' as well as anybody."

The laughter reverberated off the glassed walls and reminded us to be very careful when we spoke.

"Just tell him I'll do it—he can call me. Give him my number."

"Okay, sir. I'll handle it." This was Victoria at her finest. All business.

"Tell him I'll be speaking on the role of the media in government. Or how about this: 'Political Responsibility and Personal Convictions: Can They Marry?' You know me when I get before a mike—I won't let him down. I'll keep party politics out of it. Tell him thanks. This will be a great way to introduce myself to my temporary home."

Turning towards me he asked, "How should we promo this, Beth? Will you get the word out and cover the event for me?"

"Certainly sir–I'll work up a promo and swing it by you." I knew he wanted to wink and I held back the smile. Victoria sat there as rigid as the Calder sculptures that dotted the city's landscape.

He shook Victoria's hand warmly and then told me solemnly that he looked forward to working with me again.

"The pleasure's mine, Mr. Larken."

I couldn't look him in the eye for fear of busting up. Maybe we would all be eligible for Emmys if we got a syndicated show on TV. Or one of those Hallmark movies on a Sunday night would be a kick.

"We'll talk soon. I miss you." Victoria and I exchanged hugs. Since the place was like a morgue inside and out, Bob and I walked to the Z and left together. It wouldn't be any big deal—I *was* his employee. I sat Bowie's kennel on my lap again and stuck my fingers in for her to lick. She bit down a bit too hard with her puppy teeth and I responded with *"No no, mal perro!"*

"We'll make her bilingual yet, won't we Bowie?" Here Bob was again, talking to the dog instead of me.

"In fact," he went on, "we say 'no no bad dog' so much we could just call her B.A.D.—you know, short for Bowie Aloysia Dog?"

Oh brother. "You two are certifiable. Cute little family though, don't you think? I can't wait until we can drop our membership to that damn Fraternity."

"I know, I know." Bob's face turned serious. "It's not ideal. But there's really no choice. We're in good company. Ever wonder why some of the biggest names in politics look so happy with their wives? It's probably because they only have to be with them in front of the cameras. That's my guess. Just from my years in journalism—the politicians just never let loose—I always wondered about that but knew that was off limits. I tried to poke around during the last Senate race. That's when I first bucked up against Marty. I tried to follow him once—and was told to leave him and his personal life alone. I knew it was not an idle threat. Too many accidents that just can't be explained. Now I understand."

"Bob, do you think Glinnis had a heart attack? I mean, do you really think so?"

I had to know.

"Beth, honestly? No. No, I don't. I believe someone—or a group of people—needed him to be quiet and he refused. He was a man of great principle. I don't think he bought into the Fraternity. Rumor has it—and mind you, it's only rumor—that Billy G was the mainstream party's hope for another eight years under the dome. He was a Democrat above reproach. There were some on the right side of the aisle and some more conservative Democrats who wanted someone who would bend more. Just one theory and I don't buy the heart attack. You don't need a Ph.D. in mathematics to add it up."

"It doesn't make sense. Who would possibly want Glinnis out of office and why?"

I was about to answer my own question.

"Oh, here's a theory! Maybe someone didn't so much want Glinnis *out* but they wanted *you* in! I started in with the *doo-doo-doo-doo* "Twilight Zone" theme to lighten it up some.

"We are changing the subject and changing it right now," Bob said firmly.

I was immediately sorry I'd ever brought it up.

"Now," he continued, "Can you help me with something suitable for this lecture? If you write up a promo, fax it over to Vic for the library's approval. Or work with their PR department—you could get it out to the media to stir up interest. You'll be there, won't you? You can sit in the press row and take notes. Or doodle. Your choice."

Thank God he winked just then. It had been almost a day since I had a wink fix and it made me very glad to know he wasn't angry at my supposition.

"I'll help you. And of course I'll be there."

Over the next few days we did much more than pass winks back and forth. There were all the chores of daily life: getting phone lines in both the house and barn, having cable TV hooked up, picking Peg up from my old apartment and letting the apartment manager know I was moving out. We took advantage of being tucked away in the woods and sat outside most evenings for our deck chats. We sat for hours talking on the deck under the stars.

Of course, there was work, too. By Saturday I had written a few promos, the Ford people in GR had informed the conference participants of the change in speakers, and I had gotten it out on the AP.

Amazingly enough, Bob's nemesis, Lieutenant Governor Jim Parsons, was the speaker who cancelled out at the last minute. I didn't find out why, but was betting on indigestion. No one can eat like that and not make himself sick. Maybe all the mousse he used on what few hairs he had left had seeped through his scalp and caused some kind of internal cranial fart, I speculated uncharitably. He would be resting and recuperating in the arms of his darling little wife, of course. I'd heard she took good care of Parsons. He must have something I didn't know about because she was way too cute and apparently sweet for the likes of him. Granted, I only knew what I'd read or what Vic had heard, which wasn't much. But from that one encounter in his office, he left me cold. You know—that kind of creepy cold you get when you're at a cemetery?

Looking over what I'd written and sent out, a sense of pride overwhelmed me. Bob was still standing on his feet after what so many thought would be a serious fall.

> *Former Texas Lt. Governor, Bob Larken, will be the keynote speaker for the Michigan Republican Women's Conference to be held this Saturday, April 25th, at the Gerald R. Ford Museum*
> *Contact the Museum for further information and reservations.*

I added contact information for the library, phone numbers for several local chapters of the Republican Women and included Bob's photo, which was sure to bring out the women. I also arranged for Bob to be interviewed on ABC and NBC affiliates. Really, all I had to do was mention his name and it was a done deal.

Bob opened the passenger door to the Z. I was excited to be attending Bob's first "civilian" speech and was ready to walk in as his official liaison to the media. Luckily I looked down on the car seat before climbing in. There lay one red tulip and one yellow rose wrapped together, with a note:

> *Michigan and Texas, diversities set aside.*
> *Michigan and Texas, bound forever, side by side.*
> *I love you, my wife.*

I was touched. "I love you, too. Break a leg tonight, Larken." I kissed him before we turned out of the driveway, then leaned back in my seat. I knew we had to say anything personal now because once there, our relationship would turn mute. The Fraternity rules would prevail once again.

*Katherine Shephard*

# Chapter Nineteen

Watching Bob Larken behind a mike was magical. He would write a speech, or have one written for him, then fold it up and place it in his pocket—never to be seen again. Watching him tonight, I realized what a powerful extemporaneous speaker Bob was. He spoke off the cuff and straight from his heart. If a subject was worth speaking about, he thought, you should know what you wanted to say and then say it. You should be able to express your opinions in a way that would make others listen more intently, or, preferably, agree with you. No notes for Bob Larken. Just passion.

Amazingly, this former Democratic lieutenant governor from the South soon had two hundred Yankee Republican women eating out of the palm of his hand. He mentioned his new puppy a few times, which the women loved. He mentioned his family and his son, which I knew would always melt even the most upper-crust female. He talked about loyalty, honesty and integrity as being traits that should be shared in both the media and politics. All in all, Bob Larken played to the crowd.

He told them how he left the media because he was given a chance to put his beliefs into action—to make a difference. He talked about how presiding over the legislature of such a large and prestigious state afforded him the opportunity to see that bills and reforms were enacted that would become models for the entire nation. He then spoke in an impassioned tone about how, when his beliefs were threatened, he had to vote his conscience. End of speech. These women were now, officially, putty.

After he was done, the Republican women gave him a standing ovation that lasted several minutes. Bob shook hands and mingled while the women gathered around him. You'd think he was a pop icon or movie star. I wanted to chuckle and chime in, "Excuse me, ladies, I'd like to tell you about the jumping snorts...." Knowing that would be a bad choice but not sure I could keep a straight face, I went to the ladies room and hung out. It's amazing what you can learn from inside a bathroom stall.

"Have you ever seen his wife? I saw her on CNN. It was after he walked out of the capitol in Austin. She was so supportive and soft spoken. A real Southern lady." Okay, that made me want to puke.

"I heard his wife is staying on in Austin with their son. It's a shame he's a Democrat."

"We could use a hunk like Larken on our side. He's so rational and honest."

This mindless chatter went on for the entire time I was in the stall. Victoria had told me a lot of the insider information she'd obtained had come from ladies rooms. I could see how.

I went back into the auditorium, sat in the press row and wrote up a summary of Bob's speech for the AP. Every event at the Presidential Museum was taped—I knew that if any radio or television stations wanted some footage, it could be easily obtained. I had especially liked the joke he'd made about Bowie.

"The first night I had my new puppy," he'd said, "she relieved herself on my shoe...just when I thought I'd risen higher than a dog could lift its leg. Darn good thing it's a girl dog." The crowd had loved it. I decided to release a picture of Bowie and Bob—everyone loves animal shots. Very marketable.

An hour later, the convention attendees had all boarded chartered buses back to the Amway Grand, where they were staying. I had called in one story, faxed in another and arranged to have a few clips sent to television affiliates. I'd earned my pay tonight, that was for sure. The state was soon to be inundated with Grand Valley's latest adjunct professor. Fine with me. The more speeches he could rustle up, the more money he could earn. I was no fool.

Victoria was hurriedly approaching me just as I was standing up to leave. She motioned for me to follow her into the employee's restroom. I knew that meant she wanted to talk. In case someone had bugged the room, we immediately turned on all the faucets to cover our whispers.

"Wow he's something else, girl."

"Don't I know it." She knew exactly what I meant, too.

"I think he's found his niche—a way he can blend his media background with his fierce loyalty to his beliefs. I do believe he's married the media with politics."

I was so proud. The more I got to know him, the more I still found him absolutely amazing. The strength and conviction I'd heard on that very first broadcast came across even stronger now. I knew that on a personal level, he was filled with pride for his state, his country and his Constitution. Now he could exhibit that pride in public without compromising his beliefs.

Well, there was the fact that he was kind of married to two women—a minor moral glitch to say the least. He wasn't legally married to Margaret, just in appearances. He wasn't legally married to me, except in our hearts and before God. I figured that made me the winner.

"Hey, Beth, snap out of dreamland."

Vic poked me in the arm to shake me up some.

"Oh. Sorry. I was just counting my blessings, I guess."

"Listen, the governor just called the museum director. He just caught a clip on the news. You work fast, Missy."

She looked proud. We'd both made giant professional hurdles in the past few months.

"Governor Melvin called? Did he like what he saw? This is really my first big story to be televised or put on radio. I've only done print work."

Suddenly, my stomach felt as if a dozen butterflies were doing the Macarena on the walls of my intestines. Good thing we were in the bathroom. I might need a toilet. Nerves do that to me.

"Yes, he was very impressed. In fact, he would like the two of you to come to his office Monday. First thing, whatever that means. Bob will know, I guess."

"The governor? Well, he's a family friend of Bob's. I really enjoyed talking with him at that party you got me invited to. Mrs. Melvin is absolutely charming, too. Hey, I never thanked you for arranging that trip to Mackinac. If it weren't for you...."

"If it weren't for me you wouldn't have broken those bed slats."

The head tilt was a dead giveaway that she had some insider info. Wonder who spilled the beans?

"Vic, did Bob tell you? That skunk, he's such a brat!"

I started to laugh, glad to have another chance to talk and joke around with my best friend.

"I miss you, Vic. Thanks for understanding."

Returning to a whisper Vic smirked as she confided, "Oh I understand all about broken bed slats."

"I'm sure you do, I'm sure you do."

I couldn't help but shake my head, wondering how many bedrooms she'd trashed.

We exited the bathroom and spotted Bob. Vic motioned for him to follow and we entered the employee lunchroom. His erect posture and broad smile reminded me of the man who'd stood proudly in the Texas Senate, singing the state anthem. We were definitely living an unconventional existence but I was absolutely convinced it wouldn't be for long. Of that I felt certain.

Vic went around the corner and turned the in-house speakers up so we would have some privacy from any bugs or eavesdroppers. This was politics and you never could trust too deeply. We could now speak our hearts.

"Let's go home, Mrs. Larken. Tomorrow's Sunday and I want to spend the entire day with you and Bowie—in bed."

"Oh great, now I get to share you with a dog. She can stay in her kennel some of the time, you know. Now that our mattress is on the floor we don't need any more puppy accidents."

"I'll fix the bed when we get home. I have just the trick. Trust me."

"Why do I think that should frighten me?" I smiled over to him.

"You two lovebirds should get a move on," Vic called out. "I need to help lock the place up. We'll talk soon." We exchanged hugs one more time. Vic stayed behind and I followed a few steps behind Bob when he exited the room

On the way home I told Bob about our command appearance at Stan's Monday morning and added that I'd like to get the rest of my things from the apartment. I really needed some clothes to wear and we certainly could use everything from the kitchen.

When we entered the house, Bob flicked on the light and my heart came to an abrupt halt. There, tucked in the far corner of the living room, was my mother's ebony Wurlitzer baby grand. A big white bow was tied around the piano bench and with it, a card.

*My dear Chrissy and her beloved Bob:*
*I always promised that, when you had a home of your own, you could have Mama's piano. Remember how you use to love to play duets? Then, when you became such an artist, you would serenade us in the evenings. I've had the piano positioned so that you could look out toward the trees and river as you play. May you serenade your love for many years to come—and may the two of you share the depth of love your mother and I had for each other. Always, Dad*

On the piano was the sheet music for "The Yellow Rose of Texas" with an additional note: "April 25. Happy Texas Wildflower Day! You thought I'd forget?" And clipped to the music was "a little something" to help start our life together.

We looked at each other and said "Thorn!" at precisely the same moment. Daddy would need to have gotten Thorn's help to let the piano movers in. Movers and shakers get things done, that's for sure.

"Hey, why doesn't my wife play me something?"

How can I resist his drawl? Whenever he said *mah wahf,* I melted. Looking outside, I sat on the piano bench and began to play the sonata that started it all: Beethoven's immortal "Moonlight." Bob sat down beside me and just stared at me as I played. I'd committed the entire piece to memory years ago, and had often played it to comfort my heartache since Mama's death.

"That was *gorgeous*. I had no idea you could play the piano."

"Oh I have hidden talents."

Throwing out innuendos to one another was a favorite pastime between us. Not that we kept score, but we were pretty competitive. It was fun doing the one-upsmanship routine with Bob.

"Well, you let the pup do her business and I'll go upstairs. All those Republican women have exhausted me."

"I'll join you soon."

I should have known something was up by that grin on his face as he bounded up the stairs. Once Bowie had gone out and I'd shut down the house, I noted the eerie silence. Obviously Bob wasn't asleep or I'd hear the snoring. When I got upstairs, there he was, huge grin on his face, lying in bed. Not on the floor, but actually in bed.

"How did you fix the bed with no tools?"

"I am a man of many talents, my dear. Look underneath the bed."

He was obviously very proud of himself.

"Books?"

"Yep. I took all those books out of the closet. I'd read them on my journey from Texas overseas and back. I knew they'd come in handy somehow. Just stacked them up and propped up the bed slats. We're back in business, Mrs. Larken!"

Who could help but love a man like this?

I spent the next day finishing up promos for another speech Bob would soon be making. An officer from the Republican women's group had asked him to speak in front of the Board of Regents—that would probably lead to some commencement addresses. Most of the universities had their keynotes in place, I knew, but there were always auxiliary speeches of equal importance. We had our work cut out for us.

*Katherine Shephard*

## Chapter Twenty

Lydia, the governor's executive assistant and Dave Hawthorne's companion, knocked on our door at precisely 7 a.m. Monday morning. She was impeccably groomed with a low-maintenance haircut and wearing what Mama would have called "sensible shoes." Her appearance sang out "all business."

Mornings were bad enough. Monday mornings were miserable. Lydia was driving us to Lansing and walking us into the dome for security reasons. Why all the security? It seemed odd. I took my laptop so I could work while Bob and Stan chatted, although I was hoping I'd be included. There might be a good quote to pick up and run with. We arrived in the secured parking garage of the Olds Building and Lydia ordered me to duck down out of sight. I did, but it made me feel like either a spy or a mistress. I didn't like where that thought took me so I ignored it.

Lydia went on to explain that although it was a secure garage, a tape was made of everyone who entered. No need to have my face on tape. I'd been with Bob at the Ford Museum and if anyone started nosing around, what would we say? That's when I piped up.

"I would simply say I'm his personal PR woman. The former lieutenant governor wants to be certain that what he wants in print appears in print."

This was starting to piss me off and I'd only been doing this a week.

Just as we arrived, so did the governor and we all piled into the elevator at the same time.

"Beth, it's wonderful to see you again. I'm so happy to hear about your new job."

Lydia smiled at her boss's cryptic phrase. We all knew what he really meant. We were riding in a private, key-access-only elevator. Since the capitol was a public building, any conversation could be heard or transmitted. Anything private could be discussed at the Olds because it was as tight as a drum. I was learning. I didn't love it, but I was learning.

Once inside the Olds we walked by Lydia's desk right outside Stan's office. I smiled at the placard that greeted us: "What part of NO don't you understand?" I decided I wanted get to know her better. Bob and I went into Stan's office and I breathed easier knowing we were safe from the outside world.

"Sit down. Sit down, both of you. Bob, with just one speech you're turning into a cult hero. You stand up against an anti-voucher initiative; you give all the right answers. The public's curiosity is piqued. According to what my people tell me—they want more. The people of Michigan want to hear more from you. How do you feel about legalized gambling, Bob?"

"I can't imagine turning this state into another Vegas. There are the casinos on the reservations, but with the old-line AME Baptists in Detroit and the Grand Rapids Dutch Reform population—I can't imagine it would happen."

"Bob, this is a yes or no question. You're not a politician now. Just give me a yes or no. Would you back regulatory legislation to have legalized gaming in the state of Michigan? Not run by the tribes—but by the big boys. A simple yes or no, Bob."

"No."

"Okay. How do you feel about the inclusion of the governor's picture on state brochures? State public service announcements visitor bureau pamphlets—those types of things."

"Stan, what are you getting at? Who cares where the governor puts his photo anyhow?"

"Think about this one, Bob, and give me a one-sentence answer."

"Okay. The governor should not have his picture on any state brochure as they are to promote the state, not the governor."

"Another question—how do you feel about private airplanes and a helicopter for the governor?"

"Oh that one's easy. The governor should fly commercial—symbolically showing he's no better than his people. Sure, he'd need security but he could use state troopers. As for a helicopter? Blow the dang thing up."

He let his drawl loose on that last sentence and it made Stan and me laugh.

"Good ole Texas boy, hey?"

"Well, I do own a condo in Grand Rapids now! And I have a small place in the UP, remember? Thorn, Brad and I each bought a little fishing cabin years ago. Haven't been there in years. I've let Brad use it for business entertaining, actually."

"No, actually you have dual residency and have for years."

I squinted my eyes and Bob shook his head.

"I don't follow you, Stan."

We were both confused. That's not difficult for me, but Bob is usually right on target.

"That's exactly the point. I hope you *will* follow me."

Stan pushed a button on his phone and barked "Lydia, bring John in please."


I looked at Bob and felt like I was on an out-of-control train headed straight for hell. What was happening and why were they talking like I wasn't even here? Didn't anyone care how I felt about legalized gambling? After all, I was the one who'd lived here all her life. This was *my* state!

The door opened and in walked John Gaynor. Bob looked as shocked as I was when his mentor joined us. Standing up, the governor and Bob greeted John. I just sat there. I mean, what was the protocol when you felt like you were about to get screwed?

I nodded at John since everyone was ignoring me anyhow, and closed my eyes.

All Bob could say was, "Excuse my adorable PR lady, she's having a Catholic moment."

Finding no humor in his comment, I rubbed my temples and prayed to Teresa. She was the patron saint who handled headaches and Lord only knows, I had a headache. Correction. Make that a Texas-sized headache.

"Sit down, please," the governor commanded. I continued to pray.

"As you know, this is my last term in office. I've cut taxes twenty-three times, saving the people of Michigan billions of dollars. I got rid of the porno houses on Michigan Avenue and helped rejuvenate the City of Lansing. We have a new Civic Center and we now have a baseball farm team. We've done well and I'm proud of my service and what we've been able to accomplish."

Okay, was Stan giving his own eulogy? I hated missing a good wake.

"As you also know, Jim Parsons and I do not agree on some very key issues. If he continues on track and becomes Michigan's next governor, all I've worked for and all that I believe in will be washed down the Grand River. Gambling will take over the state, he'll live high off the hog courtesy of higher taxes and his picture will be posted everywhere."

Now that was a sobering thought.

"The only thing in his favor is that he drives Michigan-made vehicles exclusively."

With that he looked down his nose and over his glasses at Bob. I had to smile because Bob looked like a little boy who'd just got caught looking at *Playboy* in the local Seven-Eleven. I couldn't help it. I waved my index finger at him and went "*tsk tsk tsk.*"

Now that I'd broken the somber mood, John turned to the governor and said, "Stan, I told you that one was a firecracker!"

Both men winked at each other. That must have meant something.

"So, what's this all about? My Z? I love that car." Bob's trademark chuckle seemed to slip out from nerves this time.

"No." It was John Gaynor's turn, apparently. "This is about you. When you left office no one thought you'd be this high profile. You, in one speech, have already started to weave your magic. The governor, and others, noticed the comments you made to the Republican women. You sounded sincere—not like you were just talking to the crowd to get votes. You actually sounded *Republican*, Bob."

"I wasn't walking any party line, John. That's no longer my life. You know that. I have a new life."

"Well, what the governor here wants to know is—would you register as a Republican?"

"So I can vote for Parsons? Not as long as there's a breath in my body, John. He's lower than dirt. You know it and I know it."

The veins on Bob's forehead began to protrude, which meant his blood pressure was rising.

"He's also a lying sackashit, Bob, and he's about to decide not to run for governor."

"*What?*" I couldn't hold it in. "John, Governor Melvin, what is going on here?"

Just then a train sped by, its whistle blaring. The governor inhaled through clenched teeth. He pounded his desk and chose each word carefully.

"Jim Parsons can take the next train to hell. I'll be damned if I'm going to let him ruin my state! Herbert Hoover was quoted as saying 'When there is a lack of honor in government, the morals of the whole people are poisoned.' Parsons will never poison my state! Bob, Jim hasn't made any formal announcement yet, and hasn't gotten the signatures needed to run. I want to leave my legacy to someone who shares my views and values and will continue to fight my battles. Michigan needs a man like you, Bob."

Bob sat there in silence.

All I could say was "Shit."

219

*Katherine Shephard*

## Chapter Twenty-One

John Gaynor went on as if nothing out of the ordinary were being discussed.

"Jim Parsons is about to decide he needs to drop out of consideration for the governor's race due to personal matters. I'll let him worry about the excuse. I'm just going to provide the impetus."

Just as I imagined that first night on Mackinac, John Gaynor was not someone you want to piss off. And to think I'd once stolen a piece of cake from this man.

"I am out of government," Bob said. "I'm with Beth now. We made a deal."

Calmly and coolly, John Gaynor looked Bob in the eyes and simply stated, "Dump her and dump the Z. I'll handle the rest."

I sprang to my feet. "What *rest,* John? This isn't part of the package we bought in to."

"Please sit down, Beth. This is not about you."

"It is too about me!" My voice rose to a fevered pitch and I felt as if I would soon hyperventilate. "I even have a T-shirt that says 'It's all about me.' Don't you *dare* presume I'll put up with you always calling the shots with my life!" I remained standing.

"Your feeble attempt to interject humor isn't going to work today, Ms. Pullen."

"You don't get it, John," Bob said. "I don't *want* to run for governor."

At least Bob was attempting to hold his own. Is this how they felt at the Alamo? Because right now, it didn't look like we stood a chance in this battle.

"You were born to serve, Bob," John continued. "Just think about it okay? Plus the Margaret issue is just temporary."

"Temporary?" I was back in the crossfire. "Eight years is *temporary*? What do I do in the meantime? Who can answer that little tidbit?"

My voice started to rise and I was getting claustrophobic. I really wanted to break out of this conversation, this room. This had turned into enemy territory.

"Beth, you'll have a room on the twelfth floor of the Amway Grand," John said. "That floor is totally secure. Bob can get in and out without being seen. Margaret will be there, too, of course. When in Lansing, you'll stay at the Radisson. You two can meet up on the river walk. No one would see or hear you there during the campaign. All Bob needs to do is pay the filing fee. He runs and we make sure he gets elected. We need a decision within a week, to meet the filing deadline. We'll have two months to run an intense campaign. Then, as you know, an exploratory committee will check Bob out. Margaret will need to be here for the announcement and post-primary pre-convention."

Looking directly in my eyes, he continued. "You, of course, can have full press access to cover all the events. We can say you're doing a profile of his life and career. Since you were his communications director he has requested your services. That will justify any relationship."

"Bob, John is starting to sound like you. 'Relationship'—is that what you're going to allow us to become? A relationship? What about marriage? What about forever?"

It was becoming difficult to breathe. I knew I needed some fresh air.

"Gentlemen, I'm out of here. Please do let me know what you decide about my future."

With that I turned around and—security be damned—walked out. Where the hell could a girl go to fall apart around here?

"Beth, you shouldn't be alone. I'll walk with you." There was Lydia, right outside the door at her desk.

"You knew? You knew this and remained silent?" I was incredulous.

"That's my job, Beth. I've been with Governor Melvin for years. He trusts me because I've earned that trust."

"Trust. Love that word. That's choice—trust. Tell me, just who can *I* trust?" I got my answer in two words.

"No one."

Once out of the building, I just started to walk. Lydia followed, just steps behind. Aimlessly walking down Michigan Avenue I found my destination—a bench at Washington Square.

Lydia walked by and whispered, "I'll be right back."

"Where are you headed, Lydia?" I didn't really care, to be honest

"The Governor asked me to go in and buy a silk tie. They have ties with elephants on them. He wants one for Bob to wear when he goes to register as a Republican. That will be a major press event."

I could tell she immediately regretted telling me that. I turned my back and let her go on into the store. Me? I just sat there in the shadow of the capitol dome and cried my heart out. I cried for the job I'd gained and lost. I cried for the mess I'd created for Daddy. I cried for Vic. She had a great job, true, but she had to watch everything she said. I even cursed and cried for the fate of our new puppy. In just a few short days she'd become Bob's dog, not mine. I'd probably lose her, too. Mostly, I cried for myself. How could I have been such a fool to trust so blindly?

Just as I was wiping away the mascara that had found its way down my cheeks, a familiar scent approached. I knew it was Bob. There were trees surrounding the bench so we were, basically, in private. Sitting down next to me, we both looked up Michigan Avenue to the capitol building.

"Come walk me, Beth. Come back to the capitol. Let's go home."

I tried to stand up. My legs felt like I'd just gotten off a sailboat that had just weathered a hurricane but I started to walk, anyhow, right next to Bob. Damn anyone who noticed.

As we got to the grounds, Bob looked up at the dome. "You know what I have to do. I'm sorry."

"I love the way men always say 'I'm sorry.' If you were sorry you wouldn't have done it in the first place. Saying you're sorry doesn't save my heart, Bob. What am I now, your whore?"

He just stood there and took it. That's what really pissed me off. People who won't fight back.

"You're a spineless wimp, Larken. You can stand up and fight in the Senate chambers. You can preach honesty, loyalty and virtues but you can deny our marriage and our love. I love you so much, Bob, I always will. But what am I suppose to do now?"

"Beth, please. This isn't forever. Trust me, please. Trust John. And I do have a son to consider. This is where I belong. Please trust me."

"But what's next?"

I needed answers, not excuses.

"We are going in to talk with Parsons. I want you there so you know everything that is going on, first-hand. But you can't be in the room. They have placed a video surveillance system in his office, temporarily. You can sit in the basement and watch and hear what happens. Then John will contact Margaret. We'll spend the next week giving more speeches and testing the waters. John will start putting a war chest together. Then in a few weeks we'll make the announcement. I want you there, of course. Margaret will need to be here. Beth, I know it's not what we planned, but it won't be forever. Please trust me on that."

I knew I must be having a massive brain fart because I said, "I do. I'll be there. I promise." Icky as it felt, it wasn't in me to turn away now. I'd go through the motions now and figure it all out later, I decided. I turned to Bob and tried to smile.

"Okay then, let's get this over with."

Bob looked relieved. I felt as though everything had been sucked out of me like a liposuction procedure gone bad.

Lydia caught up with us and we made a handsome trio standing in the shadow of Michigan's capitol. Lydia, always the one in control, piped right in. "Lieutenant Governor Parsons has been escorted from the capitol to the Olds Building. We'll go there for privacy."

I knew what that meant. My death sentence.

Go through the keyed access door; turn away from the camera. I knew the routine..

Lydia, in her well-pressed and understated business suit, returned to her command post outside the governor's office.

Soon I was sitting in the converted closet in the basement where I'd been taken for "the viewing"—that sure sounded like a funeral to me. The room where I sat was small and dark but I could see everyone in Parson's office on a small screen and hear them through tiny speakers. Still in a daze, I occupied my scattered mind by cataloguing everybody's outfits.

In his navy pleated trousers, yellow pinstriped oxford shirt and navy tweed blazer, Bob looked distinguished yet casual, as always. He had what I call an "inviting" appearance—he always looked so accessible. John was wearing a black suit, wing-tipped shoes, white shirt, and muted red paisley tie. Conservative and in total control. Amazingly, he could swing to the left or right, depending on the cause and occasion. I wondered what his real political bent was.

What about me? I looked down. I was in a yellow skirt with a boat-neck white shell worn under a nubby yellow sweater. I definitely looked like I needed a trip to Lord and Taylor or, at the very least, Jacobsons. And to think I'd picked that outfit this morning hoping for good news and sunny skies ahead.

From my vantage point I could clearly see Parsons standing behind his desk looking smug, as usual. A gray dress shirt and a baggy black-and-gray tweed blazer accompanied black polyester-blend trousers. The corker was the tie. Bright red flowers jumped out as if to say, "Save me, save me, I need to be warped back to the Eighties." His wife must think he's cute, though. I failed to see why.

Nothing was happening yet. When I get nervous I babble and talk to myself. This was a five-star babble moment if there ever was one. I closed my eyes.

"Saint Anthony of Padua...The answer to my prayer may require a miracle. Even so, you are the saint of miracles...." Apparently he was busy with more pressing miracles. The voices coming from the small speakers cut my plea short.

"Jim, I'm sorry to hear about the family crisis you're experiencing."

John sounded sincere and soft-spoken. Jim Parsons, of course, had no clue what John meant.

"John, it's good to see you, too. Who invited Larken?"

He was trying to smile, but the moustache-chewing gave him away. Clearly, the man was nervous.

"Nothing here will go any further. The only ones privy to this conversation are Mr. Larken, myself and, of course, you, Lieutenant Governor. We are all bound by a strict code of ethics, imposed by me."

Parsons dove into his moustache like it would be his last meal. He looked like he'd kill for a cigarette. Call me sick, but seeing a grown man like him squirm was a bit amusing.

"Let me put it another way, Jim. Listen closely. You are about to develop family problems—I don't care what they are— that will prevent you from seeking the Republican nomination for governor. If that isn't clear enough, let me say it another way. If you do not make an immediate announcement saying that your name is not to be considered for the primary ballot and that you are backing Bob Larken for governor—your past will catch up with you."

"I'm backing *who* for governor? Gaynor, are you out of your mind?"

His balding head was glistening with sweat. He leaned his wide girth across the desk toward Gaynor. Parson's temper was on record as being volatile. I'd have to send him a book on anger management. Kind of a going-away present, maybe.

"No, Lieutenant Governor, I'm not out of my mind—but you are most definitely out of yours if you refuse my request."

"Gaynor, let me tell you something. I worked hard to get where I am. I am not about to turn my back on a sure thing. Everyone knows I'm the next governor. You can take that to your bank."

Damn, this was heating up and I had a front-row seat.

"That brings me directly to the point, Parsons. You did work hard to get where you are. I would hate the truth to come out and make you crash and burn."

"Seems to me the only one that's crashed around here is Larken, and something tells me his final spiral to hell—let's call it the Big Burn—hasn't even happened yet."

This was one smug guy. He was entirely full of himself. He cocked his head to the side and tried to look charming. He ended up looking like a deflated blimp.

"The truth," said Gaynor. "Let's just stick to some facts. You've been rather cagey in how you portray yourself. I'll give you that much credit. Your actual qualifications, however, seem to have been misrepresented. You say you attended U of M and held the position of an expert and specialist in the financial field. You joked and teased about CPAs like yourself. You're no CPA, bud. You're not degreed. You're a good-for-nothing flunky. Put more bluntly, Parsons, you're a lying sackashit. Is that clear enough?"

John Gaynor held the cards but I didn't think he was playing a game. Bob sat there, mouth gaping at this revelation.

"John, I've been an outstanding legislator. I've served the people of this state beyond reproach. Don't do this. I'm not proud of the deceit...."

"You know, folks don't take kindly to cheats or liars."

With those words, John stopped for emphasis. I felt as though I might be struck down at any moment, but really, I wasn't exactly cheating or lying. Bob and I were committed and we were playing by the rules. Parsons wasn't.

It finally hit me. That's what this was really about. We were really trying to make things right. Trying to build a strong foundation for a lifetime together. We might have had a weak moment or two, but I needed to trust Bob and put it in the hands of Saint Jude. This definitely qualified as a desperate situation. But if St. Jude was up to it, so was I. I would not turn my back on the only man I'd ever really loved. I would not allow them to make me feel guilty. Okay. So I felt a little guilty. But I could play the waiting game if it meant I'd be the ultimate winner. Plus, it wasn't as if Bob was being deployed overseas and I wouldn't see him for months or years. We'd still be together – we'd just have to be careful. And as for Margaret, I'm sure she would play this to the hilt. The competitor in me started rising to the surface. She didn't stand a chance.

John's booming voice snapped me out of my epiphanatic moment. Epiphanatic. There I went making up words again. Bad sign.

"You're kind of like Pinocchio, Parsons. But, instead of your nose growing with every lie, your hair falls out."

Whoa. John didn't mess around. I was glad he was on our side, even though it didn't feel like *my* side, exactly. Bob did let a small chuckle escape.

"Your deceit will, at long last, cost you. Unless you want everything I know plastered across every press medium in the state of Michigan, I'd suggest you find a family emergency and find it fast. We will be preparing a press release, just in case you decide to buck me on this one."

"You won't need one. I understand."

Parsons looked like a beaten man, which I guessed he was. Not that I felt very sorry for him. Maybe he could do voice-overs for radio or the movies. He did have a voice that would melt steel.

"And you'll fully endorse Larken as Michigan's Republican nominee for governor?"

John wanted to be certain no strings were left dangling.

"Yes, Bob, you have my full and absolute support. God help me." He extended his hand for Bob to shake. Damn.

With that, John Gaynor and Bob Larken disappeared off my tiny viewing screen as they exited the lieutenant governor's office in silence.

When a guard tapped on the door to release me from my cloistered existence, I caught up with Bob and John by the elevator door. I suddenly realized we had no car—Lydia had picked us up at the house and escorted us to Lansing.

"Excuse, me, but we have no ride and I'm starving."

"At least you're not babbling or praying. That's a start."

Leave it to Bob to know exactly what to say.

"Then let's go get something to eat and I'll see you get back to Grand Ledge," John said.

"John—just a minute," I said. "I was attempting to remain a lady back there. But let's get one thing straight. I will not be pushed around. You might be able to buy and sell everyone else. You might have bought silence here and there. You might have even been the one responsible for Bob and me being together but believe you me, I will *not* just roll over on this one. Bob is mine now, not yours."

"That is not entirely true," John said calmly. "You might have slept with him but I have him in my pocket."

"Enough! John, never, *never* speak to Beth like that again." Bob broke in. "I am not in your 'pocket.' "I know you're just trying to do what you think is best for me. You've always been there for me and I appreciate it, but you will never demean her or us again." That was the Bob I knew and loved.

"I'm sorry, Beth." John seemed taken aback by Bob's outburst. "I've been used to so much power–I guess I forget there

229

are real lives involved. You know I only want what is best for Bob. That's all I've ever wanted." He looked at me closely to see what my reaction would be.

"I know, John. Let's just get through this. If Bob truly wants to return to public service, I won't fight that. I can't. But I won't be a token back-room girl, either. I have enough guilt floating around in my soul and I'm pissed as hell. You haven't–not even once–considered my family or me. The thought of Margaret and Bob even holding hands to present a 'united front' makes me sick. But I am willing to step back because I have a feeling it won't be all that long. I'll play by the rules but I plan to make Margaret Larken's life a living inferno. Every time she looks at me she'll know the truth. Not that she even cares. She's just in it for the status and power. But who's *really* more powerful in this equation? I say let the games begin."

While the men digested my latest rant, I wondered what Mama would think if she were still here. I think she'd support my decision–to stand firm with the man I loved. I would do whatever was necessary, play whatever role seemed pertinent at any given moment to stay with Bob. We would have a life together–just not right now. But somehow it would happen.

"Beth, just be careful. If you need help–if your family needs help–I'm just a phone call away. You know I'd do anything for you."

"I know. I know." Finally, I thought, I'm learning how to negotiate.

Bob took in a deep breath and exhaled before speaking. "John, I had no idea about Parsons. How long have you had that info?" Bob was shaking his head in absolute disbelief.

"A while. I just kept it on the back burner. I have enough on back burners to ignite most of the nation."

"I have no doubt" was all I could say.

"He is morally, personally and physically reprehensible. I've never liked the fat bastard." John didn't mince many words. But apparently, his mood could turn on a dime. In an instant he dropped the anger and smugness and returned to the charming man I'd first met. "Where to for lunch?"

Smiling, I announced the obvious eatery of choice.

"I feel like a sub sandwich. I know just the place on Washington Square."

It was my turn to smirk as I said, "In honor of Jim Parsons – Blimpies."

*Katherine Shephard*

## Chapter Twenty-Two

The next week disappeared in a flurry of appointments, preliminary polls, and making sure all the t's were crossed and i's dotted. Everything had to be in perfect order when Bob made his announcement. As instructed, Parsons went on the air and told the public he would not be seeking the nomination for governor. He would make a statement, soon, as to whom he would back. This gave us time to set the stage and get everything printed and ready to run. Lydia told me to get ready to run at the speed of lightning. Unfortunately, I hated running. Almost as much as I hated mornings.

Bob was staying at the condo in Grand Rapids. For now I got to keep Bowie with me. Margaret was to arrive on the fourth. Oh, yeah. With any luck the white dog hairs would send her packing. Maybe Bowie could do a repeat performance and pee on her Bruno Magli heels, I mused. Bowie pees and Mag goes *poof!*—well, a girl can dream, can't she?

The Amway Grand was chosen as the site of the nomination speech. All the legislators would be there, of course. Key Republicans had been invited for the "you don't want to miss this speech" evening. It was being listed, officially, as a pre-primary fundraiser with Bob Larken as the keynote speaker. Anyone wanting to get re-elected would be there, schmoozing with those having deep pockets. Security would be tight.

A driver came for me, since I was part of the political elite: an invitee of the governor, speechwriter, columnist, memoir writer, PR gal, or whatever title they decided to give me on any particular day for Bob. I preferred "wife" but that was reserved for our small circle of confidantes.

Smoothing out the black silk sheath I'd chosen for the evening, I was glad I hadn't worn something long-sleeved. My beaded jacket could be removed if I started to perspire. You just never know.

Sitting in the back seat on the way to the speech, I sarcastically tallied all the ways in which I would make a fabulous wife for the governor of Michigan. I wondered if governors' wives got to pick out state china patterns like the Presidential wives did. I was an MSU grad and Michigan native, after all. I could throw a fabulous dinner party—I'd get Jill from down in Texas to cook up some of her chicken. I would even get her a damn jeweled crown since she thinks she's the Queen of Cuisine. What more could they want?

In my mind's eye I could read the headlines now. "Governor Larken Takes Trophy Bride, Former Communications Director. . . ." Well, I'm young but "trophy" didn't seem to fit my physique even at the best of times. I'd have to work on another title for the tabloids. Sadly, I imagined I'd have plenty time to think about it.

"Miss, we're approaching the entrance."

So much for that daydream. Once again I went over the written instructions that Bob had given me. "Enter via the back entrance, off of Lyon near the river walkway."

The driver held my door and I looked out from behind the Grand. The Ford Museum, the VanAndel Museum and Grand Valley University were all within sight. The blue walking bridge looked inviting—I wished I could just walk off into the setting sun.

Although the hotel had thirty-two elevators I was to use the secret stairwell. It was undetectable to the hotel's security system and would be propped open for my use. Lucky thing because otherwise, it would immediately lock. Lydia, I'm sure, did the propping. Seems like a job she'd have. I was to head to the twelfth floor—the secured floor. I had been given a key earlier in the day. Bob had received two. One for himself and one for

Margaret, since each key was carefully noted. I had Bob's key so my name wouldn't show up anywhere.

In other words, I didn't exist.

Okay, time to calm down, I told myself. I thought back through the directions to the suite. Bob hadn't written them down, for obvious reasons. Heading to the base of the staircase I spotted him. Just as he said, he was waiting for me alone. State troopers were posted in their own suite on the twelfth floor, I knew, but there was no security in this sealed stairwell.

"Oh God, Bob, I've missed you. We'll be all right, won't we?"

"Of course we will, my princess." That was what I wanted to hear. I smiled and said, "I won't be a trophy bride—I'll be a princess bride!"

"There you go, looking toward the good days. And we'll have them—tons of them. Now, remember what to do?"

"Yessir."

We climbed the stairs, not making a sound. When we got to the twelfth floor Bob opened the door, smiled, exited boldly and took a left turn. The troopers in their suite would have their door open so they could see down the hallway. I stopped and waited until Bob was out of sight down the hall. Hugging the wall, I turned right and headed through the exit door, which led outside to a fire escape ladder. After climbing a few stairs, I walked across the bricks and entered the suite through the slider into the living room—all without security having a clue. Bob was to be in the bedroom, according to the plan. I should have crawled in the bedroom window, but not in this outfit. Great. Right there in the living room, obviously waiting for me, stood Margaret. Damn.

"Well, hello *Miss* Pullen. I'm so glad you'll be joining my husband and me. How wonderful to have you back on our staff. One word of warning, though—you cross me and you'll be sorry."

I wanted to slap her silly. Her surgically drawn face showed no emotion, her posture was stoic.

"Here are your credentials, dear." She handed me a badge that read "Staff–Full Press Access."

"Thank you" was all I could seem to get out. I wished my language skills had a middle ground, but apparently it was either babble or bite my tongue.

"Excuse me."

I needed to get to the bathroom. Fast. Just as I entered the parquet hallway that led to the bedroom and bathroom, my phone rang. The readout showed Victoria's number. Here we were, together, in the eye of a political twister, I thought grimly. She was here representing the Ford Museum, since she was now on the Republican "map." More important, though, she was here for me, and for that I was grateful. Vic was always around when I needed her the most—and now was no exception. She was to "cover" me and make certain that if anyone approached, I would be deep in conversation or led away.

Fortunately, we were already pros at this well-worn routine. It had worked like a charm at the frat mixers in college. If a hot-looking guy headed toward us, whoever spotted him first would demurely say "JFK." We'd stay put and see what transpired. If he turned out to be a real loser, the spotter would announce "LBJ" and we would exit quickly to the powder room. The system never failed us, and to this day those initials meant "stay" or "retreat."

"Hi Vic. Yes. All set on my end. Going to use the ladies room, mingle and then get down to the lobby. Yes. I'll meet you in the media room." Hanging up I decided not to waste any time going to the bathroom. I wanted every possible minute with Bob. I entered the bedroom that he was supposed to have entered from the hallway, but he wasn't there. Going back to the living room, I saw that Margaret was gone as well. They'd left. Together. Damn. All there was left to do was to hug the walls and go back down the stairway, out of the state troopers' sight and away from the security cameras. I knew what to do, I just hated doing it.

The stairway also had an exit to the lobby. I took another stairway to the Ambassador Ballroom where the event was being held. It seated eight hundred and would be filled to capacity tonight.

Entering the media room at the far end of the hall, I spotted Vic. The media setup around her was impressive. AV booths, interpreter's room, sound booth, camera booth, the works. It was command central for television, radio or print media coverage. The governor had just completed his welcoming address and the salads had been placed in front of the guests.

"Vic, stay put. I'll be right back." I made an exit and headed to the left. Finding a remote spot next to the drinking fountains I leaned against the wall, wounded and wondering in silence. Where was he? Was he thinking of me? I retreated into myself and wandered back to happier times. I thought about pizza and Pepsi in bed, moonlight on the Looking Glass River, a pink bow on a little white dog, the lilac rimmed walkway at the governor's mansion on Mackinac...no, that was too close to politics and politics was what was tearing me apart right now. Someone else would be presiding over that mansion, not me.

I reached into my purse for the small heart-shaped stone I'd picked up as I left Bob's Hill Country cabin after the most magical night of my life. It had never been far from me in the intervening weeks. I turned it over and over in my hand. Under the glare of the hotel lights it didn't look much like a heart after all. Just an irregular triangle with a piece missing from one side. Right now I felt like that rough side of the triangle. The losing side. At home, I always placed my Hill Country heart right next to the crystal basket of hearts Bob gave me. His first gift sitting next to the gift I gave myself. A blending of hearts is how I saw it. Only instead of blending, my heart was bleeding.

A tap on the shoulder brought me back into reality. It was Victoria. I could tell from the look in her eyes that she was worried about me and didn't want me to be alone.

"How are you, lady?" I'm sure she knew the answer. I could no longer contain the tears that I had fought back all day.

"How did this happen?" I felt utter disbelief. "She won, Vic, she won."

Victoria didn't respond with words. She just looked down at me and took me into her arms. It felt like I'd come home. Home to a safe haven, a place where the pain did not exist—a time when all we had to worry about was whether or not a guy was a JFK or an LBJ. Whispering in my ear, my best friend finally gave her response. "He ain't no JFK, girl. All he is is an S.O.B."

I moved backwards and leaned against the tiled wall. At twenty-three I shouldn't be feeling such an enormous sense of dread and defeat. By all indications, Bob had committed political suicide once already. He'd never be an elected official again. Ever. He was mine. Forever. We had begun our life together based on the assumption that on rare occasions he might need to make a public appearance in D.C., or for a major fundraiser. Margaret would be there then, and only then. They would leave their Austin "home" together and he'd pull her along as the cameras rolled. Her face would be taut from the surgical knife, her nose in a permanent upturn and his full head of hair perfectly in place. They were Mr. and Mrs. Family Virtues with a handsome son. But he would always come home to me. To us. At least that's what I had signed on for.

Vic let me wander in my thoughts for a while before taking my arm and escorting me to the ballroom. As we approached the main door, Vic reminded me that we needed to show our credentials and sign in. Thank God she was there to make certain I played by the rules.

Staring directly into my eyes, the woman behind the registration table asked, "Don't I know you?"

I held tightly onto my portfolio, my nails digging into the leather, as I looked away. Beads of sweat trickled down my back, forming pools of dampness at the base of my spine. My heart was racing as if it were in the final heat of the Preakness. I stared at her with a false smile on my face, working hard to maintain my composure and frame an appropriate response.

As I stood there reaching for a copy of the evening's program, a commotion broke out across the hallway. The lobby was transformed, at once, into a media circus. Cameras were suddenly being jostled and hoisted into the air by eager photographers. Flashes were popping, lights were glaring, and microphones were being shoved between shoulders pressed together. Everyone pushed there way through to get a glimpse of the latest arrival. The magnitude of frenzy told me who it must be.

I glanced to my right, toward the door, and noticed that fiery red hair. It was her. Patricia. He must be with her. That was why the room suddenly lit up with feverish activity.

"Miss?" The clerk snapped my mind back to the task at hand. She continued her study of my face, taking in every sign of nervousness and apprehension.

"Oh, perhaps so—perhaps you might know me," I replied without returning her stare. I wondered if she were from Grand Ledge or Lansing.

"My name is Christine—Christine Pullen. I'm a writer. I use to be Lieutenant Governor Larken's communications director."

I didn't return her stare.

"Oh yes." Bending down to extract my program from a box below the table, she looked at me again, this time directly into my eyes. I tried to avoid her stare.

"You really do look familiar, but the name is wrong."

I thanked her, put the program inside my portfolio and hurried inside the ballroom. She knew. Somehow she knew.

Vic had gotten through the process without a hitch. I was still sweating as we took our places in the back of the room. By now the main course was being served and I felt a fresh shot of courage surging through me, for some inexplicable reason. On the stage stood a baby grand piano. There had been dinner music as the guests arrived, according to the program, and after dessert would be dancing.

"Vic, don't panic. There's something I have to do."

With all the confidence of a Texas rebel, I marched onto the stage and sat at the piano. Technicians were adjusting the podium and microphone, so I assumed Bob would be speaking soon. I looked down to the head table. Governor and Mrs. Melvin were there, of course. Bitsy gave me a wink as if she knew what I was about to do. John Gaynor gave me a smile. Bob's son, David, simply sat there. I wonder what his mom had told him. His eyes were squinting and he didn't look pleased to see me. She must have said something to him because he looked as though he wanted someone dead.

I wasn't sure what would flow from my fingers when I sat down, but it came quite naturally—the theme from the movie *Somewhere in Time*. The movie had been filmed partly on Mackinac Island. I immediately was transported back to the Island. It's a Michigan song for beautiful Mackinac memories.

As I played, the double doors opened and in walked Bob with Margaret on his arm. The crescendo of my playing paralleled the excitement of the crowd. Margaret sat down next to Bitsy and Bob took his place at the podium.

He waited until I stopped playing, then said, "Ladies and gentlemen, stand with me, please." The audience did what he asked, of course.

"I'd like to thank my former communications director, Miss Christine Pullen, for the lovely fanfare. That song brings to mind Michigan's lovely island of lilacs."

I hadn't expected to be acknowledged. I hadn't expected to serenade Bob and Margaret. Some things just happen.

"I'd like to ask Governor Stanley Melvin to join me for a moment. Stan—come on up."

What the hell was Bob up to?

"If Miss Pullen would be so kind as to accompany us, I'd like to start this evening off with the singing of our state's anthem.

While I was born and bred in Texas, I've had a home here all my life. I went to college with Stan's son, Brad, at the University of Houston but we ended up doing some graduate work together at Michigan State—their communications department is the finest around. So now, I'd like us all to join together to honor my new home, *our* state—the Great State of Michigan—in song."

Well I'll be damned.

*Katherine Shephard*

## Chapter Twenty-Three

With his television background, Bob Larken knew how to create drama. Dazzle all senses. Hit them with sights and sounds that will linger. Open with a hook and leave them awestruck in the end.

Just as he cited his intention to become Michigan's Republican nominee for governor, the curtain behind him opened. Out rolled a classic white Oldsmobile convertible with black leather interior. With a smile that would melt even the most skeptical of hearts, Bob Larken closed with "I've traded my Z in for a *real* Michigander's car."

As the applause rose to a thunderous roar, all eight hundred guests stood to give Robert Bentley Larken a standing ovation.

I knew the drill. Walk out of the building. Don't stop to talk or mingle. Turn left and walk toward the river. Wait by the fountain.

Just as I approached the walking bridge, a car pulled up to the curb. I heard the automatic back doors unlock, lock and unlock again. That was my cue.

I climbed into the back seat and was driven to Abrams Aviation in Grand Ledge. I knew the route. Bob was meeting Margaret there. He was going to take a National Guard chopper to Detroit for a midnight reception of financial backers John had already secured. Margaret would accompany him, of course. Quite the happy couple. Normally, they would have taken a four-seat Cessna, but those stopped flying at dusk.

I decided to ask the driver to stop at Saint Mary's Cathedral after the chopper lifted off. It was close by on Ionia and wouldn't really be inconvenient. More than anything, I needed the peace of a church.

Finally, I was struggling to internalize everything that had happened during the past week. My inner feelings lately had been ranging from anger and hatred through fantasies of revenge, then careening back to unconditional love and trust. The cycle repeated over and over and kept me up most nights. Was it worth it? A few days earlier I had stood in the middle of my new property—land I hadn't picked, but loved nonetheless—and watched a lone eagle fly. The sight echoed my involuntary sentence of solitude and loneliness contrasted to the peace and serenity I'd hoped to share with Bob in this beautiful place. Instead, my reality would be the moments we'd have to steal—the social events when I would be only a reporter, just like that first night back in March.

I hated Margaret Larken for what she'd done. I hated Bob, in a way, for allowing it. Some days I even despised their son David, for his very existence.

I saw myself as a strong and decent woman now caught in a maelstrom of deceit. There seemed to be only one way out, but how could I do it? Daddy had called and asked if I ever considered just walking away from it all. I told him that would be impossible. I'd always have the ghost of Bob haunting me.

I could move—but why let them win? This was *my* home, not theirs. I felt invaded, overwhelmed. Eric Clapton came on the radio. I normally listened to classical, but this felt prophetic as I listened to the words "someday. . . baby you'll be sorry."

Amen to that. But it wasn't someday, it was now.

We rounded the corner. There was the limo; there was the chopper. It was an emotional, dramatic scene; it would look glamorous to anyone looking on, but I knew better. Hell, this was my life now. Emotional, dramatic, and ultimately empty.

I stood back, as always, and watched the Guardsmen instruct Bob and Margaret in something or other. Maybe safety procedures. Who knows? Bob noticed my arrival and casually waved. As he began walking toward me, my feelings got all jumbled up. I wanted to hold him, kiss him, scream at him but all I could do was look at him, shake his hand and whisper, "I love you. I always will."

"I know. Me too. It won't be long. I promise." The chopper was positioned at an angle fifty feet away from me. I backed up and moved behind a clump of trees, hiding from sight. I didn't want anyone to see me cry. The helipad was in a clearing surrounded by trees on three sides. The fourth side was a walkway back to the National Guard building.

Bob and Margaret climbed into the tiny chopper. I thought about giving Margaret a sarcastic goodbye wave, but being so far away, she wouldn't notice anyhow.

I watched as the pitch of the blades increased and the whirling of the turbine became more intense. As the skids began to lift, it seemed like time stood still. A blinding flash split the night and a thunder of sound filled the air as the explosion tore the chopper apart. Then, silence. Burning objects whirled through the air; twisted chunks of blades flew toward me and struck the tree I crouched behind. The overpowering odor of burning fuel scorched the inside of my nose.

Oh dear God. I stayed, crumpled on the ground, afraid to stand and afraid to breathe. I began to crawl aimlessly away from the ball of flames. I was in shock. I knew I was in shock because the scent of Bob's cologne lingered in the air even though the fumes from the crash surrounded me.

I looked up to see if there was a clear path ahead and saw a figure in the distance coming from the left-from the far side of the helipad. It was probably a Guardsman sealing the crash site. My eyes were stinging and I couldn't find my cell phone. I stood up, hoping someone could help me get to a phone to call Daddy. I turned around to say one final goodbye. As I closed my eyes to pray for the souls of those on board, strong arms enveloped me.

"I love you so much," was all he whispered.

"Bob. Oh dear God in heaven."

Holding me up to keep me from falling, all Bob said was "I got off the chopper just in time."

•

From a distant cover of thicket and brush, Texas Senator Gus Bingham focused his binoculars on the helipad. As the fiery explosion pushed him back into the overgrown foliage he whispered, "Bingo."

•

As the anchorman on Detroit's NBC affiliate broke into the late evening news broadcast, Victoria sat back on her couch, wineglass in hand. Looking at the screen, her cat-like eyes squinted to see the details being shown live from the crash site. A smile crossed her face as the announcer said, "There appear to be no survivors."

•

Sitting back at his office in the Olds Building, Lieutenant Governor James Parsons had the television tuned to CNN and his radio dialed into 760 AM, WJR. When the late-night broadcasts were interrupted he placed his pen down, smiling. "There's been an accident at Abrams. A terrible, terrible tragedy." With those few words, he clicked the remote and murmured, "Done for."

•

Frank Pullen had refused to attend the gala event in Grand Rapids. At the country club in Lansing, he sat at the bar and watched television alone. The anchorman for the news broadcast looked annoyed when he was passed a piece of paper in the middle of a routine story. Frank Pullen downed a shot of bourbon as he heard "It appears that Robert Larken, former Texas lieutenant governor and heir apparent to the Michigan dome, has gone down in a...."

•

John Gaynor lay on his bed in the VanderRoth Suite on the twenty-sixth floor of the Amway Grand. He had refused the nightly turndown service—he wanted no one snooping around his belongings. The phone rang. John Gaynor heard the news over the line and slowly replaced the phone on its hook. A painful look crossed his aging face as he moaned, "My son. My son. Oh my God, my little boy."

*Katherine Shephard*

## Chapter Twenty-Four

"Beth, get down."

"Bob, oh God, what is going on?" My pleading eyes begged him to explain.

"I don't know if we're in danger, Beth. Get down and we'll crawl back to the car. Is it close by? We need to get out of here."

As we made our way back through the dense, thick brush I reached into the pocket of my beaded jacket and removed the jagged heart shape for reassurance. I could hear my dress rip as jagged pieces of downed limbs tore into the material. Breathing heavily, we reached the car. The driver was sitting there, in shock at the sights and smell of the burning remains.

"Get out. Please. There are homes nearby. Get out and give us the car. Now!"

Bob's commanding tone and glazed eyes frightened the young driver who did as he was instructed. Standing, Bob held onto the car for support and stumbled to the passengers side. Dazed and weak, he collapsed into the comfort of the leather seat. The night winds picked up and began howling ominously – as if ghosts surrounded us. I started to drive, not knowing exactly where I was to go. I needed answers.

"Bob, please talk to me. What is going on?"

"Margaret must have needed to clear her conscience and her soul. I never got the chance to find out. Margaret. . .oh dear God, Margaret. . ." As his sentence trailed off he broke down. Painful moans accompanied the flood of tears, bitter tears of grief, and he began to shake violently. He was in shock.

Pulling off onto the shoulder, I eased the car into a small clearing where we wouldn't be seen by passing traffic.

"Margaret. Margaret – she told me she was being blackmailed. John was giving her money to help pay off Patricia."

"Patricia? Blackmail?" None of this was making sense to me.

"Yes. Margaret discovered that Patricia had poisoned Billy G. Patricia wanted us all to move into what she called 'the big league.'" She had conferred with John about having me run for some county office. See what he would say. I guess John said, 'Why not something bigger?' He played right into her hand. He assured her he'd back me if that were my decision. This was quite some time ago. She did let time pass and that was that – until Glinnis had his alleged heart attack. Patricia. Patricia poisoned him, Beth."

Knowing he needed to purge himself, I listened.

"I don't know the details. There wasn't time. Margaret just said that she'd found out and Patricia was blackmailing her. She'd threatened to harm David. Margaret knew she could trust John. I didn't let her finish. I had to get to you - to tell you to get help because Margaret saw a flash in the brush. I thought maybe someone was after you. The last thing she said to me was 'I'm afraid.' Then – oh god."

"We need to go get help." I pulled the car back onto the highway. Seeing an approaching car, I waited for it to pass.

A horn blared; the car swerved and came to a pitched stop, wheels skidding in front of us.

I hurriedly opened my door, recognizing the car and driver. As my feet touched the ground he lumbered towards me. I fell into the waiting arms of John Gaynor.

"John. John, there's been an accident – maybe a murder. Bob – Bob is alright."

Running to the passenger's side of the car, the elderly man stood, crying, as he looked in to see the broken down man we both loved.

Banging on the door until Bob opened it he spoke, through sobs, "I know. I know. I saw the broadcast and knew exactly what happened. But I didn't know you'd gotten out. I called the State Troopers – went to the top. They found Gus and Patricia in the woods. The senator and Patricia were working together. The Troopers have them now. You're safe. Oh my God, my God. My boy. My son. I thought I'd lost you before you ever knew.

The men embraced as billows of smoke rose in the distance.

Bob trembled as he spoke, not fully aware of what had just been revealed. "It's over. Thank God it's over. I never want to be in that world again."

I smiled through the heartbreak, knowing that his life, our life, would never truly be free of that world.

# ~ABOUT THE AUTHOR~

KATHERINE SHEPHARD was born and raised in Michigan. An Alumnus of Michigan State University, with a degree in Criminal Justice, her experience as a political speech writer, attendance at the 1996 GOP Convention, state rallies and political fundraisers afforded her the opportunity to reseach "first hand" the life of politicians. Much of what gave her the inspiration for her book was garnered through conversations overheard in ladies restrooms! She has been dubbed "the mole in the hole."

Ms. Shephard lives in Southern California when she's not writing from her "second home" – the Texas Hill Country.

She is currently penning the second in the "Silence Series" titled *Breaking the Silence*.

To learn more about her and Fraternity of Silence, log onto www.KatherineShephard.com.